Streets

by

W. C. Highfield

Printed in the United States of America

ISBN 978-1-4507-1403-7

Library of Congress Control Number 2010907058

First Edition

To all of the *good* people
of the streets

1

Nothing I've learned from living on the streets of Key West ever prepared me for the crazy stuff that's been happening to me lately. I'm talking about some "out of this natural world" kind of things. I'm talking about going to a place that is unbelievable. But the whole thing is true, though. You are just gonna have to trust me when I tell you what's been going on. If I hadn't been through it all, myself, I probably wouldn't believe it either. Settle in, and I'll ease my way into telling you all about the whole deal. But first, I gotta let you in on a little bit about me and how we tend to business around here.

That's right, people. On the streets of Key West is where I live. Morris Scott is the name. And here in Key West is the best place I ever found for livin' on the streets. The main reason would be that it never gets too darn cold here. No chance I'm going to freeze to death like those poor bastards up north in Chicago or Detroit or New York. Man, oh man, if those sons of bitches don't make it to the shelters when the cold hits and the hawk comes roaring, they're done for. It gets so cold up there that lying on a steam grate or curling up in a refrigerator box won't save you. Your sorry ass will turn into an icy rock as hard as a turkey in the stinkin' freezer. Just like that, it will. So the weather is the major motivation for why I like Key West. If there's a possibility of freezin' my butt off, it's a chance I'm not willing to take. We may have some of the creepy, crawly critters here, but I'll

1

take them any ol' time. They're not too awful hard to deal with. Plus, Key West just happens to be crazy enough to suit me. Nothin' wrong with warm weather and foolish behavior, if you ask me. Yeah, this place has a different feel than other cities. You can just sense it in the air when you walk around—and I do a lot of walkin' around.

Now, there's something I want to get straight with you before we go any further. Whatever you do, don't go referring to me, or any other street people, as being homeless. We are _not_ stinking homeless. We all got a home, dammit. It just happens to be on the streets. What I'm sayin' here is—we all live in a city or a town, don't we? I think regular people, or civilians, as we street folks call them, believe we're just a bunch of hobos carrying a knapsack tied to a stick like back in the old days. The image of a group of us sitting around a campfire or riding in a freight train boxcar is the way most civilians seem to want to think of us. That homeless reference really gets me going. So, don't start getting me going. I got too much important stuff to tell you to get me going. Homeless, my ass. I can't stand that word.

As you might imagine, panhandling, in one form or another, is pretty much the sole source of income for us street types. It comes out of necessity, after all. Okay, I guess I do have to let you in on the fact that I've got some other little bit of money. Not a lot—just some. But I'm not gonna tell you where I get it, or where I keep it, though. At least not yet, I'm not. 'Cause you'd probably be just like everybody else and try to get some from me. Well, maybe not _everybody_ else. I do know _some_ street people who wouldn't try to get any money off of me. Maybe a *few* wouldn't. Well, at least Horace wouldn't. He's a friend of mine, who is also outdoors. I just so happen to know that Horace is not available, anyway. At least for a few days, he's not. He's coolin' his jets in the Monroe County Jail, which is located on Stock Island. It's the first land mass you hit right after you leave Key West and start up U.S Route 1. In the Keys, that road is known as the Overseas Highway. It's really cutting a path between the Atlantic Ocean and the Gulf of Mexico, but that's how they refer to it.

So, that poor bastard, Horace. He got arrested yesterday for taking a leak in front of a bunch of tourists. Now, isn't that a hoot? I can't help but hate it when something like that happens—especially to a resident of the streets. But around here, that type of stuff takes place a lot more often than you'd think. There's a whole bunch of real free spirits in this town. Seems to add to the charm of the place, if you know what I mean.

Yeah, around noon yesterday ol' Horace was just minding his own business, sleeping on the sidewalk in front of the Fidelity Bank. There was this group of vacationers sittin' around on the edge of the big planter in front of the bank. They probably thought Horace was fixing to stick up the joint or something. Stupid, transient out-of-towners. Don't you know it, just as Horace woke up and leaned over to start wizzin', Officer Keith happened to be coming by. Keith was greeted with a chorus of shrieks and squeals all going on. Bang, just like that, Horace got his poor black ass in a sling. Officer Keith is really not a bad guy, though. But what the heck could he do with all those pain-in-the-ass sightseers raising hell and going on about the pissing? Keith just had to arrest him. The cop was only doing his job. Can't blame him for that, I guess.

Tourists. Hustling a stinkin' buck off of them is practically the only thing they're good for anyway. Sometimes even just pocket change will do in a pinch. There are times, though, when I'm feeling kinda down that a word of encouragement from one of them can mean more than a $20 bill. Anyway, one of my other associates in the street-business game, Sonny, told me he heard Horace got booked on inde-cent exposure and disorderly intoxication. Disorderly intoxication, my ass. Now I don't doubt Horace may well have been drunk, but he wasn't being disorderly or anything. He was only taking a leak, for crying out loud. Guess you could say it was a matter of reliev-ing himself at the wrong place at the wrong time. Ol' Sonny and I had a good laugh about that one. Hold on a minute, I need to take a little pull from this here pint bottle. Throat tends to get a touch raw from talkin' so much......Ahh. That's better. Nothin' quite like the brown liquor to put an easing on the back of the throat. I highly recommend it. Not only is it medicinal, it's also good for the soul.

Yeah, last night my street pal, Sonny, told me about the deal that went down with Horace. Sonny said he saw the whole thing happen. At the time, Sonny was right across the street playing his gui-tar, which is his version of the panhandling routine. Sonny said Officer Keith handcuffed Horace and everything. Word is, the cops do that for your own protection. Own protection, hell. What do they think you're gonna do, punch yourself or something? Man, oh man, all this criminal justice crap has gotten a little out of hand. Horace should have told Officer Keith that he was allergic to handcuffs. That's the crazy stunt Connie Jo tried to pull off last month. She just happens to be a street person, too. Not very many women are actually street dwellers here in Key West. There are some women of the night, but that's an entirely different subject. The only street gals I know are Connie Jo and a real character named Duct Tape Sally. And she's a whole 'nother story, herself. More about Sally later on.

So, what happened was, Connie Jo got herself all fired up and stood in the middle of Duval Street cussin' her head off to beat the band. Stopped traffic and everything. When the cops came and tried to calm her down, Connie Jo started swinging her arms and spinning all around like a freakin' whirling dervish. Then, when they tried to cuff her, she used the "allergic to handcuffs" line. Didn't work, though. The cops got her for disorderly conduct and resisting arrest. Now *she* was being disorderly, all right. Carted her ugly butt right off to the Monroe County Jail. And believe me, I'm not kidding around when I make a point of telling you that Connie Jo is ugly. I'm talkin' stone ugly. To say she is homely would be giving her a huge compliment. Hardest lookin' woman I ever saw, ever. The cops were doing the general public a favor by getting her nasty-looking mug off of the streets for a while. Guess you could say the whole event turned out to be some sort of an unscheduled urban beautification project. You sure can't say the police force around here doesn't do *some* good, if you ask me.

Anyway, Horace ought to be out in a few of days even without having anybody to go his bail. They won't bother keepin' him locked up for too awful long on account of the pissing incident. In the meantime, however, he'll be chowing down on his three square meals a day and he'll be sleeping on a mattress, too. Now you might think I'd be a little jealous about Horace getting all of those comforts of home. Nope. Not one bit. I have no plans on my upcoming schedule of activities to do anything that gets me thrown in jail—unless I'm sick or something. In that case, I might go ahead and arrange my detailed agenda so as to get myself incarcerated. That would only be if I happened to need a little while to get fixed up and come back around to my normal self. As normal as normal might be for me. Jail and those damn cold-weather shelters up north tend to cramp my style. I'm more one for being in the great outdoors. I might just have a slight touch of claustrophobia in me, or at least something along those lines.

Now, I haven't lived out here on the streets my whole life. Hell, it's probably only been something like six or seven, or maybe eight years. Don't exactly know for sure. Feels like I aged twenty or thirty years in that time, though. But what the hell is life other than the blink of an eye? Right? At least that's the way I look at it.

Yeah, I started out on the streets of Philadelphia when I was somewhere in my early twenties. Like anybody else, I had to get used to livin' outside. It took me a month or so just to learn how to *be* a street person. Philly was where I grew up, but I only lasted one winter on the streets up there. Almost froze my sweet derriere off on several occasions. And, thanks to that particular winter, I happen to be minus the end of one finger and a pinky toe due to frostbite. When the cold came, I couldn't stand those damn shelters. Too crowded for my liking. Not enough elbowroom. And even though there are a lot of people in the shelters when it's cold, it's still a real lonely situation to be in. Me, I like the fresh air. Warm fresh air, in particular, is nice. Go where you want. Sleep where you want. And not have to worry about bumping into somebody every time you roll over or turn around. I need my breathing space. Don't go cuttin' off my air. You hear me?

So I said the hell with the cold and came down to Key West. I'd never been here before, but when I found out this was the southernmost city in the continental United States, I picked it right away as the place to live in the out-of-doors fashion. Being as it's completely surrounded by miles and miles of water, there's not much temperature variation between day and night. A lot of times, the difference between the daily high and low is only five or six degrees. In the summer, and all the way through September, it makes for some really warm and humid mornings. A fairly constant breeze is the only thing that keeps you from sweating your butt off. I don't mind putting up with it, though. The rest of the year makes up for the hot months. Heck, the all-time low temperature for this place is only forty-one degrees. And that was unusual as hell. Absolutely no chance it's ever gonna snow or get down anywhere close to freezing.

One creative way to cool off when it's really hot is to walk up and down Duval Street and slow down in front of the entrances to the stores. Most of them have the doors open, which allows the air conditioning from inside to pour out onto the sidewalk. When your appearance is one of a street person, you can't loiter for too awful long, though. You'll quickly get chased by store management. Our types can easily have the tendency to discourage the purchasing public from shopping at a place that looks like a deadbeat hangout. That would be especially true at one of the swanky-ass art galleries. They really crank the air conditioning, which is nice. But the clientele the galleries are catering to needn't have to rub elbows with a street dweller. Management at those joints keeps us moving on down the sidewalk.

Don't really want to say how I got down here. I didn't need anybody's help. Could've made it by myself, no problem. Okay, heck, my brother Randolph drove me. He didn't necessarily want to, but our mother made him. Just like she does when she pays for him to fly down here every now and again to check up on me. You know, make sure I'm still kickin'. Randy doesn't seem to mind making the trip, though. Especially in the winter. Can't say as I blame him, seeing as Mother foots the bill. A little winter-weather getaway to a guaranteed warm spot in American paradise can't be too awful hard to take. At other times of the year it still provides Randy with a short vacation. Specifically, a short vacation from Mother. She really likes to run the show. With her, there is only one way, and that just so happens to be *her* way.

Years back, I used to live more like the rest of you civilians. The main difference separating us is I've got this weird tick stuck into me, like most all street types. Can't seem to shake it. Whatever it is, it kinda makes us act a good bit different from regular folks, even though we're not really all that different. What happens is, you get down and you lose your confidence. You start to believe you can't make it with keepin' a job...or make it with anything, really. It's a pretty damn desperate spot to be in. Shoot, I used to have a job. Hell, I had a lot of jobs. Never could seem to be able to hold onto one, though. It must have had something to do with the drinkin'. Most everything has got something to do with the drinkin', don't you think? But I will tell you straight away, even if you took the booze out of the picture completely, most all of us street people would probably still be a little messed up in one way or another. Nice enough human beings and all. Just a little messed up. That's all. And it could be due to any number of reasons. The drinking only seems to make things worse, if you ask me. Although, I have absolutely no plans to quit the stuff anytime soon.

Well, way back when, my mother would always get me set up with a new job each time I got canned. She's got the money and connections to do it, too. Mainly because my old man made a ton of dough before he croaked. He had this trucking business haulin' stone gravel for new roadbeds. Yeah, the old man had a slew of trucks in his fleet and he even let me drive one in my late teenage years when I was working for him. That is, up until the time I dumped a load of stone gravel on a parked car. Somehow got my bearings all ass backwards. I had such a hang-over, I didn't know what the hell I was doing. I was probably cross-eyed. I went one way when I should have gone the other way. Then I accidentally hit the switch that lifted the tailgate of the truck and almost buried this teeny little Volkswagen in gravel. It just so happened that the stinkin' car belonged to a gal who was working one of those stop signs to control the traffic on the road we were widening. Man, was she pissed off. Can't say as I blame her. The company insurance took care of the repairs to the car, but that particular incident prompted the immediate end of my truck-driving career. When the old man told me I was fired, I said, "Hell, you can't fire me, I quit." That was a pretty original response, huh?

Sit tight for a second, I need a drink......yeah, there we go. I just love the soothing effect the brown liquor has on the ol' throat. Without a doubt, one of my most enjoyable activities. Real comforting. And it will get you to where you want to go quicker than most anything else I know.

So I've been hangin' around these streets of Key West, just trying to make it through life my own way. Even though I have a few friends, in general, life on the streets kinda makes you feel like a stranger. The extra little bit of money I told you about does get me by in a pinch. The problem is I only get my hands on it in bits and pieces. I usually spend most of it on the booze, though. No sense wasting good money on clothes, or shoes, or razor blades. Hell, if you buy razor blades then you gotta go and buy shaving cream. And then aftershave, for crying out loud. One thing leads to another with the regular folks' way of living. Before you know it, you end up acting like some middle-class American type. Nothing wrong with that. It's just not really for me.

Anyhow, I got a couple of extra tee shirts in my backpack. And my jeans and sandals aren't worn real bad. At least not as far as I'm concerned. Who gives a damn about underwear anyway? And it doesn't really bother me how long my hair grows. I get Sonny or Horace to hack it back a touch when it gets below the middle of my back. Are you takin' in what I'm saying here, folks? We're talking about a Spartan lifestyle, to say the least. Since you're being kind enough to listen to me, I'm going to tell it to you like it is. Not gonna pull any punches here.

By the way, I don't spend a whole lot of time worrying about washing or shampooing or using deodorant, and all the other personal hygiene crapola like brushing and gargling, either. Let's just say those aren't tasks which are very high up on my list of priorities. We street people have our own set of standards when it comes to that kind of stuff. And they're probably not the type of standards you would most likely appreciate or welcome anyway. But, then again, I'm not telling you how to live your life, so it makes us about even on that score. Let's just agree to disagree on what's important.

Now, there are times when the old stomach starts growlin' pretty bad and I'll have to go and buy myself some food with a little bit of cash. Other times I'll rummage through the dumpsters at the back door of some restaurant for something to eat. Not a very dignified method of staying alive, but look, it's survival out here on the streets. You learn a lot about survival when you play this game. And let me tell you, they got a ton of restaurants around here. And some real fine ones, too. You'd be amazed at the amount of food that gets tossed out. It would feed a mess of starvin' refugees. You got to be careful, though. Have to mix up your routine and not hit the same places all the time. Having a little variety in your choice of complimentary dining spots is a good idea or you'll end up getting busted for trespassing, or worse. Don't need that type of aggravation. Least not me.

Like I said before, I got this wild-ass story to tell you. And also like I said before, you're probably not gonna believe it. I do have to admit it's a little out there, if you know what I mean. As I think I already told you, if it hadn't happened to me, I probably wouldn't believe it myself. Hell, Sonny and Horace think I'm a little nutty, anyway. No use trying to tell them about it. I did slowly begin to let them in on it once and they got to laughin' so hard I thought they both were gonna either pass right on out or have a heart attack or something. Never even let me finish telling them the whole deal. The heck with them if they don't want to hear about it. I'd rather tell somebody who may have a little more appreciation of what's been happening to me lately. Somebody with a little more concern and interest, such as yourself.

Now, let me take a big pull on this here bottle of the brown while you just sit back, relax, and pay attention. I'll let you know when I need to take a little break so I can scrounge up some money for another pint. Throat tends to get dry, you know, when you're doing all this talking. Well, here goes…

2

It was late on a Thursday afternoon a couple of months ago and I'd gone up to Mallory Square to work over the tourists a little bit. Mallory Square is the regular meeting place in Key West where folks gather together each evening to watch the sunset and be entertained. It's considered the daily big-ass celebration of the city. Sometimes you hear all this excitement just as the sun slips down below the horizon. People claim they saw the "green flash." It's supposed to be some kind of stinkin' visual phenomenon where the light's bending at that split second when the sun disappears. I've seen my share of sunsets, and I've never seen it. Of course, I've probably never watched a sunset sober. Or maybe the whole thing is such bullshit you gotta be *really* drunk to see it. I may try that one of these days.

There's practically always a cluster of activity at the Mallory Square sunset, with a variety of performers going through all kinds of antics and gyrations to amuse the crowd. Of course, the main intention of the players, artists, and musicians is to pick up some bucks from the grateful visitors. The entertainers might seem like they just love performing and all that, but believe me, they do it for the money. I've even seen some younger kids scattered around here and there playing a musical instrument with a little tip jar at their side. Most of the time, at a suitable distance, there's an adult hanging out who is attached to each of the youngsters. I don't happen to have musical talent in the least—or any sort of talent for anything else in particular. I prefer to employ the direct panhandling approach, so as to play on the sympathetic compassion of my potential customers. I want them to feel they are lending a helping hand in uplifting a guy who's down and out. I think I am at my best playing the game when I'm really dying for something to drink.

Since it was toward the end of September, all in all, things were fairly quiet. A couple of weeks earlier there had been a Poker Run event. It's one of the motorcycle happenings that are held in Key West off and on throughout the year. The bikers make a hell of a lot of loud noise out of their exhaust pipes, but I have to say, those folks have a good sense of humor. The wild sayings they have on their tee shirts just kill me. My favorite one is the back of a guy's shirt that says, "If you can read this, the bitch fell off." You gotta love 'em.

There are a bunch of other theme gatherings, too. They've got the Pirate Festival with all the swashbuckling crap. That one's got people dressed up like pirates who walk around carrying parrots and going, "Arrghh." And there's the Ernest Hemingway look-alike contest. The biggest one is Fantasy Fest that's around Halloween. It's Key West's version of Mardi Gras. Craziest goings on you'd ever want to see at that one. Decadence and depravity at its best. If that sort of thing is your cup of tea, there are a few bars around here where clothing is optional *all* the time.

Being as it was late September, kids were back in school, fewer tourists were around, the snowbirds hadn't come down yet, and it sure wasn't the time of year for the spring-breakers. I do have to say those college students are a good distraction, though, when they show up in March and April. They get so drunk and raise so much hell that it takes up a fair amount of the attention of the law enforcement community. Those actions, in turn, tend to permit us professional street types to carry on our daily operations without being hassled quite so much by the cops. The problem is the breakers never have a whole lot of money to donate to the panhandlin' cause. What cash they do have is spent mostly on booze. Can't say there's really anything wrong with that, though, if you ask me.

So anyway, I was wandering around Mallory Square, hittin' on a few of the sightseers when I saw Sonny sitting on a low wall off to the side. He was playing a little tune on his guitar. Most all street people are thin for the obvious reason that eating is usually an afterthought—but Sonny is *really* skinny. He is also tall. Well over six feet. I'm talking about a beanpole here. Hard to believe there's enough room inside his body for all of the organs to fit. Sonny likes to strum along on the ol' six string and look forward to some welcome handouts from the appreciative tourists. You know, get a little somethin' for the effort being put forth. As usual, he had his open guitar case at his feet with a few dollars scattered around in it for bait. That particular strategy is intended to give his operation the appearance of a worthy charity. Sonny tries to make it look like some other good-hearted souls have already made a contribution to the cause. He didn't seem to be drawing much attention at all, so I went over. I wouldn't have bothered him if he had a live fish or two on the line. I stayed a little off to the side and talked quietly to him. I didn't want to scare off any of his potential customers by making it look like there was some kind of street-person gathering going on. There is a tendency to drive off the prospective clientele if we bunch up. That strategy works out well since most of us street types are loners, anyway.

"What's the good word, citizen?" I asked. "Any luck with these people?"

"Nothing so far," said Sonny. "What the hell is the problem? Where is everybody? I thought Key West was the last resort."

"That's what they say," I said, "but you couldn't prove it by the turnout today. I guess we just have to be a little patient, seeing as it's the off season."

"Well, shoot, I just may have to go on up to New Orleans," said Sonny. "That's where they say people tend to value the music more. You know, folks might be a little more willing to make a dona-tion to the program."

"Oh, I don't know about that, my friend," I said. "I hear there's way too much crime up there. I think I'd just as soon stay here and take my chances with these tourists. As nuts as it is around here at times, I'd say Key West is a lot more laid-back. I don't feel like getting rolled just for the hell of it. That's what I hear goes on up there sometimes."

"Well, Mo," said Sonny, "business better pick up or I may have to figure out something else. Maybe I'll even take up leading a life of crime."

"Now, Sonny, you just put away that thought. You don't wanna go up against the law and end up getting tossed in the lockup, now do ya?"

"If I get hungry enough," said Sonny, "anything might happen."

"Sonny," I said, "you better just cool it with that kind of talk. Here comes Officer Keith."

Keith rolled up on his bicycle and stopped near us. He is a big, blond-haired, burly cop. Officer Keith is even-tempered and all, but still the type of individual—whether he was a cop or not—that you'd want on your side if, for some reason, you were involved in a street fight. The guy is built. His sensible, level-headed manner, combined with his muscular physique, make Key West better off with him as a member of the law enforcement team. Looking out over the Gulf of Mexico he said, "Hello there, fellas. You guys hard at work, as usual?"

Like I told you before, Keith is an alright guy. He speaks to us, but he usually keeps things low-key so it doesn't look like he's really paying much attention to us. Hell, he doesn't want a stranger to think he actually talks to street people, or "those people," like a lot of civilians refer to us. That is, unless he was planning on locking one of us up for something. Keith sort of busied himself by doing some minor adjustments to his bike while we talked. It seemed like he used the tinkering as a way to take a little break.

"Just minding our own business," I said. "You know, passin' the time of day here in our fair city. How are things with you, sir?"

"Fine, just fine," said Keith as he kept fiddling with his bicycle. Every minute or so he stopped and

17

gazed out over the bright water of the Gulf. "Things are nice and quiet around here for a change. Just the way I like it. Don't you fellows go and do anything stupid to break up what little tranquility we've got. Hear me?"

"No siree," said Sonny. "We ain't planning to cause no problems at all."

"Now, come on," I said, "you know us. We're just law-abiding citizens. You can't see us doing some of the crazy stuff that people try to pull off around here, now can you? Neither of us could even think up things like they do. Don't you think, Officer Keith?"

Keith didn't answer. He just got on his bicycle and rode off. That poor ol' cop has sure got his hands full. I wouldn't want his job for any amount of money. Don't know what the city pays him, but whatever it is, it can't be anywhere close to being enough. He must have some higher calling going for him. Otherwise, you would think he'd go stinkin' nuts by having to deal with all of the wackos in this town.

I left Sonny to his guitar pickin' and fund-raising venture. Then I worked what little crowd there was until sunset, picking up a few bucks here and there. All those crazy jugglers and sword swallowers and stilt walkers and high wire walkers were doing their daily best, as usual, to attract a crowd and pick up some money for their efforts. The vendors hawking jewelry, the artists selling paintings, and the photographers peddling pictures were all hanging in there. But for them and, more unfortunately, for us street folks it turned out to be a pretty slow evening. Overall, September can be a slow month, but after being around here for a while, you come to expect that.

As it was starting to get dark, I left Mallory Square and bought a fresh pint of the brown liquor for the night. Then I made my way over to the private place in my life, which would be the Key West Cemetery. It's a pretty long walk from the Square, but I like to sleep there at night and also occasionally during the daytime hours. Unless, however, I happen to unexpectedly pass out somewhere else in town at some point. Sonny and Horace each have separate churches where they spend most nights either inside or out. The one Sonny likes to frequent is St. Paul's Episcopal Church. It's on Duval Street and it has some wild and crazy history. More about that place later on. Horace usually goes to St. Peter's Episcopal Church on Center Street. It's the black church in town, so Horace fits right in. Even though those guys have an idea of where I go sleep, I don't advertise the cemetery thing. Have my own little deal going there. Us street people got *some* secrets, you know. As a group, we are not what you would refer to as chatty social butterflies. All of us are sorta on our own personal agenda, if you know what I mean.

Man, I really like sleepin' in the cemetery. It's the quietest, most peaceful spot I know in Key West. And big as hell, it is. I heard once it covers almost twenty acres. It's gotta take up the space of four or five good-sized city blocks, with a wrought iron fence around the whole place. Not sure of the exact number, but they say somewhere between 80,000 and 100,000 folks have ended up there. According to what I've heard, the cemetery was started in 1847.

It was established just after a hurricane destroyed the previous one down on the southern end of the city. Instead of regular graves, like in cemeteries most other places, practically all of the dearly departed are buried in vaults that sit above the ground. Because the water table is so high, there's a worry about digging down very far below the surface of the ground. Wouldn't want to hollow out a hole and have it go fillin' up with water from below. Guess it's the same reason there aren't hardly any basements in Florida.

Now don't get me wrong, the Key West Cemetery is not the most pristine resting place to spend eternity. A good many of the crypts and low masonry walls around the family plots are cracked or tilting over. And a lot of the wood or metal roofs above some of the vaults have weather-beaten holes in them. So when it's been raining, or even fixin' to rain, you've got to be careful to pick out a dry spot for your night's sleep. Or day's sleep, depending on your particular schedule. Since it doesn't rain much at night around here, it would be the afternoon snoozes where you run the risk of getting soaked by a thunderstorm if you're not thinking ahead during your selection of a suitable location. But, then again, thinking ahead is not necessarily typical behavior for street folks. We kinda just live an hour or so at a time. No long-range plan. To be more specific, no plan at all.

Now, there is one fenced interment area in the cemetery I think is pretty cool. Twenty-some U. S. Navy sailors were buried in the memorial plot back in 1898. They had been crewmen on the U.S.S. Maine that was blown up in the Havana Harbor in Cuba. That particular event was what sparked the beginning of the Spanish-American War. On the center monument, there's a life-size statue of a sailor who's saluting with one hand and holding a big-ass oar in the other. It's a real American history lesson to read the plaques erected there. I think it's great to see a memorial for former veterans of the country's military service. Too bad you have to be deceased to receive any kind of recognition. It gets me down to hear about, and see, former vets returning home from overseas only to end up on the streets. People talk a good game about respect and gratitude and support for servicemen and women while they're actually serving. But once they're back here, America doesn't seem to appreciate the sacrifices they've made for the good of the country. They're just kinda forgotten about. At least, that's the way it seems to me. I think it's a shame.

There's a bunch of other interesting stuff in the cemetery, too. On the other side of the big burial ground, way across from the monument I was telling you about, there's a headstone that just cracks me up. Some woman had them put "I Told You I Was Sick" on it. She had died back in 1979 at age 50. Apparently, she had been a real hypochondriac. Another women's epitaph in the same area says, "I'm Just Resting My Eyes." Man, this town has sure got a reputation of having some citizens with a real sense of humor. It adds some charisma, don't you think? Heck, somebody's funniness isn't worth a damn unless there's someone else around to appreciate it.

Anyway, I usually set myself up for an approaching nighttime sleep session fairly close to the outer fence of the cemetery. That's where I can at least get a little light from a streetlamp on the sidewalk. But I still use a good bit of caution in picking out a spot, to avoid being seen from the street. Don't want to be getting any harassment from the cops or especially from some rowdy-ass drunks looking to rough up a poor ol' soul such as myself. I always try to make a point to avoid confrontations whenever possible. So it helps that there are a few big banyan trees in the cemetery to break up the view. Plus, there are some laurels and palm trees scattered around. You just have to use your head, as much as possible, and try to blend in with the calm cemetery ambiance. No sense standing out and making a spectacle of yourself. It's sort of similar to the concept of *not* wanting to be like the guy at a beach or a park who stands up and waves a beer around, drawing attention to himself. From my point of view, being as stealth as I can possibly be is the main objective. To carry on life as a street person for very long, you have to think about this kinda stuff. You know, be creative.

On this particular night, I took off my backpack, propped myself up on top of one of the crypts, and pulled out the pint I bought with the little bit of money I'd obtained at Mallory Square. Now here's another thing I don't go telling people: I enjoy reading for a while before I go to sleep at night. That is, if I'm not too shit-faced. So, I took this book out of my backpack. It's one I like to read before I pass out. Afraid I have to tell you it's a kid's book. Guess you could say it's a collection of children's bedtime stories. Now, don't go makin' fun and get me upset. It just happens to be something that is pleasing to me. The book is called "The Adventures of Kool the Mule." Got all kinds of neat little stories in there about this group of barnyard animals. They've got titles like, "Kool the Pool Mule," Kool the School Mule," "Kool the Tool Mule." A whole mess of 'em. And I've read them hundreds of times. I love them. They all have some kind of moral or at least something good to say. Each story has these real fine drawings of the animals. If I remember right, I read "Kool the Pool Mule" while I worked on the pint of the brown stuff.

In that story, the animals on the farm are complaining about the summer heat. Ol' Kool comes up with the idea they all should go for a swim in the pool at the next farm. Kool has the animals gather up their swimming gear, and then he tells them to load everything up on his back. He even carries the pain-in-the-ass Bandy Rooster, who's the biggest complainer. Off they go to the pool. When the group gets there, everyone gets cooled off with a swim and they all end up happy as hell. In each of the different stories, Kool has an upbeat and optimistic attitude. He always has a way of figuring things so the whole deal turns out in a positive way for his barnyard pals.

Well, I finished the story and the pint at about the same time, rolled up one of my extra tee shirts for a pillow, and put my head down. If I was gonna sleep anywhere but the cemetery, I'd always try to remember to use my backpack for my pillow. Leave it lying off to the side and you might wake up to it being gone. Make it be your pillow, so they gotta wake you up to get it. You definitely have to watch out for your stuff and not let it get stolen. I'd bet there's roughly the same percentage of bad people living on the street as there is in the balance of the general population. A good thing, though, is I feel pretty much out of harm's way in the cemetery. Before I dozed off, I heard the sound of a small prop plane overhead. It was most likely on its way to or from the Key West Airport. Now, buckle up, people, because you're not gonna believe what happened next.

3

Somewhere in the middle of the night, something made me wake up. While I was still lying on top of the crypt, I rubbed my face and eyes with both hands. I heard this whirrin' noise. It wasn't real loud, but it was a sound kinda like a big fan running. Little by little, it kept getting louder. I sat up on the vault and looked around. There was a full moon that night, so I could see pretty good across the cemetery. I kept looking and listening. I wasn't seeing anything moving around, but I was still hearing that whirrin' sound. Couldn't figure out where the heck it was coming from. As it got louder and seemed to be closer, I realized that whatever was making the noise was somewhere up in the sky. Since the moonlight was beaming, when I looked up I saw this completely dark globe lowerin' over the cemetery. It was round and looked to be about the size of a basketball as it slowly moved toward the ground.

I wiped my eyes again and strained to focus on the damn thing. After maybe about a minute of watching it, son of a gun if it didn't come straight on down and land in an open area where two of the cemetery's paved walkways crossed. As soon as it touched the blacktop path, the whirrin' sound stopped. I was really, really wondering to myself what the hell the thing was. I figured it was either some damned outer space UFO or I was plumb crazy in the head and was seeing things. I just had to get a better look at the stinkin' thing. So I took my time gettin' off the vault and then moved slowly, real slowly, toward where it was sitting on the ground. It was a tough effort, but I tried to force myself to keep calm while I was staying low and out of sight. I slipped as quietly as I could behind the grave markers and the above-ground crypts as I moved in closer. I made my way to maybe twenty feet from where the damn thing had landed, and then I peeked up over a gravestone to check it out.

Just like when it was lowering down, there still wasn't any light coming from it. It was just a dark round ball sitting at the intersection of two pathways in the goddamned cemetery. If it wasn't for the moonlight, I wouldn't have been able to see it at all. I was crouching there looking at it, puzzled as shit, but curious as hell, all at the same time. I am not ashamed to tell you that I was kinda tense. Man, the old ticker was doing double-time. To me, my heart sounded like somebody was pounding fast as hell on a big bass drum inside my chest. I was breathing real hard, too. I felt like I'd just run a couple of blocks at full tilt, or worse. I was having some real trouble trying to keep myself calmed down. What the hell is a black ball doing comin' down out of the stinkin' sky in the middle of the night and landing in the goddamned Key West Cemetery? That was the sorta stuff I was thinking about. That was what was running through my mind at the time, if you know what I mean.

After a little bit, I could see by the moonlight that a wedge on the side of the ball started to open up real slow. It was kinda like a slice being cut out of a round watermelon and then lifted up. I gotta tell you, I was figuring this was the craziest thing I'd ever seen. Seemed to me what I was staring at was straight out of some science fiction movie or something. What the hell is going on? What am I looking at? Those were the thoughts going through my head. The whole scene was pretty damn eerie.

Just as I leaned up above the headstone a little higher to get a better look, a thin beam of light shot out from the opening in the dark globe and it landed right on my freakin' face. It seemed something like what getting speared by a dart in the middle of the forehead might feel like, but without the pain. I sensed the power and grip of the ray of light lock right onto me. The next thing I knew, I got yanked out from behind that gravestone like a paperclip getting sucked to a magnet. Don't ask me how it happened, but I was pulled through the air and drawn into the open slice in the ball in no time flat. I'm talking in a stinkin' instant. Whoosh! What follows here is the way my mind and body reacted to being on the inside of the darn thing. Believe me, it's not my normal way of talking or acting. Now, you're just gonna have to go along with what went on next, because there's no explaining it. It doesn't seem to make any sense at all. I could never have figured out how to put in plain words the way I changed, but I swear this is the way it was...

At the exact instant in which I entered the sphere, I became acutely aware of a total alteration of my being. I took clear notice that my brain's functioning had been elevated to an advanced level. My consciousness was immediately enhanced and I became alert to sharp increases to my senses in perception of sight and sound. Simultaneous with my mental transformation, the entryway door to the capsule slammed shut behind me with a thunderous thud. I likened the sound of its closing to that of a drawbridge retracting back to the wall of a castle with an authoritative report. I detected a sterile, metallic odor. Amid muted lighting, it appeared I hung in a suspended state within a circular shaft which had limitless boundaries both above and below. There were no apparent physical means holding me motionless, as I could detect no sensation of touch from tangible restraint. My mind was perplexed with a dazed discernment of size. How in heaven's name could this small orb I had previously viewed externally possibly hold my body within its confines? Had my form been severely condensed or was I experiencing an immeasurable misconception of a seemingly vast interior? Any reasonable justification for my predicament defied logic. I existed in a state of complete disorientation. Had all mental faculties abandoned my awareness of reality, thereby reducing me to a state of severe bewilderment? Was I hallucinating or was some superior authority or influence deceiving me?

The dim illumination within the shaft lasted for only a mere moment, at least as it seemed. Suddenly, from all sides, bright white lights began revolving in a circular fashion around me. With unmistakable clarity, it occurred to me I was the subject of an analysis being conducted by a sophisticated scanning device. No rational explanation existed for me to have such knowledge, but know it I did. After several seconds, I was released from the inexplicable means by which I was held and began descending through the illuminated shaft. What now had become multi-colored lights streamed by me at ever-increasing velocity. The passing lights provided the impression of reaching a downward speed of perhaps one hundred miles an hour. Faster. Five hundred miles an hour. Faster yet. A thousand miles an hour. The speed continued to accelerate exponentially. Down, ever down, the shaft I plunged. I dropped what seemed an infinite distance within the circular tube.

At the beginning of my plummet, the lights on the sides of the shaft appeared to beam from individual sources. However, as the speed of my fall increased, they became connected streaks that trailed off above as I fell farther and farther. My body spun and rolled. I maintained not even the slightest command over it. Enduring a totally perplexed concept of time and space, I existed in a rapidly descending state of utter panic and confusion. How would I ever find purchase upon some safe haven from this tumbling madness? I speculated as to when my uncontrolled free-fall into this eternal abyss would come to an end. I craved for it to cease. Within my mind, I pleaded to the unknown source of power reigning over me to bring the insanity to an end.

With no forewarning whatsoever, my ever-accelerating descent ended with a flagrant flop upon a massive padded chair. To my astonishment, I landed in an upright sitting position. With the speed at which I had been traveling, coupled with the abrupt halt, it was pure folly to believe I had not sustained some form of bodily harm. But for some inexplicable reason, I endured the fall without any noticeable injury. The lack of physical wounding left me in a puzzled frame of mind. To suggest that I was dazed and perplexed would have been an enormous understatement. The entire event had terrified me to the core and my heart raced and pounded in a manner I had never experienced. I expected it likely to explode from my chest with each succeeding beat.

With uncommon concentration, I willed my mind to regain command of my shaken body and spirit. Upon achieving a minimal amount of control over myself, I observed that I sat in the middle of a ring-shaped room. Spaced around the circumference of the room was a vast array of video monitors with varied images emanating from each screen. Several of them displayed views of me from a variety of angles. I took immediate notice of a dramatic change in my outward appearance. Vanished were both my worn clothing and my unkempt grooming. They had been replaced with a white jumpsuit-style uniform coupled with neatly trimmed hair and beard. In addition, my physical condition had been converted to one of strength and dynamism. I sensed an uncommon, robust fitness about my body. There had been an absolute transformation of all aspects of my life form.

Other monitors on the circular wall projected technical data, the significance of which I hadn't the faintest clue. My native intuition, however, led me to believe the displayed information and statistics were concerned with the aforementioned analysis of my being, which I had suspected upon my initial entry into the capsule. At the very least, it was an unnerving assumption.

4

After what seemed like an eternity, a blank panel in the circular wall lifted and a striking woman with brunette hair entered the chamber. She was resplendent in a pure-white, strapless gown. It was difficult to accurately judge her age, but she had beautifully chiseled features and a tall, slender physique. Her long dark hair was worn in a twirled up fashion upon her head, appearing as a stunning, lustrous brown mass. Her emerald eyes sparkled in the bright lighting of the room. She immediately captured my complete and undivided attention. She was, without a doubt, a veritable vision of beauty.

"Greetings, Morris," she said, "my name is Cassandra. Welcome to our vessel, which is known as Holidaymaker. I trust your entry and subsequent admission process has not caused you any ill effects. It is not our intention to harm you in any manner."

"I return the greetings, Cassandra," I said. "I believe I am unharmed, but I must admit that the whole experience here within your craft has certainly been a touch on the volatile side. If it would not be too much of a difficulty, I would respectfully request that you provide me with an explanation as to who you are, why I am here, and what this whole affair is concerned with. Enlighten me, if you please. To begin, how is it that you know my name?"

"All in good time, Morris," she said. "We happen to know a great deal about you. And as we proceed, you, in turn, will learn much about us. Alleviate yourself of any qualms or fears. We want you to know we are a peaceful society and mean no harm to you or any others. Here on Holidaymaker we are devoid of violence, hostility, and misdeeds. However, the most important feature, of which you will gain generous knowledge, is that our entire way of life is based on portraying a positive mood and rendering an optimistic environment. To explain further—no negativity or pessimism, in any form, exists here whatsoever. We have analyzed your character and spirit and, in doing such, we have determined you are capable of behavior consistent with this guiding principle. Had you not been, you would not be here at this moment, or ever, for that matter. Any being that seeks, embraces, or dwells upon the negative is not welcome here, nor is tolerated in our midst. Such individuals deprive themselves of the opportunity to realize their full potential by harboring an attitude and creating an atmosphere which manifests itself in failure. Morris, those are not the type of characteristics we see in you."

"Well," I said, "I must say I am reasonably relieved by what you have said. Nevertheless, I am still in a quandary over the purpose of my visit. Speaking of which, is this, in fact, just a visit? What is the intended length of my stay, may I ask?"

"Time, Morris, has a relative value," said Cassandra. "One must quantify time to one's given set of parameters. By that, I mean you are only bound to our time definition while you are in the confines of our craft. It is not our intention to deprive you of the due course of time passage you are familiar with in your customary way of life. One might say we have merely *borrowed* you temporarily."

"All you have said is very compelling, but I remain at a loss as to the purpose of it all. Why have you chosen me and why am I here?"

"You will be educated in our ways and capabilities," she said, "but I would advise you to make every effort to retain your patience and tolerance throughout the learning process. Here on Holidaymaker we recognize our guests' unique abilities. Although, in many cases, these hidden proficiencies have long gone without being considered, attempted, or attained. We see in our visitors, such as yourself, the capacity to accomplish what you might never have imagined. Our mission is to facilitate the opportunity to realize these latent talents. We seek to enable you to achieve the aptitudes which you already possess. Allow me to provide an example."

Cassandra turned and pressed a keypad on the chamber wall. A panel elevated and she withdrew a tray from the cavity in the partition. On the tray was what appeared to be a disassembled mechanical device. Numerous gears, pulleys, rods and other un-identified pieces of metallic equipment lay scattered about in disarray. She placed the tray in front of me and secured it to the arms of the large chair in which I sat.

"Morris," she said, "sitting before you are the components of a complex mechanism, which re-quires assembly. I dare say you are unfamiliar with its design, construction, or end purpose. Using your intuitive engineering skills, proceed to bring together the dissimilar components so they are converted into a working apparatus."

"Why do you deride me so?" I said. "I haven't the faintest notion of where or how to begin, and even if I did, how then would I be knowledgeable of the process to continue? Cassandra, it is an impossible undertaking to consider."

"It is not my intention to deride, disparage, or ridicule you," she said. "Actually, quite the con-trary. I wish only to demonstrate a learning experi-ence by way of the task before you. I implore you to commence the assembly process. Free your mind of any apprehensiveness or pangs of doubt. In ad-dition, please bear in mind the customary approach by which we conduct our affairs here. Only positive thoughts and actions are tolerated. You are capable of the undertaking, Morris. Please proceed." With that, she turned, moved to the far side of the room, and maintained a position facing away from me. She ap-peared to busy herself by noting and recording vari-ous data from one of the numerous wall monitors.

Without forethought of reason, I lowered my eyes and studied the scores of unrelated parts strewn about before me. Where a moment before I existed without a clue in the universe as to how to initiate a course of action, in a virtual instant I possessed an insightful state of mind, coupled with a growing feeling of confidence. I selected two of the parts and secured them together. This action occurred with what seemed the absence of both mental and physical exertion. I then attached two more parts. And yet another two. My mind flowed ahead of the movement of my hands, which glided with nimble ease over the parts in a continuously adroit assembly process. With methodical and meticulous precision, the scattered pieces came together by my hands, with the outcome resulting in a functioning operational instrument. Gears meshed. Pulleys revolved. The movement of small rods heated a series of thin metal plates. The increased temperature of the plates caused a miniature belt to expand and rotate, affecting yet other mechanisms in an intricate gearbox. In turn, the whole process was repeated and the procedure continued over and over again. With no rationale to have such knowledge, I realized I had, in essence, assembled a fundamental perpetual motion machine.

The ability of my eyes, mind, and hands to move in coordinated unison, as well as with such precision, confounded me to the point that I became overwhelmed. A chill shuddered through me and I became short of breath. Emotion filled my eyes and I fought back impending tears. How in heaven's name could I have completed an undertaking so complex?

As I sat staring at the device in stunned disbelief, I sensed Cassandra standing by my side.

"Well done, Morris," she said. "You have reached a successful conclusion to your initial challenging experience here on Holidaymaker. What is your reaction to this accomplishment?"

"My mind is a bewildered muddle," I said. "How can it be? By what knowledge could I have possessed the capability to comprehend such a complicated procedure?"

"For one," she said, "you demonstrated the foremost trait that is essential on our vessel. You maintained a positive attitude and approach to the task. Beyond that, who is to say there are not hundreds or even thousands of alternative means of bringing the very same components together to form a working model? Morris, your achievement is unique to your own personal skills, abilities, and aptitudes."

"I am inundated with confusion," I said. "I am baffled by the entire matter."

"Put your mind at ease, Morris," said Cassandra. "This is but one simple example of what is achievable here. There is a vast and truly limitless horizon of potential for you while you are in our midst. In time, you will reach a level of comfort with what you are capable of attaining. Please be patient with your puzzlement. It is my purpose to be of assistance in alleviating any reservations or doubts you may encounter while on Holidaymaker."

"Well, Cassandra," I said, "your words have granted a calming influence on my being, which would otherwise exist in a state of total mystification. I put secure trust in your capability to guide me during this complex indoctrination process. I feel confident and self-assured in your midst."

"Very good, Morris," she said. "It appears you have faired well with your preliminary adaptation to our methods. You possess the attributes that will grant you successful opportunities with us. Emblazon this event in your memory, as well as the related thought process you attained. It will serve you well as we proceed in the future. Now, please relax as I place you in a condition of absolute repose until the appropriate initiation of your next positive experience here on Holidaymaker. Be at ease."

She approached me with her left hand extended. With the tips of her index and middle fingers, she gently touched my eyelids with a slight downward motion and immediately I was a million miles away.

5

The next thing I remember was opening my eyes to some real dim daylight. It had to be just barely before dawn. Looked around and son-of-a-bitch if I'm not lying on the pavement where two pathways crossed in the stinkin' cemetery. Right exactly where I saw the spaceship thing land. My mind was doing cartwheels and my stomach wasn't doing much better. I was thinkin' to myself, holy shit, what the hell was that all about? I kinda felt myself over to make sure I was really alive and still in one piece.

Seemed to be. Couldn't find any bleeding or bruises, and nothing hurt. Damned if I wasn't lying on the ground in the freakin' Key West Cemetery and it was starting to get light. I looked back across to the vault where I had set myself up to sleep the night before. There was enough light so I could just barely see my backpack and my rolled up tee shirt sitting on top of it where I'd laid down. I told myself again I was really lying right where the black basketball had landed during the night. I took my time standing up, started looking around, and it all came back to me real clear. I'm talkin' really, really clear. The waking up from the whirrin' sound, seeing the dark ball lowering down, getting sucked into it by the beam of light, and then everything else that happened while I was on the inside of the thing. I remembered the whole crazy deal. Holy shit, I thought. Holy freaking shit.

I checked out the spot where the ship had been sitting on the paved pathway, but I didn't see any sign it had been there. I looked around a little further for scorch marks or burnt pavement or any other clues, but there was nothing out of the ordinary—just headstones, vaults, and green grass. Then I just stood and stared at the ground in a half-daze for I don't know how long. I finally went over and sat down next to my backpack. I noticed I was wearing my regular clothes and my hair and beard were long, as usual. While I was trying to get myself back together, I put my nighttime reading book away in my pack. I put the empty pint in it, too. I made it a point to never leave any empty bottles around the cemetery. Didn't want to spark any interest from the cops or the folks that looked after the property. No need creating any trouble for myself by littering up the place. I'd toss the bottle away later. I felt so spaced-out that I wasn't doing things consciously. I was just going through the motions.

After I sat there focusing on nothing for about ten minutes, I decided to go get some coffee. My head was still buzzin' from what I had been through. And it sure wasn't the type of buzzin' my head was used to. I walked, but it was more like an absent-minded shuffle, down a couple of blocks to Truman Avenue where there's a little breakfast joint. It's a place I patronize from time to time. I went down the alley next to the café and sat down. All of a sudden I couldn't keep my eyes open. I put my head down and went into siesta mode. Not sure how long I was out. When I came to, I got up and went into the place. I bought a sweet roll and a cup of coffee. A little splash of the brown liquor in the java would have helped to doctor it up. But I was out of the brown and, for some strange reason, I felt like keepin' my head clear instead of clouding it up like I tended to do.

I guess the funny last part of the whole thing was my mind kept running over the lines of an old song that goes, "Hey, Mr. Spaceman, won't you please take me along, I won't do anything wrong." Couldn't seem to get it out of my head. I had to laugh out loud just thinkin' about it. Later in the song is the line, "Won't you please take me along for a ride?" Man, some real crazy stuff is going on around here, I thought. I figured I'd have to try awful hard to block that song out of my head. I already had enough to think about. Didn't need to be bugged over and over by a stinkin' song on top of it all.

Something else that hit me when I was thinking about being on Holidaymaker was how small it was on the outside. If I had actually been inside the darn thing, I would have thought I'd have gotten a really bad case of the claustrophobia I told you about earlier. But I hadn't. Everything seemed normal size, life-size. I hadn't gotten any sensation I was inside some teeny tiny space. That would have freaked me out big-time. A cramped feeling never came over me at all. Okay, maybe for a little while, when I was in the cylinder at first, but not real bad. The way I hate being in confined places like shelters or jail, man, oh man, I would have gone stark raving batty if I felt I was stuck inside something the size of a basketball. The whole deal was practically too much to think about.

I went out and around the corner of the little café, sat down on the ground, and started to enjoy my breakfast. There were a few chickens milling around to keep me company. The damn things are everywhere in Key West. Especially around places that serve food. Off and on all day around town, you can hear the roosters wailing out their cock-a-doodle-doos. It's the worst when they start up early in the morning while it's still dark. Sometimes they don't even give a good rendition of the stinkin' cock-a-doodle-doo. It's almost like they don't give a shit—like some of the rest of us—and just let out some half-ass screech. In general, the chickens are an annoying nuisance, but nobody seems to do much about the issue. For some real entertainment, you ought to see a rooster hop on a hen underneath a chair, try to pin her in there, and then start to go to town. Man, if you want to see all hell break loose, you have got to witness an act like that firsthand. Thrashing and screeching and banging around and all. It's a real scene. Damn chickens, feral cats and dogs. For crying out loud, this place is a regular menagerie around here, if you ask me.

While my coffee was cooling off, I made another effort to remember everything that had happened during the night. I kept going over and over all of the particulars. Holidaymaker. Cassandra. Putting the model together. It all seemed so, so real. There was one downbeat thought that went through my head. How the hell could I tell anybody about what happened? People already looked at me funny anyway 'cause I was one of "those people." The civilian types think you got a screw loose 'cause you live on the street. I figured if I went and tried to tell any of the normal-type people what happened, I'd get myself committed to the loony bin quicker than shit. Even street folks were out. I decided, at least for a while, I would just keep quiet about the whole wacky experience. I knew it was gonna be tough, but I also knew it was what I needed to do. I'd just have to think of it as my own little personal secret.

I finished up the roll and coffee and told the stinkin' chickens it was tough shit but they weren't gettin' anything. I needed to keep up my strength, you know. When I was tossing my breakfast trash in the garbage can next to the coffee shop, I remembered the empty pint in my backpack and let it go, too. The next brilliant thought that hit me was it would be a good idea to go over to Duval Street. That venerable thoroughfare just happens to be the main drag of Key West. I was figuring if I got myself moving around with a bunch of other people, maybe I would be able to get my mind off of Holidaymaker and get settled down some. Making an attempt to get back into the flow of being an upstanding street person in this fair city was the plan. At least that was what I was hoping for.

Not long after I turned the corner off Truman and started heading up Duval, I heard a commotion coming from an alley next to one of the storefronts. I thought I recognized the voices of the two guys who were arguing. Damn if I didn't look down the stinkin' alley and see Sonny and Horace in the middle of a full-blown quarrel. I got the impression they had been arguing with words, but now they were actually startin' to wrestle around. It was the craziest thing to see Sonny, tall and skinny as he was, getting into it with Horace. Horace had these massive, matted dreadlocks and he was a lot shorter than Sonny.

41

"You black sonofabitch," yelled Sonny, "I'm telling you, the rest of the wine is mine."

"The hell it is," shouted Horace. "It's mine. You want it? Then you just try and take it from me, big boy."

Sonny grabbed onto Horace's left sleeve while Horace started swinging the wine jug around at arm's length with his right hand. They were tottering around in such a way that it looked like some kind of a drunken, street-person tango. In reality, they probably were not capable of doing too much damage to each other. I'd seen my share of fights before where the winner went to jail and the loser went to the hospital. This was not one of those kinds of fights. It was anything *but* a battle royal.

"That's just what I'm gonna do, homeboy," slurred Sonny. "Just watch me."

"You keep it up," said Horace, "and I'm gonna hit you up side the head."

"You just go ahead and try, cornbread."

"Get ready," said Horace, "'cause you gonna end up flat on your poor lily-white butt."

I'm hearing all of this as I was moving in on them to try and break it up. "Yo, hey you guys knock it off!" I hollered, taking hold of each of their shirts above their shoulders. Gripping hard, I tried to push them apart but made little progress. "You two wanna end up in the slammer this morning? Sonny let go. And you, Horace, put the damn jug down."

"Morris," said Horace, "this sorry honky is trying to take the last little bit of my wine."

"Put the jug down now, Horace," I said. "And Sonny, you let go of him. What are you two doing fightin' over that little ol' bit of wine for? You guys usually *spill* more than that much anyway."

After some more grabbing and pushing, they managed to cut loose and ease away from each other, and then I let go, too. We were all out of breath when Horace leaned down and set the nearly empty jug on the ground. Without any warning, Sonny took a staggering step forward and kicked at the jug. Missing, he lost his balance and fell backwards on the ground with his long-ass legs ending up in the air all over the place.

Horace lunged forward toward Sonny saying, "Why, you dirty bastard, you *did* end up on your pansy white butt and now you're gonna get it."

I caught Horace by the sleeve and said, "Hold it right there, man. No more fighting. You got it?"

"He tried to break the damn bottle," said Horace, gasping for air

I was pretty winded myself when I said, "Look, here's what we're gonna do. Horace, you take a swig of the wine, but not all of it. Leave some in there for Sonny. You guys are going to share what's left and I'm going to go get another full one we all can split up between us. Now, you do what I say and get yourselves calmed down. I'll meet you guys behind Steamers Restaurant by that little grove of trees in twenty minutes. Got it? And throw that jug away in a garbage can. Let's not give the man a reason to hassle you. Hear me?"

"Yeah, yeah," they wheezed at the same time.

Horace and Sonny each took a sip of what little wine was still in the jug and order was restored.

Once the wine was gone, they were right away back on good terms. Although Sonny and Horace were known to tangle occasionally, most street folks aren't much for arguing and fighting. Takes too much effort and energy. Booze tends to be about the only thing any of us would want to make a fuss over anyway. Take it away and the problem is over. Or get a hold of some more and everything is fine. At least for the time being.

6

I went out to the sidewalk and turned back up Duval Street. I was laughing right out loud, thinking about those two guys fighting. The whole event was a match-up of complete opposites, at least in their builds. It was just plain funny to see them tusslin' around. Horace is short and he has a much stockier build than Sonny. Well, as stocky as a street person can be. But Sonny is a real beanpole, though. Mostly, we're all pretty slim. You don't come across hardly any street folks who are overweight anyway. Seeing as how eating tends to be way down in the pecking order, a stout, chunky physique does not fit the standard profile for a citizen of the street, if you know what I mean. We all stay in sorta decent shape by all the walkin' we do. But the many deficiencies we have in our diets don't help at all.

As soon as I was sure I was out of sight of the boys, I cut across the street and went into the Southern Trust Bank. There was no sense in letting Horace and Sonny know what I was up to. No reason to give them too much information regarding my personal affairs. Where I was going was to check in with my twice-weekly money source. At that particular bank, my mother had an account set up that I could withdraw from two times every week. I could only get twenty-five dollars at a time and I couldn't tap the account two days in a row. It was kind of a strange setup but, believe me, I knew the rules and so did all of the tellers. Fifty bucks a week wasn't much to live on, but it sure did help to supplement what I could make at the panhandlin' game.

I went to the counter in the lobby area of the bank and filled out a withdrawal slip. I just happened to have the account number memorized. Since there was nobody in line, I took dead aim at the one teller who made coming into the bank just about as rewarding as the cash I was about to get out of it.

"Good morning, Mr. Scott," said the tall, attractive, young lady teller.

"Hello there, Suzanne," I said, handing her the slip. "How are things going with you today?"

I always try to time my spot in the rat maze customer line so I have Suzanne handle my banking business. I will even let other people go ahead of me until she's available for the next customer. It's the same sort of technique you can use at a barber shop when you want to wait for your favorite barber even though you're next up. I remember that deal from when I was growing up and actually went to a barber shop to get my hair cut. Thinking about something like that now seems like a whole different lifetime ago.

Man, Suzanne is a really pretty gal. And right friendly to me, too. Especially when you consider the fact that my outward appearance isn't, what you might say, consistent with the bank's normal clientele. She does business with me like she would any other customer. None of that condescending crap just because I look different. Suzanne has long and full dark hair and a tall, slim figure. She has a sweet face, a perfect smile, and beautiful green eyes. Really easy to look at, if you ask me. Now, I'm no lecher or anything, but to me, she is a real knockout. Problem is, she's a nice, hard-working, regular-type girl and I am your shabby, indigent—*don't you just love that word?*—street person. I don't have a snowball's chance in hell of ever making it with Suzanne. There is not a chance in the whole wide world it would ever happen. Because all of that is true, it seems to make dealing with her a little frustrating at times. Although, from a realistic standpoint, I still consider myself a pretty lucky guy just to be able to know her and talk to her and look at her. Suzanne is really something. She's number one as far as I'm concerned.

"Just fine, Mr. Scott," she said. "Anything else today besides your withdrawal?"

"No thanks," I said, "I think this here twenty-five bucks should hold me for a little bit. That is, unless you want to take me out on a date or somethin'." Before she could react, I said, "Just kidding, Suzanne, just kidding."

I grabbed the money, shoved it in my pocket, and put my head down 'cause I felt silly for what I had just said. As I started to turn and walk away, she called after me, "Oh, Mr. Scott, I almost forgot, a letter came for you a couple of days ago." As she handed the envelope to me, Suzanne said, "I believe it's from your brother who's on the account here with you and your mother."

"Thanks," I said, "Probably letting me know when he's coming down here next."

With a smile she said, "Have a nice day, Mr. Scott."

"You do the same, Suzanne," I said, smiling. "See you in a couple of days."

I made a mental note to tell her to call me by my first name the next time I came in the bank. I'd known her for a couple of years but she always seemed to want to keep things on a formal, business-like level. That was her way. I do like to think she kinda cares for me. Well, as much as an attractive girl can actually like a scruffy, grungy bum like me. Chances are, she is just being polite, but there sure aren't any doubts in my mind that I'm sweet on her. Nothin' much I can do about it, though. It's just one of those drawbacks in the long line of occupational hazards of being a street person.

On my way back to meet the boys, I stopped by a liquor store and bought the biggest jug of wine they sold. It was a low-grade, recent vintage of Italian red table wine. Cheap Chianti, Dago Red, call it what you want, but it sure was a hell of a lot of wine for nine dollars. I had the clerk bag it for me. No sense in attracting too much attention on the street, if you know what I mean. Although, I would bet that nine out of ten people could have still guessed what I was carrying. The only thing the plastic bag managed to do was hide the brand, whatever the hell it happened to be. The jug might as well have had one of those black and white generic labels that just said "Red Wine." You see, us street folks don't get caught up with all that name-brand recognition bullshit. We're a whole lot more concerned with the economics and effect of the product being purchased. Maximum bang for the buck is the general thinking. It makes beer pretty much out for us as a beverage of choice. You learn real fast you can drink more beer than you can carry. I hear that's what people who go hiking like to say, too. Plus, with beer you gotta drink a hell of a lot of it to get to the desired plane you're aiming for. And you also have to take a leak way too often, which cuts into valuable time.

As I was walking back down Duval, I opened the letter from Randy. He and my mother both knew the bank was the only place in town with an actual address where they could send me a note. Plus, they knew I stopped by the bank twice a week. The letter was short and sweet. Randy was coming down in about three weeks for one of his yearly handful of visits. There was no need to think about it for a while, so I stuffed the letter in my backpack. I had plenty of time later on to prepare for the details of his pending arrival.

I went down the alleyway beside Steamers Restaurant, which led to an empty lot that was overgrown with trees and bushes. In the middle of a dense ring of seagrapes, hibiscus, and climbing bougainvillea was a clearing with some grassy spots here and there. An overhead canopy of some humongous palm fronds completed the secluded feel of the place. Near the rear of the vacant lot sat a rusted-out International Scout with weeds growin' up through the wheel wells and broken windows. The cozy lot is one of those spots here and there in Key West that seems like somebody, or most everybody, has forgotten about. But, at the same time, you learned to not abuse that particular hideaway, or others, by using them as an everyday hangout. No sense in drawing unwanted attention, pissing somebody off, and getting into trouble.

Sonny and Horace were waiting for me, sitting on the ground in the shade of the overhanging foliage. They seemed relaxed and back on good terms as I approached.

"Now, have you boys made up from your little tiff?" I asked.

"Everything is copasetic," said Horace.

"We're doin' fine," said Sonny. "All calmed down and everything. Just waiting on you, Mo. We were wondering where you'd been. We were getting ready to send out a search party for you. And what sort of treat might you be packin' in that there plastic bag?"

Pulling the jug out of the bag, I said, "Oh, this here's some fine, first-class wine I brought along. Figured we ought to have ourselves a drink and relax a bit."

"Well," said Sonny, "I'd say that's just what the doctor ordered. You go right ahead and dole it out as you see fit."

I cracked open the twist-off cap. Supporting the weight of the jug with my forearm, I took several big gulps. I was thinking to myself that I needed to simmer the old nerves down a touch from what had happened the night before. You know, level out a little bit.

I passed the jug to Horace. As he hoisted it to his mouth he said, "Here's to you, partner. Top o' the mornin' to ya."

"Yeah," said Sonny when it was his turn, "appreciate it. You're a real gentleman and a scholar, Mo."

"And, by golly, there aren't too many of us left," I said.

We proceeded to pass the jug around until an hour or so later when we finished it off. We each chipped in three bucks apiece and I went and got another one. During the drinking of the second jug, the conversation became both more open and more philosophical. Consuming a whole lot of wine usually tends to have that effect.

"You know," said Sonny, "this street life is just a temporary thing for me. I know some day I can get back to being the regular kinda person I used to be."

"Sure you can," said Horace. "Sure you can. You mean ya might try to get back with the telephone company up north? You had a good job with them, didn't you?"

"Damn right I did," said Sonny. "A damn good job. I was makin' enough money to buy a house and provide for the wife and kid. I had things going good... going good. Had a couple of cars and everything.

And a damn good job. Hell, I know I can still do it. I just got to get myself back together a little. That's all."

"You can do it, my friend," I said. "If that's what you want. Nothing stoppin' you. We all can get out of this street life if we put our mind to it. Guess we're all just a little down on our luck at the present time, huh? But we can't give up hope altogether. What we could use is some kinda avenue off the avenue, so to speak. What's even a bigger problem overall is there are a whole lot of people in this country who are only one or two missed paychecks away from being on the streets like us. It's a sad thing."

"It's a hard fate," said Horace. "A real hard fate."

"A damn good job...a damn good job," said Sonny again. "Then the wife up and leaves me because of the drinkin', at least so she said. And then I lost the job at the phone company. Then it was the house and the cars down the drain, just like that. I know I could still get back to that way of livin'. I just gotta get things together. That's all. I hit bottom. I just hit bottom. All I'm lookin' for is a second chance."

"Sure enough, brother," said Horace. "That's right. It's just a matter of time. You could do it. We could all do it. You know what I mean. When you see somebody who does it, then it makes you think you can do it, too." Then after a pause, "Me, I know what I'm gonna do one of these days. I gonna get me a piece of ground up in the Mississippi Delta. I got some kin up there. But any land I get hold of has gotta have a pond on it or be right next to a stream or something. I'll just sit right there on my own land

and catch them ol' catfish like it's going out of style. Maybe I'll even start me one of them catfish farms. Raise a bunch of 'em and sell 'em off to some food distributor. Make me a mess o' money. I'll be sittin pretty. Just kickin' back and takin' it easy at my own place up in the Delta. Yeah, my own place. That's right. It'll be nice."

"That sounds great, Horace," I said. "And I'll come up and see you. You can teach me the finer points of how to catch catfish."

"You come on up any time, my friend," said Horace. "We'll have us a good ol' time. Have a few drinks. Do us a little fishin'. And listen to some blues. The Mississippi Delta is the home of the blues, man. From when I lived up there a long time ago, I remember goin' down the road—sometimes dirt roads— and listening to the blues at a local juke joint. A lot of times the place was really just somebody's little ol' house that had been converted to a place where you could listen to the music and get something to eat and drink. Morris, you come up and visit anytime. You know, we'll just take it easy." Then after a pause, "And the best thing of all about goin' up there is I'll get me a young soul sister to live with. If I'm not feelin' so good or I get old and don't get around too good, I'll have somebody to look after me. That's what I'll do."

"How the hell are you gonna get a woman?" said Sonny. "I mean, what woman would want your sorry black ass?"

"What are you talkin' about?" said Horace, "I'll get me one. You had one didn't you? I'll get me one. And a young one, too. Just you wait and see.

There's a mess of single soul sisters up there in the Delta. All I'll have to do is just give one of them sweet young gals a little peek at the big guy and it'll be easy pickins. Yeah, baby. Them young ones won't be able to resist me. Yeah, baby. Heeee."

"Yeah, give the guy a break, Sonny," I said. "Horace will do just fine, if that's what he wants to do." Then after a minute I said, "I don't know about me. Got to figure something out here sometime, some way. Just not sure what I want to do. That's been the deal all along. My whole life, I've never been sure what I wanted to do."

"You'll figure out something, partner," said Horace. "You can do anything you want. Any of us could. It's just a slow process gettin' back to being a civilian."

After the second jug was polished off, the balance of the afternoon passed quietly as we each took ourselves extended siestas. Can't remember much more about the rest of that day and early evening, but I feel sure we really enjoyed what you might refer to as a street-folk wine fest. Sonny and Horace were back on good terms and the morning's squabble was a distant, if not forgotten, memory. When it comes to dealing with a falling out among street people, grudges usually aren't held onto for too awful long. You never know when the person you had bickered with earlier would come through for you in a neighborly fashion somewhere down the line. Even though it's a lonely life, it's sort of like we're all on the same team, at least most of the time. That is, unless somebody happens to start being a real ass-hole. I don't have that kind of problem with Horace, and only with Sonny every now and then. They have their moments with each other, but they're okay guys to me.

When the sun started to go down, the boys decided to go up toward Mallory Square to see what handouts they could scrounge up from the tourists. It was sort of like a new day for them. Street people tend to get the nighttime and daytime all jumbled up on a fairly regular basis. It's especially true if the drinking starts a little too early in the day, like we had done. For Sonny and Horace, it was just the beginning of a new work shift.

"Now, you boys mind your manners this evening," I said. "You hear?"

"Sure will," said Sonny. "We're just going to check and see if any of the flaming faggots got some bucks to spare."

"Now why do you have to go talkin' like that," said Horace. "Ain't none of them homosexuals ever done you no harm. Not a one."

"Horace is right," I said. "We got a mess of gays and lesbians around this town, but as long as they mind their own business, we got nothing to complain about. No sense makin' fun of them. They all seem to have money and they're as good a bet as anybody to help us out with a little cash."

"You're right," said Sonny, "but I'm still gonna think of those gay guys as being just plain old faggots. They give me the heebee geebees. And for the lesbos, I sure wouldn't want to get into a fist fight with any of them. Them dykes are liable to knock your lights out. You know they say that, by and large, the women around here are bi and large."

"You know, Sonny, you sure do have a way with words," I said. "But why not start trying to think of it this way. If you're talking to a gay guy just imagine you're talking to a girl. And if you're talking to a lesbian, just figure you're talking to a guy. It's as simple as that. Give it a try. You might start to take on a whole different outlook on the subject."

"Thanks for the advice," said Sonny. "But they're still faggots and dykes as far as I'm concerned."

"Now don't go being so sensitive and getting your bowels in an uproar, brother," said Horace. "Ain't none of them ever bothered your poor white butt."

"Yeah," I said, "open up that narrow mind of yours just a touch. It could do wonders for you."

"I'll think about it," said Sonny, "but don't hold your breath."

"There's a Gay and Lesbian Center on Truman," I said. "It's just a couple of doors from the place I like to get breakfast every now and then. One of these days I may just take you over there and acquaint you with this group you seem to have a problem with. Maybe they could straighten you out a little on their lifestyle and what they're all about."

"You'll be making that trip on your own, Mo," said Sonny. "I wouldn't set foot in the place."

"Suit yourself," I said. "I'm only trying to help you out, pal."

After saying goodbye to them, I started on over to the Key West Cemetery. On the way, I picked up a pint of the brown liquor. Thought I might need a little nightcap to help me make it until sleep time.

7

Since I had snoozed away the better part of the afternoon, I wasn't very sleepy. I read a few of my children's stories and worked on the pint until it got dark. When I finished the bottle I still wasn't drowsy so I decided to see if I could stay awake as long as possible. If the damn spaceship was coming back, I wanted to make sure I was conscious and not get caught off guard by being asleep. I sat with my back propped up against a vault that was listing to one side. I made a strong effort to keep my eyes open. But ain't it the darndest thing when you want to try and stay awake, it's lights out before you know it. A better way to doze off than any sleeping pill in the world. Reminds me of when I was younger and was making a long drive during the middle of the night. Man, I'd start to doze off behind the wheel, so I'd pull off at a rest area or a gas station. I'd try to get a little sleep when I stopped, but I'd sit there wide awake while the car wasn't moving. Then I'd start driving and damned if I didn't start to pass out again right away. What a pisser that was.

So, I guess at some point I fell asleep. And darned if sometime during the night they got ahold of me again. No warning or nothin'. I snapped wide-awake while I was flying right through the freakin' air. That freakin' beam of light had locked onto me like a set of big ol' vise grips. I didn't even have time to let out a stinkin' peep. Just like that, zap, my sorry butt was airborne and the next thing I knew I was inside the ship. My way of thinking and acting changed just like it did before...

My return to the interior of Holidaymaker differed from my initial experience. On this visit, the tractor beam which seized me from outside, delivered me directly to the large chair where I had been seated during my original stay. Bypassed were the lighted cylindrical shaft and the precipitous plunge of my earlier trip. Yet, I arrived, as I had before, with my attire and grooming significantly transformed. Once again, I was clothed in a white jumpsuit uniform. In addition, my hair and beard were neatly trimmed. Beyond that, I took notice of a general cleanliness about me, the likes of which I was not accustomed. I existed in an orderly state of mind, complete with a physical condition of extraordinary fitness and exceptional hygiene. Surprisingly, I noted that my finger, part of which had been lost to frostbite, had returned to its natural state and was functional. I concluded that the portion of my toe which had also been a victim of frostbite had been replaced inside the tapered white boot I wore. These modifications may well have occurred on my first encounter on Holidaymaker, but I had not perceived them. Other, more consuming, concerns had monopolized my attention the previous time, to say the least.

I reflected on the significant transformations of my person and determined they had a distinctive appeal to me. Whether I had assumed an overall higher comfort level because of my familiarity with the surroundings, I wasn't certain. However, I was convinced I maintained an increased degree of poise and confidence. As opposed to my first visit, I felt far more comfortable and at ease with my situation and my being. I was delighted to be returned to the ship.

Time had a way of playing tricks while on Holidaymaker, and although it could have been hours, after what seemed like a brief moment, Cassandra entered the room. She appeared yet more tall and striking than my previous recollection. She was dressed, as before, in a white gown with her toned shoulders exposed. I took greater notice of the healthy glow of her light almond-colored skin. Her facial features were even more delicate than I recalled. Cassandra's radiant complexion was devoid of the slightest of flaws, and the jade shade of her eyes sparkled from the surrounding bright lights. She was everything that was beautiful. I was fascinated. I was captivated. There was nowhere else I desired to be except in her company.

"Welcome back, Morris," she said. "It is indeed good to have you here once again on Holidaymaker.

"It is a pleasure to be back," I said. Fumbling for the ideal comment to make, I merely repeated, "It is a pleasure to be back." I was so mesmerized by her attractiveness that a warm wave came rushing over me. Even though I conjectured that I was blushing, I did my best to remain at ease and mask my self-consciousness. In view of her considerable allure and charisma, it was a challenging task.

"Our plan for your second visit," said Cassandra "includes a tour of our Science Department, in addition to a further exercise to display your underlying abilities."

"I am prepared," I said, "to follow whatever

course of action you have in mind. I am eager to commence with any and all undertakings."

"It is reassuring to hear you respond so enthusiastically," she said. "However, please bear in mind our primary tenet of maintaining an optimistic attitude. As we proceed, you will encounter difficult and demanding assignments. Do not allow them to discourage you. A positive mind-set will be your greatest ally."

"I am ready," I said. "I intend to put forth my best effort."

"Very well," said Cassandra, "let us proceed. Please accompany me."

I rose from the oversized chair and faced Cassandra with steady eye contact. The fascination I felt toward her helped brace and prepare me to pursue any endeavor she could have possibly suggested. Turning away and toward the circular wall, Cassandra placed her outstretched hand on a recessed keypad next to one of several door panels. After one of the panels opened, we walked through the doorway and into a complex maze of hallways as the panel closed behind us. Identically appearing corridors split off in a myriad of directions with no apparent pattern of design.

Turning from one hallway to the next, we passed a seemingly endless number of doorway panels, each controlled by a blank handprint keypad. The combination of the labyrinth of similar-looking halls and the lack of any signage denoting each doorway's designation or purpose left me in a lost and confused mental state. There was zero probability I would be capable of accurately retracing my steps.

Cassandra, however, strode confidently, yet casually, as we walked on. I thought it best to not become separated from her; although I reflected that with her competent manner, she would see to it I was kept in close tow. The prospect of that particular scenario continuing, I considered fantastic.

Cassandra slowed her pace and then stopped in front of one of the countless unmarked doorways. She placed her hand on the adjacent keypad and, after the door panel opened, we entered a vast scientific laboratory. In every direction, and as far as my vision permitted, men and women attired in white laboratory coats milled about at various stations. They were all attentively occupied with projects in a variety of mediums. Some groups were conducting chemical experimentation while others were engaged in mechanical and aerospace projects. Yet others were busy with electrical tests. Agricultural projects, as well as medical research, ran the gamut of technical variety which was underway. The range and intensity of the activities being performed was overwhelming to me.

Once again, I was struck with the complexity of comprehending the relative concepts of time and space while aboard the craft. How could all of this action and all of this cavernous volume of square footage possibly be contained on a ship which, on the exterior, appeared no larger than the size of a basketball? Although entirely dumbfounded, I remained determined to avoid being consumed by the predicament. I was far too enamored with the prospects of my tour, not to mention Cassandra, to allow my concern for a logical explanation to get the best of me. I resolved to follow the ancient credo, "When in Rome, do as the Romans do."

A tall, stout, elderly gentleman with long, flowing white hair and beard approached us. He, too, wore a white lab coat and was smiling as he greeted us saying, "Welcome Cassandra, so nice of you to join us." Then turning to me and extending his hand, "And you must be Morris. We have awaited your arrival with great relish here at the laboratory. I am Bernard, Director of Science."

Shaking his hand, I said "Morris Scott. It's a pleasure to be in your company. This is indeed an extensive operation you have in progress."

"All in a day's work, Morris," said Bernard, chuckling. "We strive to leave no stone unturned in our pursuit of scientific knowledge. Allow me to show you around our facility."

Cassandra turned and touched my arm saying, "Morris, I must take my leave of you for a segment of time. Bernard will escort you from this point. Be at ease and do your best to absorb all we have available to you. Your potential for success is unlimited."

"Thank you, Cassandra. My aim is to press on and do my utmost to excel."

"Very good," she said. "Put forth your best effort."

I meant the words I had spoken and was truly inquisitive as to what knowledge and experience thus intended for my comprehension lay ahead in the immense laboratory. Yet, before she even departed the room, I experienced a sinking, crestfallen feeling in my chest. Although I was confident I could successfully continue the tour without Cassandra present, I already yearned for her return. To satisfy my longing, it could not occur rapidly enough. I was infatuated with her beyond all belief.

8

"Morris," said Bernard, "I am aware of your previous visit and of your successful completion of the intake exam. It comes as no surprise that you possess the capacity for adhering to a positive approach with your mental processes. Our background investigations are nearly flawless in our quest to select viable candidates to experience Holidaymaker."

"Thank you, sir," I said. "I tried—"

"Pardon me for interrupting, Morris, but it is not our practice to use the term "sir" here. In addition, I took note that you stated your last name when we just met. On Holidaymaker we care to use only first names to identify ourselves. There is uniqueness in each individual which does not require further definition by the use of surnames. I trust you will find this policy suitable."

"I certainly find no difficulty in being compliant with your customs," I said. "Additionally, I aspire to study and learn all you have to offer, Bernard."

"Very well, Morris," he said with a smile. "The opportunity to engage in unique and exceptional experiences is what we desire to make available to our visitors. We are a society in which each individual's abilities are fostered and nurtured in order to allow them to achieve their utmost. As we proceed, I trust you will repeatedly find the aptitude-related aspects of the process are already contained within you. That potential, coupled with an affirmative approach, will permit you to be released from the bonds of negative thought and underachievement. Come with me and I will exhibit and demonstrate the concept."

As we made our way through the laboratory, I couldn't help but be intrigued with Bernard and all he represented. Here was the director of an immense scientific facility, and he was giving me a personal tour. It was readily apparent he was both intelligent and scholarly, in addition to possessing the administrative and managerial skills necessary to be in charge of such a massive technical venture. Furthermore, he had an openhanded and personable style. A benevolent demeanor virtually radiated from him. I was profoundly awed with the opportunity to be in his presence. Being a touch on the portly side, and with his long white hair and beard, I equated him to a scientist-like, yet taller, version of Santa Claus.

As we continued our methodical tour, I was amazed how the length and breadth of the laboratory appeared limitless. With a high ceiling and bright lighting, the space seemed infinite. I also observed every conceivable genre of research in progress. The variety of the multitude of personnel ranged from biochemists to botanists, geologists to geographers, astrophysicists to astronomers. At one point it struck me that everyone appeared to be approximately the same height, the stature of which was significantly less than the height of Bernard and, for that matter,

Cassandra. Another constant among the diverse assortment of both male and female scientists and technicians was the cordial salutations they extended me throughout the tour. As we passed by a bevy of chemical engineers I was met with, "Welcome, Morris" or "Greetings, Morris." Observing a group of mathematicians deeply involved with what appeared to be a complex problem-solving project, they paused from their task at hand with "Glad to have you aboard, Morris" or "Nice to see you, Morris." Perplexed with their familiarity of me, I reminded myself over and over, "When in Rome...when in Rome."

After an extensive excursion around the lab, Bernard led me to an empty drawing table located in a recessed corner. "Now then, Morris," he said, "it is our understanding you have previous work experience in the field of civil engineering."

"Please," I replied, "do not go to the point of referring to my work in road construction as having been any form of engineering. I merely drove a dump truck for my father's company, and it was only for a relatively short period of time. I must make clear that I lack any formal education or training in civil or any other type of engineering, whatsoever."

"Ah, to the contrary, Morris," said Bernard, "we believe you possess an underlying talent in that realm of study, which has simply remained dormant for a period of time. Let me pose a specific exercise for you, which is intended to reinvigorate your ability to design and plan."

"I will attempt any test you may have in mind," I said, "but I have serious doubts I can complete one with any level of expertise that involves engineering."

"Here, here, Morris," cautioned Bernard, "positive thoughts and only positive thoughts. You know the required approach."

"Very well," I said. "I am ready. Positive thoughts it is."

"All right then, Morris," said Bernard as he pulled several large sheets of paper from a drawer in the drawing table. "On this first paper you will note a topographic map of a parcel of real estate, complete with contour lines of equal elevation. An existing road is shown on the lower portion of the tract. What I would like you to do is redesign the designated property by adjusting the gradients, or slope, indicating areas requiring cuts or fills. Your plan should include a parking lot with a capacity of one hundred seventy-eight vehicles. Incorporate into your drawing a retail shopping center, exterior detail only, to be located at the northern section of the parcel. In your design, be sure to include a drainage plan as well as entrances and exits to the shopping center. Be creative, but be sure to bear in mind standard accepted design parameters."

"Bernard," I said, "before I begin such a daunting task I must ask you to help me with one of the perplexing and confounding issues I have been struggling with while on board Holidaymaker."

"Certainly, Morris. As you wish."

"How is it that you and everyone else here are so familiar with, not only the English language, but also the terminology and vocabulary which are indigenous to my country and culture? How do you have the specific knowledge of these things as they apply to me?"

"Morris," said Bernard, "it is our standard practice to do extensive background research of all of our candidates, such as yourself, well in advance. We become thoroughly acquainted with our clients' language, mores, traditions, and way of life. By learning all there is to know about a particular society and individual, we, therefore, become able to converse with our guests in the vernacular with which they are accustomed. Consequently, our interactions are transformed into one of familiarity."

"Very interesting," I said. "So, for example, as a result of your prior investigation, if I were a native of, say, a particular region of China, would I then be conversing with you and everyone else here in the specific Chinese dialect which was native to my point of origin?"

"Precisely, Morris," said Bernard. "We like to think of ourselves here on Holidaymaker as being, shall we say, flexible."

"Forgive me, Bernard," I said. "I am learning your ways slowly but surely. Most of what I am experiencing here is not only unfamiliar, but is also a tad bit confusing to me."

"No need for concern, Morris. You are doing just fine. Now without further adieu, please proceed. Your exercise in civil engineering awaits you."

Bernard then excused himself and left me to embark on the task. Before beginning, I lowered my head and closed my eyes for a moment while rallying all of the encouraging motivation I could generate. Positive, be positive. I can do this, I thought. When I once again fixed my eyes on the plot plan it was as if I had devised such a project a thousand times before.

Grabbing a pencil and right angle square, I feverishly attacked the assignment. On the plan I drew a cut for a drainage swale to run parallel with the existing road. I marked two locations for entrance and exit bridges to span the swale and connect the road with the parking lot. On a separate sheet of drawing paper, I designed the bridges with both plan and section views. My mind raced at such a swift velocity it was difficult for my hands to keep up. Moving to the parking lot, I sketched in a rough layout. For whatever reason, while analyzing the general gradient of the property it occurred to me that cuts were preferred over fills in areas where the weight of cars and buildings would be located. With the soil acquired from the necessary cuts in other areas, I formed berms on the east and west sides of the property. At strategic points in the parking lot I marked the location of catch basins to collect rainwater for the storm sewer. The speed and precision with which I worked was beyond belief. I consciously decided to not be caught up with the unexpected accuracy of my efforts. Uplifting inspiration fueled my labor.

Continuing on at a furious pace, I marked out exactly one hundred seventy-eight parking spaces. I added islands in the parking lot to contribute to smooth traffic flow. Moving to the shopping center itself, I indicated its location on the plan and then drew, on separate schedules, front, rear, and side elevations. I completed the undertaking with a landscaping schedule which specified the position of trees and shrubbery. The notion flashed briefly through my mind that an architectural scale model of the entire site—including buildings, trees, and cars—would be a fitting culmination of the assignment. However, I exercised restraint by limiting my efforts to the requested drawings. I was literally beaming from ear to ear when I hailed Bernard to examine my work.

"You have completed the assignment, Morris?" asked Bernard.

With firm conviction, I said, "I feel confident I have done what you requested."

Scanning the pages of drawings with a skilled and experienced eye, the hint of a smile crept upon Bernard's face. "Nicely done, Morris. Very nicely done, indeed. Your drawings are detailed and precise. Your initial misgivings regarding your engineering expertise were evidently unfounded. You have clearly demonstrated with exacting thoroughness that you possess a talented proficiency in the genus of civil engineering. It is clear you adopted a positive attitude in addressing this assignment. This is an excellent example of what you are capable of achieving. Be pleased with yourself."

"I am not a conceited individual," I said, "nor one who is caught up with ego and self-importance. However, Bernard, I must admit I feel a strong sense of satisfaction with what I have just completed. Are those feelings acceptable? I have no desire to offend you or anyone else here. I aspire to comply with whatever is the approved, customary behavior."

"A sense of satisfaction is absolutely acceptable," said Bernard. "Taking pleasure and delight in the fulfillment of a difficult undertaking is not only acceptable, but is a natural and expected product of successfully completed complex work. Pride can be tremendously energizing. We would not have reached our current elevated level of scientific expertise on Holidaymaker without the enduring drive that pride can provide. It is a source of motivation and inspiration, which encourages a dedication toward excellence. The positive approach to matters we espouse here, coupled with a sense of satisfaction within our staff, is the impetus for extraordinary achievement. The sensations you are experiencing show, to this point, you are flourishing in our midst. To use a colloquial term from your world, you are 'catching on' in quite a satisfactory manner."

"Your kind and complimentary observations are indeed heartening," I replied. "There is an amazing joy I feel within me."

"Your response," said Bernard "is indeed encouraging. Thus, step number two in your indoctrination has reached a triumphant conclusion. To continue any further at this juncture would be premature. We will continue with your growth and development at a later time. You should feel good about yourself. You have done well. You have coupled your fundamental core abilities together with a positive mindset and it has resulted in what I'm sure you would acknowledge were astonishing results. There are more enlightening experiences on the horizon for you here on Holidaymaker. Now, Morris, please relax and I will proceed to place you in a condition of absolute repose. Be at ease."

As Cassandra had done on my first visit, Bernard approached me with his left hand extended. Then, with the tips of his index and middle fingers, he lightly touched my eyelids with a slight downward motion and I departed instantly.

9

I came to and it was dark as hell. I was sweating like crazy all over my whole damn body. I'm talkin' soaked from head to toe. It wasn't really all that hot, so I didn't know what was going on with all the sweating. I was lying down next to the cock-eyed crypt where I had started out the night. I heard two cats fighting. Really fighting like hell. They were wailing their stinkin' asses off. The shrieks they were making could have raised the dead. So they just happened to be in a good place for it, 'cause they sounded close enough to be inside the cemetery fence, somewhere off to my left. I couldn't see them but I could hear them just fine. Way too fine, to be honest with you.

I leaned over and felt around on the ground for something to throw at them. I was lucky enough to come up with a couple of stones next to the base of the vault. Man, those damn cats were screeching and going on like mad. Even though it was real dark, I got a pretty good idea of about where they were from all the noise they were making. So I stood up and threw a stone as hard as I could toward their sounds. I didn't hear the stone hit anything, so I threw again. It felt like I pulled a muscle in my left shoulder after the second heave. It hurt real bad, but it was worth it. The second rock must have hit a headstone square on, right near the fracas, because it made a big popping sound and the bawling noises from the cats quit. Wasn't sure where they got off to, but the god-awful catfight was over, at least for the time being.

I sat back down and peeled off my drenched tee shirt. I laid it out over a grave marker and pulled on a dry one from out of my backpack. I'd bet I was reeking up a storm, but when you're a street person you become sort of immune to those types of body odors. I was kinda shell-shocked by the whole deal, what with getting back from the spaceship so quickly and coming around in a pool of sweat—and then the damn cats and all. I was pretty stressed out.

Being as it was still dark, I figured I'd try to get a little more shut-eye. I sat there on the ground, pulled my feet up toward my butt and laid my head down on my arms that were crisscrossed on my knees. I wasn't cold but I was shaking all over. I felt like I didn't have an ounce of energy left. Whatever little bit of oomph I normally had was drained out of me. I was weaker and more worn out than I could ever remember. To give you a rough idea of how bad I felt, this was coming from a guy who drank a hell of a lot of booze and only ate every now and then. It wasn't like I normally had much energy anyway, but for some reason I was completely exhausted. So I dug around in my backpack and found a half-eaten bagel. I took a bite out of it but it was stale as hell. It was like trying to chew a thick chunk of cardboard. A paste formed in my mouth that I eventually managed to force down. I sure could have used something to drink but I didn't have anything in my backpack and I didn't feel like going over to the maintenance building of the cemetery where I knew there was a water faucet. I didn't think I had the strength. Instead, I just sat there and put my head back down.

I couldn't fall back to sleep right away since my mind kept running over all of the stuff that had gone on while I was on the ship. What the hell was it all about? Everything seemed so damn real it shook the livin' shit out of me. Cassandra and Bernard, for crying out loud. I felt like I knew them as well as I knew Sonny or Horace. And what about the freakin' civil engineering test. Boy, I nailed the piss out of that sucker. How could I have done it? What the hell has been happening to me? Somebody or something is really messing with my ass, I thought. I just sat there shaking and quaking until I guess I finally dozed off.

When I woke up, it was broad daylight so I figured it was the middle part of the morning. I felt so hollow I knew I had to get some food or I wasn't going to make it. I hobbled on down to Truman Avenue and my little breakfast spot. On the way, the song "Space Cowboy" kept running through my mind. It's the one that goes, "I'm a space cowboy, bet you weren't ready for that." Over and over it went. I was thinkin' I had to get myself squared away or sooner or later I was going to go completely off the deep end. I got enough problems as it is, I thought. The last thing I needed was to go stone raging nuts. Although, I was beginning to think there was a strong possibility something like that might just happen. It was putting a crazy new twist on the whole wacko deal of living on the street, if you know what I mean.

When I got to the breakfast joint I threw away my empty pint bottle from the previous evening's nightcap and then checked my money supply. I saw I still had ten dollars left from my withdrawal from the bank the day before. I was so damn hungry I got two stacks of pancakes. I loaded on gobs and gobs of butter and drenched the whole deal with about a pint of maple syrup. I went out around the corner of the place and sat down in the alley to eat. I always liked to have a little bit of privacy at eating establishments. No sense sitting inside and having the customers take turns staring at me the whole time like I was some kind of wild animal. That reaction by the civilians tends to make me a little uncomfortable sometimes. Not all the time, just sometimes. Actually, they are probably the ones who are uncomfortable 'cause of me. I guess I am just doing them a favor by getting lost. Thinkin' on it that way, I gotta take a second to mention how I really appreciate you folks hanging in there with me and listening to what I've got to tell you. You're doin' much better than the regular types usually do in dealing with street people. Way to go.

I was so starved I put away every last bite in no time. Then I washed it all down with a big ol' cup of coffee. My coffee-drinking style is a strange one. I don't like to do the sip-sip routine on a hot cup of java. For one thing, with the warm weather in Key West, I'd get all hot and sweaty, especially after I had eaten some food. I prefer to let the coffee get cooled down to just below lukewarm. Then I guzzle the whole cup down in two or three big swigs. Drinking it that way, the caffeine kicks in a lot quicker and stronger. Makes for a fast, cheap speed-type buzz. I like the effect it gives.

Boy, did I feel like a new man after the breakfast. All energized. The only thing about my body that bothered me was my sore left shoulder from throwin' the rocks at the fucking cats. Those little bastards.

They show their mangy, flea-bitten asses near me in the cemetery and they are gonna get it, I thought. I had more than enough mind-blowin' crap to be concerned with than to be bothered by a wailing cat fight. Only thing cats are good for is to keep the rodent population under control, if you ask me. My apologies to any of you folks who happen to be cat-lovers. That's just the way I feel. Besides, the cats I end up dealing with are not what you might refer to as "domesticated." Most of the ones I see have quite an attitude.

I decided I needed a little change of scenery for the day. I wanted to do something different to get my mind off of Holidaymaker and everything. So I started to make the long walk over to Smathers Beach, which is near the Key West airport. I figured I might be able to pick up a little cash here and there from the sunbathing crowd. I've found it's a good idea to mix up my spots a little when I play the panhandling game. At the very least, I figured I could watch the planes landing and taking off at the airport. I always get a kick out of that. Don't know why I feel that way. I've never been on an airplane in my life. But I've been on a spaceship, though. A couple of times.

On the way over to the beach, I slipped in the side door of the Kokomo Bar. There's a men's room I'd used there before that you can get into without going all the way inside to the bar. That was good, 'cause there was no sense in alerting management to the fact I was using their facilities—seeing as how I wasn't going to be a paying customer. I was just quietly passing through and was making a quick pit stop to use the facilities.

When I first got in the restroom, I couldn't help but notice these two mirrors on the wall that came close together in one of the corners. I'd never really paid any attention to them on my previous stops. When I looked toward the corner I saw my reflection, but because of the angle of the mirrors, my body was kinda distorted. It was weird because from just below my chest on down I looked super lean and trim, but my upper body and arms and shoulders looked all big and broad and muscular. It was an image that seemed sort of strange to me. Something like a cartoon-character version of the way my body had changed to being in shape and being fit, like when I was back on the spaceship. The view freaked me out a little bit since I was really pretty scrawny, muscle-wise. It was like the mirrors were playing games with my head.

After I took care of relieving myself by way of the basic bodily functions, man, I felt like a hundred bucks. As possible as it was for me, I had come around and was feelin' pretty okay. The rest stop also gave me a chance to rinse my sweaty tee shirt in the sink. I figured I could let it dry out when I got over to the beach. We street people need to be sort of imaginative when it comes to that kind of stuff. You know, be sure to take advantage of all the readily available resources.

I even took that thought process a step further when, on my way out, I went around the back of the Kokomo and salvaged a half-eaten fish sandwich and a handful of fries from one of the open dumpsters. The food couldn't have been in there very long 'cause I only had to scatter a couple of flies off of it. I dropped the vittles in my backpack so I'd have something to eat in case I got hungry later on. Starting to turn away from the dumpster, I noticed part of a stick of pepperoni hiding under the edge of a paper plate. I grabbed that bad boy, too. Never did know when I might be in need of a little snack. Just as I stuck the pepperoni into my backpack, a man's rough-sounding voice bellowed out from inside the screen door of the kitchen.

"Get the hell out of there and get off the property," he yelled. Then, sticking his head out of the door, the husky cook roared, "You come around here again and I'll have you arrested for trespassing, ya bum. Get out of here!" The guy was built like a barrel and had absolutely no neck. His forearms were as thick as telephone poles and I figured he could easily snap my poor ass in two if he got a hold of me. The cook went on, "Go on and get going. Go do your garbage picking somewhere else, dirtball."

"Yeah, yeah," I said, walking away, "I'm moving along. I was just trying to help you out."

"Yeah, sure," he said. "Beat it. We don't need your kind of help, you stinkin' slime."

I just waved my hand and kept on going. I didn't feel like having any kind of confrontation with that burly fella, or anyone else for that matter. I made a mental note to avoid the Kokomo for a while. At least in broad daylight.

10

The next couple of days cruised by quietly. I had slept real sound all the way through several nights at the cemetery. No return trips to Holidaymaker. In the back of my mind, I was thinking maybe I was all through with that crazy jazz. I gotta admit, though, I was starting to miss the whole far-out deal in an odd way. One thing I did know for sure was I missed seeing Cassandra. Damn, she was somethin'. I had drifted off into daydreaming about her more than a couple of times, I can tell you. I still had the clearest vision of her in my head. Couldn't seem to get her completely off of my mind for any decent length of time.

Seeing as how the finances were beginning to run a little short, I decided to ease my way on over to the Southern Trust Bank and make a little withdrawal. And being as it was Friday—well, I was pretty sure it was Friday—I figured they'd be kinda busy. It turned out I was right on both counts. When I walked in, the single line to wait for the tellers had to have twelve or fifteen people in it. And when I was filling out my withdrawal slip I saw "Friday" and the date on the back ledge of the customer counter.

I got in the end of the zigzag line and spotted Suzanne at her regular window. She was looking as good as ever. There was just something about her tall, lean figure and pretty face. And her green eyes absolutely knocked me out. I never wanted to come off looking like a pervert or something while I was waiting in line, but I couldn't seem to stop staring at her, if you know what I mean.

She was dealing with some loud-talking, big-shot guy in a fancy-ass, expensive suit. Even I could tell that about the suit. You know the type. Thinks he's got the world by the balls and, therefore, everybody and their brother had better know about it. You got the impression the guy's ego was about the size of Montana. He was acting arrogant, mighty arrogant. Apparently, there was some kind of mix-up with his account and he was not happy at all. Suzanne, in a calm manner, was doing her best to explain the bank's policy regarding the situation. She was speaking in hushed tones, so I couldn't really hear what she was saying. But I sure didn't have any problem hearing the asshole's voice booming out loud and clear.

"I'm telling you," he hollered, "I deposited those checks this morning. What are you talking about? You're saying I can't make a withdrawal of my money that's in your bank. I put it in here and I want to take it out. Am I getting through to you?" Then after Suzanne spoke quietly to him, he said, so that everyone could hear, "I've had an account at this bank for ten years." Suzanne continued, softly, to explain further and he interrupted her in an even louder voice by saying, "Sis, you've got to be out of your little pea-brained mind. Give me my damn money."

I couldn't take it anymore. As I was starting to step over the velvet cord that kept customers in line, I called out real loud, "You can't talk to her that way." I got my front leg over, but my back foot got hung up on the cord and I tripped. I went down hard on the tile floor and so did one of the silver metal poles that supported the cord. There was a hell of a crashing sound as the pole banged on the floor at least a couple of times. Even another pole ended up getting pulled down in a chain reaction. To me, it sounded like a big ol' tray of dishes got dropped out of an airplane and hit the deck with a crash, boom, and bang! Well, with all the noise, I sure got everybody's attention in the whole stinkin' bank in a big hurry.

I came up off the floor and went straight for the loud-mouthed asshole. I'm no fighter, but I was fighting mad. I felt like taking the guy's head off. I wasn't thinking, I was just reacting, I guess. I got to the jerk at about the same time the security guard got to me. The guard was middle-aged but in good shape. He had that look like he could have been a retired cop.

I was pointing my finger at the big-shot and hollering, "You hear me? I'm talking to *you*, man. You can't talk to her that way." The guard stepped between the asshole and me, grabbing my shoulders with both of his hands. "Hold it right there," said the guard. He had a real stern look on his face. If there was going to be a brawl in his bank, there was no doubt this guard was gonna lock onto the scrawny street person right off the bat. No way was he going to lay a hand on the customer in the pricey suit. He'd leave it up to one of the officers of the bank to calm that son of a bitch down.

"What's the problem here, mister?" said the guard. He was fairly new, because I'd only seen him maybe a couple of times before. I don't think he knew I was a regular customer at the bank—just like El Jerko apparently was.

"The problem," I said, "is with this *gentleman,* if you wanna call him that. He was being awful rude to Suzanne, your teller there."

"Everything's okay, Ernie," Suzanne said to the guard. "We've just had a little misunderstanding with Mr. Paulino's account. You can let Mr. Scott go. He was just trying to help out."

By then, one of the young male officers of the bank had come out of his office to find out what all the commotion was about. He huddled briefly with Suzanne and then the bank officer escorted the hot-shot jerk away from the teller window and back into his office. Dealing with Mr. Asshole was now the young guy's predicament. The guard finally turned me loose and told me to go back to the end of the customer line. I straightened my tee shirt and ran my fingers through my hair on the sides of my head. Ordinarily, I couldn't care less if I looked a little mussed. But after that particular encounter, I felt like making myself seem a little more presentable. The whole deal had gotten me kinda pumped up.

Order had been restored, but the people ahead of me in line kept turning around and shooting glances like I was some kind of a criminal or something. To no one in particular, I repeated out loud what Suzanne had said, "I was just trying to help out." Then after a pause I said, "You can't talk that way to a teller in here." I guess I was trying to explain my actions, but I didn't think the other customers were buying my side of the story. They kept taking turns looking down their noses at me. It really didn't bother me much, though. For years, I had been used to getting those types of looks just because of my general appearance. You know, 'cause I was one of "those people." But I can't say it had ever been due to me starting a ruckus. And especially since the ruckus was started in a bank. It wasn't my normal style.

By the time I got up to the front of the line, things had calmed way down and the place had cleared out some. When it was my turn in the front of the line, I let a couple of customers who had come in behind me go ahead to the next available teller. I was making sure I wasn't going to do my business with anyone but Suzanne. When her window was open, she called, "I can help you now, Mr. Scott." I marched over to her with a little bit of a proud stride. Proud for me, that is. How could a low-life like me have a proud stinkin' stride?

"Is everything okay, Suzanne?" I asked.

"I was going to ask you the same question, Mr. Scott. Fortunately or unfortunately, I've had quite a bit of experience dealing with customers like that. But it was very nice of you to step in. I just don't want you to get in any trouble here at the bank."

"I don't want any trouble either," I said, "but I just couldn't stand back there and have the jerk treat you that way. He had no business talking to you like that. It was wrong and I just couldn't take it. You shouldn't have to put up with that kinda lip. And, by the way, Suzanne, the Mr. Scott routine sounds way too formal. Why don't you just call me Morris?"

"Fair enough," said Suzanne, "Morris it is. But next time, if there is a problem in the bank, why

81

don't you just let the employees handle the irate customers."

"Fair enough, yourself," I said.

I completed the transaction, put the standard withdrawal of twenty-five bucks in my pocket and said goodbye to Suzanne. She called me Morris again when I was leaving her window. Man, oh man, that was really fine. As I left the bank, I was feeling pretty good about myself. I guess I had a little bit of a swollen head about the whole experience. There I was, someone who normally steered clear of any kind of confrontation, going ahead and jumping into some rich guy's face to save the beautiful girl. And now she was calling me by my first name. I was about as close to feeling like hot shit as I could get. I couldn't ever remember having any feelings like pride or confidence in my entire adult life, but I could sense them starting to creep over me a little bit. Imagine that, coming from a stinkin' street person. What the hell is this crazy world coming to, I thought. As I went up Duval Street, instead of my normal slow shuffle, I thought I noticed a little bit of a spring in my step.

11

Several nights later, my third visit to Holidaymaker began as my last had, with a direct transition to the large chair in the circular room of the interior of the spacecraft. Yet, the duration of the peaceful portion of the transfer lasted only briefly. Whether there had been some form of technological difficulty with the transition of my body from the cemetery grounds to within the confines of the capsule, I did not know. A dilemma, however, was rapidly evident due to the fact I was sporadically cast from what had become familiar surroundings, into delirious and chaotic spells of hallucination. I endured a series of intermittently varying sessions which originated with seemingly being on the ship, but which then interchanged into an aggressive visual bombardment of kaleidoscopic streams of color. The transitions back and forth were so striking, they continually altered my perception of reality. In effect, deception had become my reality. It was as though the conversion from my ordinary life to the one on Holidaymaker had somehow been short-circuited.

There were moments, or hours—there was no way of telling—where I was sitting in the large, familiar chair in the circular room, which was lined with the monitor screens. Then, with no justification or warning, I was elsewhere, surrounded by a multicolored phantasm of surrealistic aggravation. What began as a dazzling, yet exasperating, barrage of rainbow-hued light, proceeded to deteriorate into a torturous optical assault by grotesque, gargoyle-like beasts. The fiendish images of these monsters descended upon me from all directions. There was neither audible sound nor bodily contact from their attack, but what suffering I withstood. I struggled, oh, how I struggled, to free myself from the incessant onslaught. Indeed, it was an onerous and daunting travail at best. From a physical, as well as mental, standpoint I was powerless to restrain or diminish the mayhem-causing assailants and their unyielding torrent of hostility. It was as if all of my faculties were lifelessly paralyzed to the point of complete immobility.

The brief intervals in which I would be transformed back to Holidaymaker were my only respite from the wretched ordeal I experienced. To my increasing dismay, the occasions of relief were drastically reduced with each succeeding cycle. The time on the ship became minimized to only a mere flash and continued to lessen until finally no lull from the flood of ghastly forms and overwhelming light existed whatsoever. I remained incapable of impeding the maddening assault of the hideous creatures. Over and over the streaking monsters persistently harassed me. The outlandish bedlam and pandemonium continued unchecked. The distress and misery I endured was completely debilitating as the unbearable offensive blitz of fierce, brightly colored creatures continued at will. As bizarre and repulsive as they were, the airborne gargoyles, at times, appeared to be fleeing in fear from one another.

I was the recipient of visual and mental torture the likes of which I had never experienced or even imagined. With great effort, I struggled to cry out, but to no avail. Not a scream, a shout, or even a simple sound could I generate. Nor could I produce any physical movement whatsoever. I commenced to presume I was losing the entire authority over both my mind and body. It was as if I was restrained in a frightful asylum and the inmates were staging a horrifying revolt. I futilely attempted to consider what cause or intent was the basis of the malevolent havoc I was undergoing. But I was unable to spawn any explanation as to the source of such a horrid and macabre event within the hellish netherworld in which I existed. It was pure unadulterated agony that was outrageously amplified to an immeasurable degree. I was defenseless and overwhelmed. The tormenting anguish seemed without end...

"AHHHH....AHH...Ahh...Oh   Man...Holy Shit....What the hell was that all about?"

I was sitting bolt upright in near-darkness on top of a vault in the cemetery. I was soaked in sweat and my hair was all wet and matted on the sides of my face. I wasn't just breathing hard, I was heaving. Chest was pounding like hell. Felt awful. Was thinkin' I might puke. I just sat there for a few minutes until I could even get enough control of myself to come up with a clear thought. It was a bad few minutes. I was a mess.

After my body settled down some, my mind started working again. I couldn't figure it out. It was the first time a visit to Holidaymaker had turned out like that. The two times I'd been there before had been great experiences. Well, I guess I was sorta forgetting about rocketing down the shaft the first time and plopping in the chair. And I was also forgetting about flying through the air and getting sucked into the ship a couple of times. But man, the trip I'd just gone through was some really nasty shit by comparison. Folks, I gotta tell you, the screwed-up connection with gettin' onto Holidaymaker about blew me away. I felt like I'd been roughed up by the

Devil himself, along with a gang of his best pals. And I believe they'd thought it was fun, if you know what I mean.

With only a little glow from a streetlight, I looked around and didn't have a clue what time it was, what day it was, or what the hell was going on. I felt like such crap I figured I must have really had a hell of a drunk on from the day or night before. Couldn't remember a thing about it, though. That sort of stuff can occasionally happen to us street people. At some liquor store I had, quite possibly, been over-served. Or maybe somebody I knew had let me have way too much of their hooch. Couldn't tell you. The entire day before was a complete blackout. Zero.

I didn't have the slightest idea of when or how I got to the cemetery. And to add a little intrigue to the whole deal, I noticed there was a hole in my jeans over my right knee. I could see through the opening that my knee had a scrape on it with some dried blood. And both of the palms of my hands were scuffed up. Some nice little bloody rips in the skin where they must have hit the pavement. My head was pounding like hell but I wasn't sure if it was from banging it around on the ground or from a whole lot of too much booze. Couldn't find any lumps or blood on the ol' noggin so I guessed it was the booze. Damn, I must have really tied one on, I thought.

I dug into my backpack to get a dry shirt and came across a pretty good-sized muffin and a half-eaten cheeseburger. They were both kinda smashed out of shape. No hint at all where the food came from. I changed shirts and took a few bites out of the muffin. Man, my mouth was really parched dry as hell after I forced myself to swallow the lump of dough down. Figuring I might gag or choke to death, I hobbled over about fifty yards to the maintenance building of the cemetery that had an outside water faucet. I drank like hell out of it and splashed my face. On the return trip to where I'd been sleeping I took a leak and then almost threw up from all the water I drank. By the time I got back to my spot, the queasiness had passed a little bit. The sky was still dark, so I curled up like a fetus on top of the vault with my backpack as a pillow. I was kinda quivering and shaking for a while. I felt like absolute pure shit. I guess I finally calmed down and fell asleep, because the next thing I knew, it was daylight.

12

Even though I'd had the messed up outing to Holidaymaker, afterward there was an odd similarity to the earlier trips. Just like the first two times, when they were much better experiences, there was a song I couldn't get out of my head. This time it was "Ride Captain Ride." It's the one that goes: "Ride, captain ride upon your mystery ship, be amazed at the friends you have here on your trip." Round and around it kept going in my mind. Couldn't seem to shake it. I can tell you I sure was *amazed* by the horrible incident, but those freaks who were torturing me sure as hell weren't my *friends*. Then, in my head, the song kept going on to the verse: "On your way to a world that others might have missed." What's with this song stuff, I thought. It was definitely a world I wished *I'd* missed. Don't think I would wish that deal on anybody I could think of. Had to get the stinkin' song out of my poor ol' pounding head.

After I got myself together with a little food and some coffee at my breakfast spot, I decided it was a good day to have a bit of a timeout. The best place I knew for that was the library on Fleming Street, so I made my way up there. Seeing as how life on the street is not very mentally stimulating, I take advantage of the reading material and other available facilities at the library on a fairly regular basis. The place was only closed on Sunday so, even not really knowing what day it was, I took a chance it was open. On the way, I asked a guy what day it was and what time it was. He said it was Monday and it was a little before 9:00. So when I got to the library it would only be about an hour until it opened at 10:00. Since I didn't have any urgent appointments scheduled for the day, I sat down on the side of the building and waited. I was still not feeling very good and I think I dozed off for a while. Not sure how long. The library was open when the cat nap was over, so I shuffled inside.

The official name of the place is the Monroe County May Hill Russell Library. It would be real easy to walk right by and not even notice it as being the library. It's a long, one story pink house that was built back in 1959. Over the entrance is a symbol of a book with the Lamp of Learning above it. There's a sign on the outside front wall that always kills me.

It reads, "Please do not feed the chickens—they spread disease." People, there isn't a chance in hell I'm going to feed the stinkin' chickens. I *eat* whatever food I get my hands on. The hell with the chickens. But there are always some of them wandering around outside the place anyway. Guess they can't read. Or maybe it's the nut cases who feed them that can't read.

Now, the rules and regulations of the library are pretty strict and pretty extensive. So, to save me from telling you folks about them, and then maybe forgetting something, I'm just going to list them roughly the way they're written on the wall when you walk in the front door. I think you will notice that some of the library policies seem to be specifically aimed at the target group of us street people. See if you pick up on that, too.

These are things you can't do, or do not do, or who won't be admitted, or what won't be tolerated:

—without shirt or shoes, smoke, food or drink, sleep, loiter, solicit, harass patrons or employees, drunk or disorderly (such as: patrons who are intoxicated will be asked to leave), feet on tables or chairs, bring in bedrolls or backpacks or parcels; in bathrooms: no shaving, washing clothes or bathing—And for this last little gem, I'm going to give you a direct quote. It's my favorite: "Library patrons, whose bodily hygiene is offensive, so as to constitute a nuisance to other persons, must leave the building." Now what particular group of patrons do you think the library administration might possibly be referring to with that one? Can't blame them for listing the darn rules, though. Gives them a whole bunch of reasons for kicking out any real assholes who are trying to take advantage of a free, clean place to hang out and kill some time.

So they have everything pretty much covered with the rules. There is even a guard inside most of the time to keep an eye on things. The one guard named Bill that I usually see when I go in is real nice. He's an older black guy, maybe in his sixties. He's in good shape and is always looking sharp in his uniform. I never have any problem with him. The trick, for us street folks, is to leave your backpack outside around the corner in the weeds. Then you stuff your pockets with whatever you want to take in. But you have to be cool about not taking in too much and end up getting caught violating the stinking rules.

It's kind of a street person honor system when it comes to the backpacks. There might be a bunch of them hidden all close together in the underbrush, but there's rarely any problem with your stuff getting ripped off. It's sort of like the same thing as camping or going to the beach. There is that unwritten rule: You don't mess with other people's shit. Us inhabitants of the street do have *some* principles, you know. At least most all of the ones who frequent the library. It's kind of a special haven in that respect.

As I came through the front door I spotted Bill, the guard, at his post near the checkout desk. We each nodded hello, but I decided to keep moving. The first thing I wanted to do was get to the men's room and clean up the scrapes on my hands and my knee…and maybe take care of other basic functions, too.

When I went through the reading room I saw a few street types sitting around. Most of them were looking at some reading material and quietly passing the time. I noticed Duct Tape Sally with her head buried in the stinkin' Wall Street Journal. Looking at her parked there reading away, I was thinkin' she's a heck of a hoot. Sally got the Duct Tape nickname for a reason. I swear she always has miles of silver duct tape wrapped around practically all of the clothing she wears. Her shoes are wrapped up completely with the stuff. It makes her look like she's always wearing some kind of crazy silver slippers. Her bag, her jeans, and usually the shirt she's wearing each have various amounts of duct tape stuck to them. It seems like the stuff is keeping ol' Duct Tape Sally held together, if you ask me. She kinda reminds you of a walking, talking silver mummy. And there she was, reading the Wall Street Journal, of all things. Guess she was checking up on some of her investments. I don't know how old Sally is, but her hair is gray and she has a bunch of wrinkles on her face that make you think she has some years on her. But, then again, most street people tend to look a good bit older than they really are anyway.

In the bathroom, I got the scrapes cleaned out and generally freshened up, as you regular-type folks might say. I came back into the reading room and sat down at a table across from Sally. Her face was still tucked behind the Wall Street Journal.

In a quiet voice, I said, "Boning up on some new financial strategies today, Sally?"

She lowered the paper, recognized me and, keeping her voice just above a whisper, said, "Hey there, Morris. I'm reading about this new Mutual Fund. It's a highly informative article. It's good to keep up with this kinda stuff. If you happen to require any personal financial advice, just let me know."

"I'll do that if I'm in need," I said. "Figured you'd be in here. Thought I saw your shopping cart outside near the other backpacks on my way in."

"Yeah," she said, "I opened up this place today. When I first got here, I saw you around the side taking a little mid-morning siesta. Oh, by the way, I happened to pass by Sonny on Duval Street when I was coming over this morning. He told me about the big plans you guys were making yesterday for when your brother comes down the next time."

"Uh, really?" I said. "Plans? What kind of plans?"

"Oh," said Sally, "Sonny said that you and him and Horace were cooking up some big scheme for a kick-ass party when your brother comes down."

"No shit."

"Yeah," said Sally, "Sonny said you guys spent most of yesterday afternoon planning it out."

"Man, that's news to me. I don't really re-member anything from yesterday."

"Well," said Sally, "I guess that's no surprise considering Sonny did happen to mention that yes-terday you were shit-faced in a big way. He said you seemed to lose it right from the start of the brain-storming session. Sonny told me that as soon as he and Horace started talking about your brother coming down next time and wanting to have a party and all, you kinda kicked it into a higher gear with the drinking."

"Oh, boy."

"And, apparently, when it got later on you just got up and wandered off and left your boys. Sonny said neither him or Horace could talk any sense into you. By the way, what's with the damage to the palms of your hands there?"

"I think I may have had a horizontal collision with the sidewalk somewhere along this foolish yarn we're piecing together. It's not so awful. I'll be okay. But it sounds like I was kind of in a bad way, huh?"

"Hey," said Sally, "all of us guardians of the street have our moments every now and then. It happens. I wouldn't worry about it. You might want to check with those guys and see what the hell you were planning."

"Thanks, Sally, I'll look into it." Then after a pause, "So how are things with you?"

"Oh, I've been better," she said. "I haven't eaten anything since yesterday morning....I'm starting to feel a little washed out....Kinda hurtin' for some cash. I'm not completely broke, but I am very badly bent. Pretty much down to just change."

I reached in my pocket and sorted through a few bills that were crumpled up. I unfolded a five dollar bill and handed it across the table toward Sally. "Here," I said, "stick this in your pocket and go get yourself something to eat. I don't want you starving to death on me. It would not be a good way to go."

"Thanks," said Sally, "I guess I've been letting myself down some with the panhandling game. You know things are going poorly when you're getting handouts from another street person."

"Look, it's no big deal. Those of us in this loyal fraternity have got to stick together, you know. Next time, maybe you'll be helping another one of us out. It gets spread around."

"Well, you're right," she said. "Matter of fact, last week I helped Connie Jo with some money when she was down and out."

"She hasn't gotten thrown in jail again, has she? No more telling the cops she's allergic to handcuffs or anything?"

"No," said Sally, "she was just havin' a bad couple of days. She's doin' better now. Look, Morris, I appreciate the cash. I've just gotta get my motivation perked up again."

"My pleasure," I said. "It's the least I could do for you, considering you helped fill me in from my, uh, little blackout episode."

Duct Tape Sally folded up the Wall Street Journal and placed it on the periodical shelf. We said goodbye as she was leaving. What a sight it was to see her shuffling out of the library with all that silver tape wrapped around her clothes. A little bit more coverage and she would have almost looked like a female version of The Tin Man from "The Wizard of Oz." And seeing her on the street pushing her shopping cart only adds to the total look. She claims she needs the cart to carry all of her stuff because she's a gatherer. No telling what the hell she gathers to put in that cart. I really don't care to know. You have to see her to believe her, if you know what I mean.

13

I spent the next few hours reading through some newspapers and magazines. Also, I began to feel somewhat better from the effects of the bender I had apparently tied on the previous day. Recovery from those sorts of ultra-excessive imbibing episodes generally comes down to just being a matter of time. While I was reading, I came across an article in the New York Times that kind of shook me up a little. The report said some guy up in New York, who lived on the street, had passed out in the middle of a heap of crates and boxes near a trash collection site. Son of a gun, if he didn't get scooped up by a front-end loader and dumped into a compacting machine. He must have come around late in the process and started screaming, but it was too late. They sorted through the compacter and found his body all crumpled up like a tossed out piece of paper. Done. History. Sayonora. There was one less street person wandering around the Big Apple today, I thought. I figured it was another good reason not to live up north in one of those big cities. I'll take Key West any day. But I did remind myself to not actually climb into a trash dumpster when I was rooting around the back side of a restaurant for some leftover food. Might somehow get stuck in there and end up like the poor ol' bastard in New York. What a hell of a way to go.

The library is a great place to spend some time during the day since it's out of the sun, plus it is comfortably cool from the air conditioning. On top of that, you can obtain some culture and education from all the various stuff which is available to read. It keeps a street person's mind a good deal sharper than it would be otherwise. The best part of all is the whole deal is free. Of course, I never can check anything out 'cause I don't have a library card. Can't get one because I don't have a driver's license or any other form of identification on me which has an address. That would be because I don't happen to *have* any specific address. One time, I did hear a good one about this guy who was outdoors like the rest of us. He applied for an ID card and for his address he just put "streets" on the application form.

Didn't work, though. When you live on the street and don't have an ID, it's pretty assured you can't get a library card. Or more importantly, I guess, a job. It is another one of those occupational hazards associated with life on the street. But it's okay, I can still come in the library and stay as long as I want, and read anything the place has if I follow the rules, which I always do.

I love the library. Looking back to when I was growing up makes spending time there now seem kind of funny. As a teenager, when I was going to school off and on, you wouldn't catch me dead in the stinkin' library. I guess, as an adult I've matured and expanded my mind a fair amount. Street life tends to stir up a little creativity in your style. Helps you to take advantage of different opportunities that become available. As limited as those opportunities may be. For me, the library is one of them.

After a while, the Holidaymaker situation started creeping back into my mind. There has got to be some rational and reasonable explanation to it, I thought. What the hell was the cause of all of this? I was convinced it was real. And I was convinced I wasn't imagining the trips. To me, it wasn't *like* I was there. I felt for sure I *was* there and nobody was going to talk me into thinking otherwise. Not that I was planning to let anybody in on it. But I'm telling you, the whole deal was way too real *not* to be real.

So, seeing as I was at the library, I decided to do a little research into the matter. I went into the card catalogue and looked under UFOs, as in Unidentified Flying Objects. Man, is there a bunch of stuff on that subject. I poured through it like a madman. The information seemed almost endless: vehicle interference cases, physical trace cases, radar cases, pilot sightings, electro-magnetic effects, government studies, scientific studies, it goes on and on. There are reports from all over the world on the topic, including the history of UFOs. Plus, there are articles and books by the skeptics who give their arguments against the existence of UFOs. After reading and reading, I hit right on what I guess I was looking for—abductions. Stinkin' abductions is what I'm talking about, people. My poor ol' butt had been abducted on three occasions, and I felt like getting to the bottom of it.

There have been all kinds of studies done on the subject of UFOs. Depending on which article you read, it is estimated that between three and four million Americans have been abducted by UFOs. Well, that made me feel a little better about not just imagining the Holidaymaker trips. In fact, when hypnotists and other scientific types have examined and interviewed people who have supposedly been abducted, the witnesses include a very low number of people with mental illness. So, I figured at least I had that going for me. I mean, I'm a street person and all, but that doesn't necessarily mean I'm certifiably crazy. Although a good many of us may be a little off their rocker in one way or another, if you ask me.

Some of the information said that people had experienced bright colored lights and had ended up in a small circular room. I was pretty encouraged by reading that kinda stuff. I knew what it was all about. But a lot of the reports talked about the aliens on the spacecraft being short, maybe only four feet tall, with big, pear-shaped heads and huge, dark oval eyes. Most times it said they only have three fingers and had no hair on them at all. They are referred to as "Grays." Well, the people on Holidaymaker all looked like regular human beings to me. So that part didn't fit. Some of the studies did mention that the leader or leaders of the UFOs were taller than the rest of the individuals who were encountered. It struck me that Cassandra and Bernard were taller than the others in the group on Holidaymaker.

Then I read where the majority of the abductions happened at night and in sparsely populated places. Okay, for me, it had always been at night when they showed up. That part worked. And although Key West has a pretty good-sized population, the island is a freaking speck of land a long way out in the water where the Gulf of Mexico and the Caribbean Sea meet. And as I told you before, the Key West Cemetery is a huge-ass piece of ground, the inhabitants of which are no longer among the living. It would seem like a perfect dark and vacant landing area. At least, that was what I was thinking while I was reading all the info. Some of the reports said people who had been abducted had been physically examined by the aliens. I hadn't been probed with anything I could recall. But I told you about when I was suspended in the entry cylinder it seemed to me the light beams were scanning and inspecting me. At least it was the impression I had gotten.

I pored over a ton of reports on the subject with an eager interest that I couldn't remember I'd ever had about anything. Some of the information talked about hearing a humming or buzzing sound and a bright beam of light and being "floated" or transported to the UFO. Man, I kept getting this growing feeling I could really identify with a lot of the stuff I was taking in. I mean, this was pretty darn close—at least close enough—to what had been happening to me. I was starting to feel like some kind of knowledgeable, firsthand authority on the subject, if you know what I mean.

I checked on some of the associated topics for UFOs which were listed in the reference materials. The Bermuda Triangle caught my eye. I'd heard of it before but I didn't know any of the details of what it was all about. I found out it's an area in the western Atlantic Ocean where many ships and airplanes have been lost. Sometimes ships have been found but without a trace of their crews. There are varied descriptions of the Triangle's boundaries, depending on which report you read. The three tips of the area are roughly Miami, Bermuda, and San Juan, Puerto Rico. But some of the articles suggested the eastern part of the Gulf of Mexico is included. One of the main things that kept coming up in everything I read, were reports of strange and bizarre compass readings that pilots and ship's captains would get at some point while they were in the Triangle. The first person to document that sort of activity was none other than Christopher Columbus. I knew for sure he was a guy who lived a hell of a long time ago and was supposedly the first European to discover America. And he's got a holiday named after him, for crying out loud. He must have known what the heck he was talkin' about.

Of the many different explanations for the history of wacky behavior in the Triangle, the one that jumped off the page for me was "activity by extraterrestrial beings." Now, knowing a little bit of geography, I figured Key West could possibly be included in the stinkin' Triangle. And, since I vividly remembered the details of having been on Holidaymaker three times—well, really two times—I was thinking Cassandra and the other folks on board could most likely be described as extraterrestrial freakin' beings. I'm talking about a UFO here. I'm talking Bermuda Triangle. I was all over this stuff now. I was fired up. Knowledge is power, right? I might be getting the power from learning everything I could, but what good was it going to do me? Who the hell could I talk to about it? I was figuring I was pretty much on my own with this particular issue. Of course, I knew I'd have to pace myself with the research I'd gotten started. There was no sense in getting overwhelmed all at once. I knew I'd have to just take it a step at a time. But I felt sure I'd eventually nail it.

I looked up at the clock and saw it was almost 4:30. Man, did the day fly by. I hadn't thought about my hangover for hours, and now I realized it was gone. All the studying and learning had taken my mind off it. I needed to relax a little, find Horace or Sonny, and get a little bit of Happy Hour underway. I was thinking maybe they could fill me in on the previous day's activities, too. I put all the books and articles back where they belonged and then made one last pit stop in the men's room. Taking a leak and making another quick treatment on the wounds was a good idea.

On the way out, Bill was still on duty near the checkout desk. He looked as fresh and alert in his spotless guard uniform as when I had come in. He could be tough on street folks who broke the rules, but if you acted right, he was easy to get along with. As I walked by I said, "Bill, it's amazing how much there is to learn in this place."

"Yes, indeed," he said. And then after a pause, "Lots to learn." Then another pause, "A fella could sit in here and learn and learn all day long… all day long."

"You know, that's exactly what I did today. I'm doing some research on this subject that I got interested in recently. It's some real complicated-type stuff."

"Well," said Bill, "you come on in here any old time and do all the research you want. That's what this place is here for. Anyway, you don't cause any problems, so it's just fine with me."

"Thanks, Bill. I'll be back one of these days real soon. I got more learnin' to do."

"You take care, now," said Bill.

"See you."

I went over to Duval Street and started making my way up to Mallory Square. I was figuring I'd run into Horace or Sonny at the Square or somewhere along the way. Off and on all day at the library I had been using paper towels from the men's room to dab the bloody spots on my hands and my knee. I'd gotten the immediate problem of the bleeding under control, but I knew I was going to have to put up with with some scabs for a while. Spending what little money I had on buying stinkin' bandages was an expense out of my limited budget which really couldn't be justified. The money would be put to better use by purchasing some wine or maybe a bit of the brown liquor. It would be an ingenious method of treatment to help me medicate internally. Having a few scabs, and they'd probably ooze some off and on, was yet another one of those conditions that came with the territory of living life on the street. I could handle the matter. It was no big deal.

14

As I headed up Duval Street, I did a quick check on the finances. Even though I'd given a five to Duct Tape Sally, I still had eight bucks left in my pocket. And when I shook my backpack I could hear some coins rattling around inside. Whenever I got change, I made a point of trying to remember to put it in the backpack. It seemed like whenever I put coins in my pants' pocket, I'd pass out somewhere and they would fall out and end up getting lost by some unknown means. If I remembered I'd had some change in my pocket and then it was gone, it would get me kinda upset. I always looked at it as an unnecessary and preventable loss of valuable drinking funds. The backpack kept my change in one place. This sensible practice would be still another thoughtful and useful concept coming from the practical mind of the street person. Important stuff, people.

Actually, I was a little surprised I had as much money as I did, seeing as how I had no recollection of the previous day's activities whatsoever. Remembering nothing, and based on what I had heard from Duct Tape Sally—not to mention the unexplained scrapes and cuts I woke up with—it wouldn't have surprised me if I didn't have any folding money at all. I figured it could have been a lot worse. I looked at it as eight dollars gained. The five bucks I'd given to Sally didn't even count. She would have done the same for me if the situation was reversed. I made a mental note to mention to her, next time I saw her, to stop spending her money on stinkin' duct tape and buy some food for herself instead. Food is key. I was thinking I needed to help her out a little with her priorities. You gotta be careful with that stuff, though. We're all individuals out here on the street. You have to respect that fact and not go alienating any of the group by being too overly instructional with advice and recommendations. You know, live and let live. We've all got our own reasons for why we do what we do to survive. Don't want to come off sounding like a know-it-all and then piss somebody off, if you know what I mean. It's important for street folks to stay on good terms with each other. Never know when there might come a time when some help could be reciprocal.

I crossed over Duval Street 'cause I was thinkin' of stopping at the Southern Trust Bank to make my first withdrawal of the week. But then it hit me that the bank closed at four, so I was over a half an hour late. As I passed the front doors and started to cross Eaton Street, I heard a big-time argument in progress in the little parking lot behind the bank. There was a guy's voice doing a lot of yelling and a girl's voice kind of half screaming and half crying. As I kept walking, I turned back and got a look at the couple involved in the argument. Damn if the girl wasn't Suzanne having it out with a tall, slim, dark-haired guy. He was dressed real nice but he sure wasn't acting real nice.

"I'm telling you," he said with his voice raised, "you don't go out with your girlfriend when I call you and tell you I'm coming over. You tell her something came up and you can't go. Got it?"

"Look, Curt," said Suzanne, her voice breaking up, "last night was the only night she was going to be in town. We'd made the plans to go out over a week ago."

The guy grabbed her arm and yelled back, "Listen, when I call you and tell you I'm coming over, you wait at your place until I get there, see."

"You don't own me," screamed Suzanne, "You don't own me, Curt." With that, he slapped her hard on the side of her face.

That did it. I took off on a beeline back across Eaton Street, going right toward them yelling, "Hey, hold on there. Stop that." By the time I got to them, Suzanne was crying full out and Curt, the jerk, was still holding onto her arm saying, "You do as I tell you. Hear me?"

I dropped my backpack on the ground and as I started to grab the guy's shoulder from behind, I said, "What are you doing? Let go of her."

He turned and pushed me away with his free hand, his slapping hand, saying, "Get out of here ya bum. Stay out of it."

I came right back at him. "Get away from her. Stop it!"

He let go of Suzanne's arm and wheeled around with a short, stiff punch to my stomach that felt like it went all the way through to my back. It happened so quick, I never saw it coming. It knocked all of the wind out of me and doubled me over. While I was hanging there, barely standing, he fired two quick blows to the left side of my face. I went down in a heap. I couldn't get my hands out in time and banged the right side of my face on the pavement of the parking lot. I wasn't completely knocked out, but I couldn't get any air at all and my head was in la-la land.

The next few minutes were a little fuzzy. But I do remember hearing car tires squealing close by. As I was coming around, I looked up and saw Suzanne's face. She was sitting down on the ground and had my head propped up on her leg just above her knee. When I could get enough air and sense to speak, I managed to get out, "Is he gone?"

"Yes," said Suzanne, stroking my forehead, "he's gone. I am so sorry this happened. Morris, I'm so sorry."

"Well, I couldn't let him hit you like that."

"Oh, Morris," she said, "this is really a shame. When you think you can, I'll help you stand up. We have to take care of your face."

Suzanne pulled a handkerchief out of her purse and put it on the right side of my face where it had hit the ground. My cheek had drawn some blood from the bounce off the pavement. As I started to get up she held my arm and steadied me while I got my sea legs. If I wasn't so busted up I would have thought the contact with her was pretty darn great.

"Morris," said Suzanne, "come on with me. I've got to do some first aid on you. I'm taking you to my apartment."

"Uh, okay." I was in no condition to be disagreeable. Whatever she thought was a good idea was fine with me.

After she grabbed my backpack off the ground, Suzanne helped me over to her car and put me into the passenger seat of her compact coupe. I held her hanky on my cheek and matted the blood from the scrape. My face was throbbing on both sides and I still wasn't thinking too clearly, but I had enough consciousness to realize I was about to be chauffeured by a beautiful gal I had admired for a long time. The way things were turning out, it made it almost worth the beating I had taken.

We drove down to Truman, went over to Grinnell Street and turned south for four or five blocks. Heck, I didn't give a hoot where the hell we were going or how long it took. I would have ridden all the way to Miami with her if that's where she wanted to take me. But it did occur to me, in such close quarters in the car, she was probably getting a good quality whiff of my general lack of personal hygiene. Another one of those occupational hazards of street life. But even if she noticed any bodily odors, Suzanne was kind enough not to bring up the subject.

She parked on the street and we got out and walked about a half a block past tightly spaced houses. As we moved slowly along, several times Suzanne gently patted me on the back without saying anything. She pointed out her place, and we climbed an outside stairway up to her second floor apartment. As soon as we went in, the first thing I noticed was how freakin' neat everything was. I mean, it was unreal how every single thing was arranged just so. It seemed like a full-sized doll house with all of her stuff positioned exactly the way she wanted it. On top of that, I could tell the place was clean as hell. It was so spotless, I was afraid to set my backpack on any of the furniture. I just put it down on the floor near the door. Like many of the overly-civilized folks in Florida are known to do, I even took my sandals off. When I bent over, the blood rushed to my head and made it pound like hell.

"Morris," said Suzanne, "sit down there at the kitchen table. I have to do some doctoring on you."

"Okay," I said. "You're the boss. Wow, you sure keep your place all tidied up, don't you?

"Oh, yeah, I like to keep things organized," Suzanne said as she put a handful of ice cubes in a zippered plastic bag. Then she grabbed a bottle of water out of the refrigerator. "Here, hold this ice on your cheek while I get some supplies. And have a drink of cold water."

While she was gone, I did what she said. Man, did that cold water taste good. Sort of flushed things down a little bit. Can't say it hit the spot as much as a good long pull on a bottle of the ol' brown liquor would have, but at that particular point in time it was close. Suzanne had turned on the ceiling fan, and the air from it had a cooling effect that felt good, too. On the kitchen table, I couldn't help but notice a number of stacks of various coins. They were set in such a way, it was obvious they weren't just random piles. The precise sorting had to have been done intentionally. Man, all of her stuff was put in such order it was amazing. I wouldn't have been surprised if she categorized some of her belongings alphabetically.

The ice bag was starting to numb-up the side of my face, but at the same time it was producing the pounding effect like one of those ice cream headaches you got as a kid. Overall, my head had a big throb going on. It was different than the hangover head-pounding I'd woke up with in the morning, but, by comparison, it was just as bad or maybe worse. I was responsible for the first one, and the asshole, Curt, was to blame for number two.

Suzanne came back with armfuls of shit that looked like the entire first aid section of a pharmacy. I'm talking bandages, peroxide, cotton balls, antiseptic spray and pretty much everything else you could think of to fix up a wound. You name it, she had it. She even gave me two aspirin that I washed down with a couple of big gulps from the water bottle. While she was working on the scraped up side of my face, she also noticed the cuts on the palms of my hands and then my banged-up knee from my unexplained tumble the day before.

"What's with these other injuries, Morris? What else happened to you?"

"Uh, the hands and the knee got a little messed up yesterday or maybe last night. But I'm not really sure where or when. I think I had a little spill at some point. I worked on those particular dings in the bathroom at the library today."

"Well," said Suzanne, "let's get them taken care of, too." She proceeded to clean out all the breaks in the skin, previous and current. I alternated hands to hold the ice bag on the left side of my face where the bastard had popped me hard twice. That area had swollen to the point where it felt like I had either a huge chaw of tobacco or a baseball inside my cheek.

"Thanks," I said "I really appreciate you helping me out like this."

"It's the least I can do for you trying to stop Curt. I'll say it again, Morris. I'm so sorry you got hurt. Curt has a terrible temper."

"You have a little bit of a red spot on your cheek there yourself where he slapped you. Are you okay?"

"Oh," she said, "it's fine. It's not the first time it's happened."

"It's none of my business, Suzanne" I said, "but why are you hanging around with a guy like him? I mean, he shouldn't be treating you like that. You're a nice girl. He doesn't seem like he'd be your type."

"Oh, I don't know, Morris," she said. "I do know he's very possessive and controlling, but he usually treats me nicely. I guess there's just something about him I'm attracted to. He's a lawyer and has also worked in the mayor's administration here in Key West. He just has this thing about being the one in charge and he's used to getting his way. He's a good bit older than I am and he just recently got divorced. I'm ashamed to say it, but I've been seeing him for a couple of years. I couldn't help myself. But I think it's over now. I've just got to get up the gumption to tell him. He's so domineering. I have been dating another guy a couple of times and I like him. He's closer to my age and is single. We've gotten along really well so far. I've got to break it off with Curt. It's just that he's so jealous."

I didn't say anything for a few minutes while she continued to patch me up. The silence was broken briefly when the cuckoo clock mounted on the wall just outside the kitchen cuckooed six times. I sat there thinkin' to myself, what the hell kind of advice can I give Suzanne? Life on the street sure didn't qualify me to be any kind of relationship counselor. But there I was, in the apartment of this attractive woman who I'd been pretty much in awe of for quite a while. Not only that, she was mending my various wounds, and she was basically pouring her heart out to me. I took a deep breath and tried to figure out what to say next. Counseling Suzanne on love life issues was not part of my normal job description. Anyway, I was thinking it was still really cool I was just sitting there with her while she doctored me. And that was even though I had taken a pretty good pounding for the whole situation to be happening in the first place.

"Look Suzanne," I said, "I don't have a whole lot of experience with this sort of thing. I'm not sure what to say. Other than it seems to me you deserve to be with somebody who doesn't treat you like that guy does. I'd just say things probably have a way better chance of working out for you if you were with somebody else. Anybody else, really."

"Thanks," she said. "I don't mean to bother you with all this. It's *my* problem. I guess it's just my way of trying to explain why he hit you. It shouldn't have happened. I'm sorry you ended up getting in my mess."

"Aw, it's okay. I'll be fine before you know it." Hesitating for a second and then half laughing, I said, "Well, as fine as somebody like me can manage to get."

After Suzanne finished bandaging the pavement-bouncing side of my face, she said, "Alright, Morris, I think I've got you all patched up. You may want to change some of these bandages every day or two."

"Uh, sure."

Shoot, I was wearing more first aid shit at one time than I had in my entire adult life—altogether. My knee, both hands, and the right side of my face had been dressed. It occurred to me that with a few more spots covered with gauze and tape, I might start to look like a male version of Duct Tape Sally, only in white instead of gray. Didn't need that. All of the bandages Suzanne had applied would have to do until they fell off for good. The left side of my face didn't need any bandaging anyway since it was pretty much just one big bruise.

Suzanne started digging in the refrigerator, saying, "How about a snack, Morris?"

"Uh, yeah, sure. That would be great." I was feeling kinda hollow, and furthermore, it wasn't a policy of mine to turn down food when it was offered. Especially if it was complimentary, if you know what I mean.

As she was getting things together, I went into the living room and started checking out the array of stuff that was on display. On what seemed like a million shelves were all kinds of statuettes, carvings, and ornaments. Plus, there were a ton of framed photographs. And, not that I really ought to have noticed these types of things, there wasn't a speck of dust anywhere. The whole room was like a stinkin' museum.

"You got some real nice figurines here," I called into the kitchen.

"Oh, yeah, I like to collect things."

"And a bunch of pictures, too. Are they of your family? I see you with the same people in a lot of them."

She came out of the kitchen, stood next to me and said, "Yes, this is my family, but things really aren't the same anymore from when these pictures were taken." Pointing at one of the photos, she said, "That's my dad. He died three years ago. And that's my mom. She lives up home in New York but she has cancer and the prognosis for her recovery is not good. My sister there, Lynn, doesn't miss a chance to remind me that I'm down here in Key West and she's up in New York taking care of all of the details for Mom. She likes to rub it in about having to handle everything. And that's my brother, Ken." She lowered her head a little and paused for a second. "He's in jail for dealing drugs. My whole family scene is really not very good at all."

"I'm awful sorry to hear that," I said. I had only wanted to make some type of cordial and positive conversation, but now I didn't feel so good I'd asked about the photos. Suzanne seemed to have everything so together when I saw her working at the

113

bank. Now I realized her family life and her personal life were not nearly as perfect and under control as I thought they would be. Appearances could sure be misleading.

"Well," she said, "we all look pretty good in the pictures. But it was a few years back when things were different. Come on, let's have some nibbles."

When we went back into the kitchen, the table was full of snacks of all kinds. Suzanne had fixed up, in practically no time, what you regular folks might refer to as a big ol' Happy Hour spread. There were bowls of nuts, crackers, grapes and carrots. She had sliced up a block of cheese and there was a small container of mustard for dipping. It all looked mighty fine. Particularly for someone such as me.

"Would you like a glass of sherry?" she said.

"Sure. That sounds great."

There wasn't a chance I was going to say no to a little ol' snort. Even though sherry was not my normal beverage of choice. Too much on the sweet side. But it would have to do. I did my darndest to hold off from digging into the snacks until Suzanne came back to the table with the glasses of sherry. Growing up, I had been taught *some* manners that had stuck. I figured this was a chance to put one of them to good use. I showed good restraint, and waited to grab a slice of cheese 'til she sat down.

We ate and made small talk for a half an hour or so. I had to make an effort to take my time eating so I wasn't shoveling the food away. Everything tasted so damn good. What helped control my pace was the fact that every time I chewed, my face hurt, regardless of which side of my mouth I was using.

Plus, my stomach area was aching from the body shot the asshole had delivered at the beginning of the so-called fight. As I expected, the sherry was really sweet so I just sipped on it. Plus, I didn't want to look like some kind of a lush in front of Suzanne.

At one point, she excused herself and went back to her bedroom. I quickly gulped down my half-filled glass, reached over and grabbed the bottle of sherry off the counter and filled my glass all the way up. Then I fired down half of it so the sherry was back to the same level as where it had been. I even took a quick pull off the bottle before I put it back on the counter. Since I didn't really care for the taste, I thought while she was gone, the quicker I drank it, the better for several reasons. I didn't want her to see me doing it and, in addition, I was really just going for the desired effect anyway. She didn't seem like much of a drinker, so I was hoping she wouldn't necessarily take notice of my slick maneuver.

It started creeping over me that Suzanne and I really didn't have anything in common. She had done all the nice things for me and we had talked, but I wasn't so naïve to think anything more of it. I figured she was just trying to make up for the beating I had taken from her supposed boyfriend. She had her neat, organized life even though she had her personal issues. Me, I was a stinkin' street personality. It struck me that it was time to be making a polite and timely exit.

When she returned from her bedroom, I said, "Well, Suzanne I want to thank you for all of your doctoring and all your hospitality, but I think I'll be going."

As I finished saying that, I thought I almost saw a little look of relief in her eye. I'd bet she probably had been wondering how she was going to get rid of me without just coming out and courteously suggesting that maybe I ought to leave.

"Well," she said, "let me put together a container with the leftover snacks. You might get hungry later."

She proceeded to individually bag each different item we had been nibbling on and then put those smaller bags in a large, zippered plastic bag. While she was at the counter putting everything together, I noticed she put a $20 bill in its own little plastic bag and then dropped it into the larger one with the other bags of snacks. I took the opportunity to discreetly finish off my sherry in one big gulp.

I picked up my backpack near the door and slipped my sandals back on. When I leaned over to connect the straps, my head pounded like it did when I took them off. Maybe not quite as bad 'cause of the doctoring, and the aspirin, and the food, and the sherry. As Suzanne brought out my "care package," she said, "Here you go. Beside the snacks, I put a few extra aspirin in the bag. Plus, there's a little something in there you can use for a nice meal when you want."

"I always heard you shouldn't say 'you didn't have to do that,' so I won't. I'll just say thanks."

"It's the least I could do for you helping me out. You know, you probably ought to report this to the police. Curt shouldn't be able to get away with doing what he did to you."

"Curt," I said, "shouldn't be able to get away

with doing what he did to you, either. But there's not a snowball's chance in hell I could press charges. Look at him. He's some big-shot lawyer. He'd say he was just defending himself from some grubby street bum who was trying to shake him down. Who do you think the cops would believe?"

"Well, I know what happened. And I don't think of you in that way, but I guess you're probably right. Anyway, stop in the bank and let me know how you're doing. Do you need a ride somewhere?"

"No, no. Walking is fine with me. I have a couple of things I need to check on. I'll be over to the bank in the next day or two, for sure. As you know, it's a regular part of my weekly schedule." I stopped for a second and then said, "Look, Suzanne, I hope things work out for you. For you and for your family, too."

"Thanks. I hope so. Take care of yourself out there. No more fights, okay?"

"I'm not planning on any. See you," I said, starting down the outside stairway.

I heard and saw the cuckoo clock tweet seven o'clock a little before I left Suzanne's place, so I knew it wouldn't be light very long. I walked back up Grinnell to Truman and stopped in a little hole-in-the-wall liquor store. Needed to pick up a pint of the brown liquor. My face and stomach were still hurting, so I figured there was a requirement for something stronger than the sherry. I'd only had a couple of glasses of that anyway. I remembered I had eight dollars when I checked after leaving the library. Along with the twenty Suzanne had slipped me, I was flush with funds. The liquor store wasn't very far from the cemetery, and that was a good thing because the cemetery was where I was headed.

After I left the store, I heard some live music coming from a corner bar. Just before the place, I stepped into the alleyway and cracked off the cap of the pint of brown that was inside a small paper bag. After taking a deep breath, I fired down a good-sized gulp. I was always careful about being out of the sight of the general population when drinking anywhere along the streets. Attracting attention was never my intent with that sort of thing. The band in the bar was playing reggae music. I recognized the song was the Bob Marley tune, "Three Little Birds." It has the repeated lines, "Don't worry 'bout a thing, 'cause every little thing's gonna be alright." As I went on to the cemetery, I thought about those lyrics. After what had happened with the fight, and feeling pretty sore from it, I sure was hoping every little thing *was* gonna be alright.

15

Hanging out in the cemetery just as it is getting dark is one of my favorite times. Not much of a view like at Mallory Square when the sun is setting and afterward, but I like it. Even though I was kinda busted up, nobody was bothering me, I was out in the open air and, most importantly, I had a fairly full pint of the trusty brown with me. I got set up on one of those above-ground crypts near the edge of the grounds where a streetlight on the sidewalk had just come on. Under the circumstances, I felt pretty comfortable. Hurting some, but comfortable.

I grabbed my book with the children's stories, took a couple of good pulls on the bottle, and broke out the big plastic bag of goodies Suzanne had put together for me. Man, I'd found out more about her in the last few hours than I'd ever known or even imagined by only seeing her at the bank. All of her organization and neatness and attention to detail were really hard to believe. For someone like me, she was tough to figure out. Just keeping my folding money and change under control was a big enough responsibility for me to keep in order. Heck, just *being* a street person is a full time job. At least it is for me. Suzanne kept a hell of a lot of other things straight besides just working at the bank. But, at the same time, her life wasn't exactly as perfectly managed as it appeared. She had her hands full with problems and issues that were way beyond me. To my way of thinking, she had more troubles than I did. More good stuff, you could say, but more troubles, too.

I knew there was never, ever going to be anything between Suzanne and me. But, boy oh boy, being with her at her place and all, well, it made me feel kind of sexy. I have to admit it. I hadn't felt like that in a long time. It wasn't a love thing or a passion thing. It was more, I guess, some kind of crazy, foolish infatuation. At least that's the word I heard used when I was a teenager. I remember dating a little in high school and stuff. But it seemed mostly like a lot of work and expense for not much reward, if you ask me.

But, there was one girl back in school I seemed to hit it off with. The problem was we were way too much alike. We liked hanging around with each other but we both were very bad at keeping up with any sort of a schedule or being serious about most anything. Plus, we both liked to drink too much. You combine two people who are similar in that way, and there's a darn good chance it's not gonna last. I guess you could say neither of us tried very hard to make it work. It wasn't a high priority for either of us. And I will tell you—during the times we were together, we broke a lot of rules. Underage drinking and getting into some other kind of trouble were pretty much the only things we had going for us. No Dean's List or college plans for either her or me. With the way she was so much like me back then, I wouldn't be surprised if she was a street person somewhere now, herself. I wouldn't blame her. It's an honorable profession, at least for the circle I travel in.

During my street career I haven't bothered to dabble much in dealing with the opposite sex. That is, in terms of a one-on-one relationship. I've just never had the urge or motivation to bother with women, and the extra responsibilities that come with them. That is, in a traditional kind of dating arrangement. Of course, the hooker option has always been available. But, in general, I've tended to not view that alternative as a worthwhile endeavor. As a result, I have avoided the prospective opportunity as much as possible. And I do believe I've been better off for it in a lot of ways. The main one being, when you go tapping such available female resources it most definitely tends to decrease valuable drinking funds. And this is not to mention other potentially negative consequences. So, as you can clearly see, I do indeed have my priorities. Maybe a little screwed up priorities from the normal person's point of view, but priorities nonetheless.

I nibbled a little more on Suzanne's Happy Hour travel bag, but I wasn't really all that hungry. I had put away quite a few of the snacks at her place and, anyway, when you don't eat much food on a regular basis, you tend to get filled up fairly quickly. So I stashed the plastic bag in my backpack. It was good to know I had some provisions in the reserve inventory for the next day or so. My immediate plan was to kick back, read a little, and finish off the pint of the brown liquor. Plus, I thought I'd check out the stars and enjoy breathing in the fresh air. Being on a fairly small island—which is surrounded by an enormous amount of nothing but water—makes for a practically pollution-free atmosphere. No smokestacks spewing out all different kinds of junk—none of which can be good for you. In Key West, the stars are brighter and the air is cleaner than anyplace up north. At least anyplace that's near a city. Those poor bastards on the streets in northern cities have it bad all the way around with the cold and the air pollution. Don't they know they're killing themselves?

It had been quite a day for this tired ol' puppy. Coming around from an awful hangover, having the heavy research session at the library, and dealing with multiple bodily injuries had made things way more eventful than I was used to handling. I was pooped. If the folks from Holidaymaker just happened to show up and grab hold of my sorry butt, it would have been fine with me.

16

I woke up and it was daylight. I had tried to stay awake for a while and keep an eye out for Holidaymaker, but it didn't happen. I guess I was just plain exhausted from all the previous day's activities. I'd slept like a rock. I was hoping I hadn't missed my outer-space folks. But I figured they would have gotten me if they had landed in the cemetery and really wanted me, whether I was sound asleep or not. My face was still sore and kind of puffy on the left side when I felt it over. But the rest of the bandages Suzanne had applied on the other side of my face and elsewhere were still firmly in place. I thought about Duct Tape Sally again. Never thought I'd start looking like her with all the tape. That was a scary thought.

I decided to look at my existing situation as a new day with new challenges to confront. The main one being, making an effort to find out what the hell I was supposedly planning with Sonny and Horace a couple of days earlier. Now, I will admit I get a little stressed and antsy when my brother, Randy, is going to come down and check on me. But when the subject came up this time, I'd apparently drunk myself into a total blackout. I needed to relax and settle down a touch on the subject of Randy's upcoming visit. Heck, Suzanne had a whole lot more worries going on about stuff with her family and her love life than I ever did. And she had been pulling it off to where you'd never know that anything was a problem, at least from what I saw. Maybe that's why I lead the tension-free life on the street. My personal makeup generally fits the advertised job profile for being a street person. Getting some wine or a touch of the brown and maybe something to eat was pretty much the extent of my concerns on a daily basis, if you know what I mean.

I left the cemetery and walked over toward Duval on Olivia Street. When I got to Center Street, I hung a right and went up to St. Peter's Episcopal Church. I knew that's where Horace usually crashed for the night. The priest of St. Peter's let him sleep in a storage area in the rear of the maintenance building. Horace was coming around from the back of the grounds as I was walking up.

"What's the good word, Horace?" I called.

"Mornin' to you, Morris." As Horace got closer, he said, "Good to see you out and about, but what the heck happened to you? Your face is looking pretty banged up, brother."

"Oh, it's no big deal," I said. If anybody asked me, I had already decided to blame the facial damage on the fall I must have taken a couple of nights earlier when I was wasted. I didn't want to get into the story of the beating I took from Suzanne's asshole boyfriend with any of my fellow citizens of the street. No sense in burdening them with that whole deal. It was far more information than they needed to know. So I just said, "I believe I had a bit of a fall the other night."

"Well," said Horace with a smile, "I can believe it could have happened. You were pretty far out there the night before last. I'd have to say you were pretty darn close to speaking in tongues, my friend."

"Yeah, I really don't recall much of anything. It's a big blank."

"Oh, I wouldn't worry about it," said Horace. "It happens to the best of us from time to time. But sorry you got hurt anyway."

"Thanks, man. What do you say if we go find Sonny and reconvene our meeting? I'd like to get a clearer picture of what we were talking about. Duct Tape Sally told me it had to do with my brother coming down."

"Well," said Horace, "Miss Sally would be right on that score. I'll walk up there with you to where Sonny sleeps, but I get the creeps being around that church. All them stories about ghosts and whatnot seem awful scary to me."

"It's alright, pal," I said. "Stick with me and you'll be fine. Nothing to worry about."

We went out to Duval Street and headed up town. During the four or five block walk I thought back to the various tales having to do with St. Paul's. It was the other Episcopal Church in Key West where Sonny hung out to sleep. As legend has it, back in 1866 the wife of the priest of St. Paul's was having an affair with the Deacon of the Baptist Church, which sat across an alleyway from St. Paul's. Apparently in a fit of rage, the priest set fire to the Baptist Church while his wife was conducting a Sunday school class there. She and all of the seventeen children in the class died in the fire. The story goes that ever since that day, the voices of the children can be heard all around the area, and especially in the courtyard behind St. Paul's. In the courtyard there's a small cemetery where interments were made prior to the fire. Some believe a sea captain buried there has been known to chase visitors from the courtyard. The more recently built Club Chameleon, which is located on the sight of the Baptist Church, has sat empty for years. They say, construction workers left their tools and equipment in the building and refused to go back inside because of supposed supernatural activity. Talk about some crazy stuff going on in Key West. Man, we have everything here. For me, if you add in my Holidaymaker experiences to it all, you can start to believe practically anything.

When we got to St. Paul's, Horace and I went around to one of the gates that leads into the rear courtyard. There's an overhead trellis along the length of the side of the courtyard that's covered with trailing plants. It makes for a real private feel. We looked through the gate and saw Sonny sleeping on one of the benches with his guitar case sitting on the pavers underneath him.

I turned to Horace and said, "Well just look at our boy, Sonny. It looks like he's sleeping in a little late today. Must have had a big night."

There was a chain around the gate with a padlock on it, but Sonny had showed me where the key was hidden in a little fake rock on the ground. It was right next to the gate, so Sonny could reach through, get the key, and let himself out in the mornings. He had told me the gate was then normally left unlocked during the daytime. Sonny had quite a setup by having a safe place to spend his nights.

"Go ahead and wake him up," said Horace. "This place scares the heck out of me. I got the chills all over. Let's get out of here real quick."

As we walked over to where Sonny was lying down, I said, "Hang in there, Horace. Everything's fine. We'll be out of here in a few minutes."

When we got to the bench, as if on cue, Sonny opened his eyes and was instantly wide awake. "Hey there, Mo. What happened to you, man? Your face is a mess. And don't look now but there's a freakin' black ghost standing right next to you."

"That's not funny," said Horace. "Come on, Morris. Let's get out of here, now."

Sonny sat up on the bench and looked right at Horace. "You're not scared of little kids' ghosts are you? They really don't bother anybody much around here. Except for *that* one," Sonny said pointing just to the side of Horace.

Horace jumped about a foot off the ground and spun around to see nothing. "I don't like that shit, man. Cut it out. I'm leaving."

"I'll tell you what," I said, "let's all go on up to the lot behind Steamers. I'm calling a meeting. Come on."

Horace turned and scooted out of the courtyard and through the gate to lead the way. I followed, while Sonny grabbed his guitar case and brought up the rear. With Horace still within hearing distance, Sonny called ahead, "Did you hear them just then, Horace? Did you hear their voices? I think those kids were calling your name. I think they want your sorry black butt to come on back. Maybe they want to play a game of hopscotch or something with you. Hee, hee."

Horace, who was walking ahead at a brisk pace, called over his shoulder, "The hell with you, you stinkin' redneck."

On the way to our rendezvous, I told Horace I was picking up a jug of red wine and I would be along directly to our meeting place. I figured it would be a good idea to have some liquid refreshment available while we revisited the prior planning session, which had completely escaped my memory. Plus, it was probably just the right elixir to get the boys back on good terms. It seemed to most always work with them.

17

When I got to the overgrown lot behind Steamers Restaurant, both Sonny and Horace were sitting there, but they weren't talking to each other. As I walked up, I said, "I've got just the ticket here to raise your spirits, fellows. Some fine red wine."

"Well," said Sonny pointing at Horace, "this poor ol' boy over here definitely needs something to drink. I thought for sure he was gonna turn pure white back there at the church. Wouldn't that have been something? Those little kids' ghosts 'bout drained all the color out of him. Guess you could say they spooked a stinkin' spook."

Horace lunged right at Sonny, yelling, "Why, you poor white-trash sonofabitch."

Horace was all over him, knocking Sonny backwards onto the ground. They started rolling around with arms and legs swinging and flailing everywhere. There was a whole lot more contact going on than the time before when they were drunk and had tangled over the last dregs of wine. I set the unopened jug on the ground and went in after them. For a second, I had half a mind to let Horace work Sonny over a little for being such an asshole. But I thought better of it and dove in to be peacemaker.

The three of us were in a big heap, rolling back and forth on the ground.

"Come on, knock it off you two," I yelled as I struggled to separate them. "You guys want to get us all thrown in jail? Stop it. You hear me? Just stop it."

With much effort, I finally got them apart. We were all a heavy-breathing, dirty, grass-stained mess. But because we were attired in our standard street-folk garb, the soiling of the clothes probably wasn't particularly noticeable. At least peace had been restored. Unfortunately, the bandages on my hands were now blood-soaked from all the grabbing I had done. And the patch on my knee was oozing blood, too. I'd had enough physical banging around in just a couple of days to last a real long time. And I was only making my condition worse by trying to stop a stinkin' fight between those two clowns.

"You guys have got to cut this crap out," I said. "Next time I'm just gonna let you go on fighting and then see who ends up in the hospital or jail or both." Sonny and Horace both started to speak at the same time. I didn't know whether they were going to try to blame each other or only say they were sorry. I didn't care. I didn't want to hear it. I cut them off. "Just stop right there. Both of you. No more talking until I say so. Nothing. I'm pissed off at you guys."

"But—," Horace started.

"You heard me," I said. "Nothing."

I picked up the jug of wine, cracked the screw-off top, and took a long pull. Then I reached out and passed it to Horace saying, "Nobody says anything until the jug makes it around a couple of times."

After about ten minutes and a few gulps of wine for each of us, I said, "Okay, it's over. No more fighting. You guys keep fightin' and I'm not going to hang around with you anymore. It's over. Got it?"

"Alright, alright, Mo," said Sonny. "We're going to start havin' some peaceful coexistence. It'll be Kumbaya and all that happy horseshit. So what the hell happened to your face? And your hands are all bandaged up. Did you get yourself into a brawl or something, Mr. Diplomat?"

"Naw," I said, "I do believe I had a spill the other night after I'd been with you guys. Not exactly sure what happened, but I guess I just banged myself up pretty good. That's all. I'll be alright."

"Thanks for the wine, Mo," said Sonny before he took a gulp. Then he passed it to Horace and turned back to me saying, "You sure were kinda out of control. No doubt about it. But I have a funny feeling you may have had a head start on us that day to begin with. So maybe it's why you went straight off the edge. Sorry you got hurt, man."

"Yeah," said Horace, "appreciate the wine. Tastes real good right now. Hope you're doing better." He raised the jug for a second pull and nodded at me, "Here's to ya."

As I had suspected, it didn't take very long for the two of them to calm down. After a couple of snorts they both were back to normal. Well, as normal as any of us could really be. Anything was better than the fighting, as far as I was concerned.

"Okay," I said, "so what the hell were we planning anyway? Let's go over things again while I got my wits about me."

"You told us," said Horace, "your brother is coming down here next week from up north. So, we all got to figuring we oughta have some kind of party for him while he's here. Sonny and I don't know him because we've never met him when he comes here to see you."

"Yeah," said Sonny. "He always stays up there at the highfalutin' Pier House and you go and see him. But we thought it would be a nice thing to do. You know, throw a little party so we could get to meet him and all. Something real nice."

"How the hell are we gonna do that?" I said. "Where would we have a party? How would we put that together? We couldn't have it here in this stinkin' empty lot. Now, I know we pool our money every now and then to get a crappy little motel room so we can shower up, but I don't think one of those kinda joints would work out as a good place for Randy."

"Well, fine," said Sonny. "But you've told us before he sometimes lets you use his room to take a shower and whatnot when he goes out around town during the day. We were figuring we could all come up to the Pier House and get things set up while he's out. Then, when he came back, we could surprise him with a nice party."

"Yup," said Horace, "a real nice party. You know, do it up fine. Me and Sonny could meet him and have a real nice party. First class....first class."

"I don't know, guys," I said, "I don't think it's such a great idea. It's no wonder I got shit-faced right away the other day. If this was what we were talking about, I can see how something like that would happen."

"Oh, come on," said Sonny, "you said your brother's not a bad guy. And this would be a chance where we could all get together. We'd do it up right, Mo. It'd be a good time. We wouldn't mess anything up. Just a little party for a little while. I bet he would think it was a good thing we were thinking about him and wanted to meet him and all."

"Yeah," said Horace, "it'd be a fine thing. We could do it up right. What do ya say, Morris? We'd really like to meet him. Everything would be all right."

"Well," I said, "I'm gonna have to think about this. I mean, Randy is a lot different than us. He's even different than most civilians. Kinda likes to be on his own. Especially when he's down here. I think he's just glad to be away from our mother for a while. She's always bossing him around. It's a vacation for him."

"He's single isn't he?" said Sonny.

"Yeah," I said. "Always has been."

""Well," said Horace, "that's even more reason for us to meet your brother. Show him we can be real friendly and sociable. A little party would be just fine. Come on Morris, what do ya say?"

"Uh, I guess it would be okay," I said. "But not for long, okay? Not for very long."

"Sure," said Sonny. "Not too long. It'll be a good time."

"So, how are we gonna pay for this?" I said.

"Well," said Sonny, "we all are just gonna have to work on savin' up here and there for the next five or six days. We'll have enough money to pay for it. I just know we will. It'll all work out fine. The only other choice is we could always hold him for ransom while he's here. You know, ask your mom for some big bucks so's we'd turn him loose when we got the cash. That would get her fired up, I bet."

"What?" I said.

"I'm just kidding, Mo," said Sonny. "Just kidding around. We'll have a real nice party. It'll be a good time. A real good time."

"Yeah," said Horace, "we'll all have a heck of time. How about another round of that wine there, Morris. We need to celebrate, don't you think?"

"Uh, yeah," I said, "let's celebrate...I guess. Randy does get the same room at the Pier House every time he's down here. It's on the first level and it's around the side of the place toward the back. His room is sort of tucked away from the other rooms. And there's a ton of shrubs and trees. Seems real secluded. But we can't be makin' a lot of noise, anyway. It's the freakin' Pier House, for cryin' out loud. Big time swanko. But at least we wouldn't have to go through the main entrance. I think he always gets that room because I can get to it without having to run into hardly anybody. I guess he doesn't want me to get any harassment from the staff. Or maybe it's 'cause he doesn't want anybody who's working there to think he associates with a stinkin' street person. I'd bet that's a big part of it, too."

"Well, heck, it all sounds just great," said Sonny. "We got a few days to pull everything together. I know we can do it. Mark my words. It'll be a good time."

"Sure it will," said Horace. "A real good time."

We sat quietly while the jug of wine made a few more passes between the three of us. I still wasn't completely convinced that having a party was really something we ought to do. The Pier House is a very upscale hotel. I figured we were going to have to be awful careful not to get Randy, or any of us, in trouble. A couple more gulps of wine and the idea began to grow on me some. If the boys wanted to have a party for Randy, maybe we could work it out. But it would have to be for just a little while. Not a big deal. Just a small get-together to talk and have a few drinks with Randy was all it would be. I started thinking it would probably be all right. Wouldn't cause any harm.

After a bit, Horace broke the silence. "Yeah, it'll be a good time. A real good time."

18

Over the next few days, I had some up and down feelings about the party for Randy. But every time I ran into either Sonny or Horace they were really upbeat about the whole deal, so I started to feel better about it. They each told me they were working hard to save up money for the party provisions. I'd even put aside some folding money in a pocket of my backpack. It was shaping up like we were actually gonna throw the little get-together.

The twenty Suzanne had contributed to the cause had helped to tide me over for a few days. Her cash, coupled with my regular panhandling income meant I was a little delayed in making it to my trusty financial institution. I was hoping to talk to Suzanne when I went to the bank, but she must have been off that day. Even though I was familiar with the other tellers, and they knew what the arrangement was with me, I didn't particularly like dealing with any of the rest of them. Not one of 'em was nearly as friendly as Suzanne. Not even close. I was real sorry I had missed her. My injuries had improved to pretty much just scabs, and I wanted to share that good medical report with her, seeing as she had been so nice to bandage me up. Even though, by then, all of the stuff she had dressed me with had fallen off.

The teller I dealt with was on the ball enough to remember to give me a letter that had arrived a few days earlier at the bank. It was from Randy. The second advance note was the standard method he used to communicate with me a few days before he got to Key West. Randy wrote that he was due in on Friday and was leaving on Monday. It was the normal length of time he stayed on his visits. He was staying in the same room as usual at the Pier House. He told me to come over to #108, early in the afternoon on Saturday so I could see him and then use his shower and other facilities. He would be going out for a few hours, as he generally did. So the timing was perfect for having the party in his room later that afternoon.

I had seen Sonny and Horace at Mallory Square at Thursday sunset and we arranged a meeting in the vacant lot behind Steamers on Friday around 2:00 or so. We needed to tally up the money we'd saved and make our final plans for the party. On the way over to the meeting, I decided to pick up a jug of red wine. I figured we'd need a little refreshment while we discussed the last-minute details for the gig. When I got to the lot, the boys were already there. Right off, I could tell that they were in a good mood.

"Good afternoon, partner," said Sonny as I walked up. "And what's the package you got there under your arm?"

"Oh," I said, "just a nice jug of high quality Dago red. I thought we needed a touch of some fine wine while we finish up our plans."

"Well," said Horace, "that was real thoughtful of you, Morris. Real thoughtful."

We each took a few good pulls on the jug before we got down to business. For some reason, I was starting to have a fairly positive attitude about the party. Both Sonny and Horace seemed to be on good terms and I wasn't nearly as anxious about how everything would turn out.

"First off," I said, "we need to talk about the financing of this deal. How much money have you guys come up with? I've got $30 to contribute."

"I did pretty good with the guitar-playing the last few days," said Sonny. "Here's twenty five."

"I guess," said Horace, "I'm low man on the totem pole. I just got twenty."

"Well," I said, "that's seventy five bucks between us. I think it'll be plenty."

"By the way," said Sonny, "Duct Tape Sally said she'd kick in ten dollars."

"Wait a minute," I said, "I thought it was just gonna be the three of us and Randy."

"Well," said Sonny, "I got to thinkin' Sally

could help us out with her shopping cart. We gotta pick up the fixin's for the party and get them to the Pier House somehow. Me and Horace can't carry everything ourselves. We'd look pretty obvious trying to haul all the stuff over there by hand. Sally said she'd help out. We can put everything in her cart and cover it up. That way we wouldn't be so noticeable, don't you think, Mo?"

"I guess that would be okay," I said. "But nobody else, you guys. Just us and Sally."

"No problem, Mo," said Sonny. "It'll be great to have her cart to use."

"Yeah," said Horace, "it'll be good to have Miss Sally helpin' us out. She's good folk. I just know this party is going to be real fine. Real fine. I just know it."

"Now," I said, "let's meet tomorrow at about 11:30 at Nutter's Package Store on Greene Street. It's not far from the Pier House. We can pick up all the things for the party. They have snacks and stuff like that, too. I can point out how to get to the room without any of you being seen by the front desk staff. I'm meeting Randy at his room around one. We usually talk for a little bit and then he'll be going out for a while. When he leaves, I'll put the Do Not Disturb sign on the door handle. That way you'll know he's gone. We can get everything set up before he comes back."

"Sounds like a good plan," said Sonny. "I'll let Sally know. I usually see her most mornings on Duval Street."

"This is gonna be a wonderful time," said Horace. "A real wonderful time."

We sort of let the afternoon drift by. Over the next few hours some of our funds were depleted slightly since we picked up a couple more jugs of wine. When it got a few hours before sunset we all went up to Mallory Square. The idea was, maybe our panhandling efforts there would replenish the expenses of the afternoon drinking. Plus, I wanted to stay in contact with both Sonny and Horace. I didn't want them squandering any of the money they had saved for the party. After all, we had a budget to work with. I was actually a little surprised they had come up with as much money as they had. With street folks, having extra cash on hand can sometimes turn into a recipe for disaster, if you know what I mean.

19

Saturday morning came and almost went before I woke up at the cemetery. As a result, I was late in starting up to Nutter's Package Store. But seeing as we outdoor folks have the advantage of not taking a lot of time with personal grooming or primping, I was on my way pretty quickly. It was still sometime after twelve when I managed to drag my butt up there. The good part was that Sonny, Horace, and Duct Tape Sally were all late, too. Lateness is practically never an issue for us street types to be concerned with, due to the fact that we really never have anything to be on time for anyway.

We ended up pooling together $82 for the purchase of the provisions we deemed necessary for our little gathering. We spent about twenty bucks on snacks. The rest went to pay for liquid refreshments and Florida sales tax. We got three big jugs of red wine and one of those huge bottles of brown liquor. There was even enough money left over to get two pint bottles of the brown. We were careful in our selection process to make sure we picked out the least expensive brands. It wasn't like we were being cheap or anything. We just wanted to maximize the volume of liquid refreshment.

All of us agreed that we had acquired the proper amount of supplies for the party. In fact, we felt there was maybe even an excess of the wine, considering it was going to be a short social gathering. So we finished off one of the jugs in the alley next-door to Nutter's before I went to Randy's room. I think each of us happened to be a little uneasy about the prospect of our group descending on one of the nicest, swankiest hotels in Key West. We all needed to relax and unwind a bit. On my way to Randy's room, I started getting a little worried that the boys and Duct Tape Sally might carry the relaxation process a step or two further. After all, they had a mess of booze in Sally's cart and they were going to be without my supervision for a while. I decided to make the initial visit with Randy as short as possible.

I used my regular outside path to #108 and knocked on the door. Randy opened it and said, "Well, hello little brother. You made it. Come on in."

"Hey there, Randy. Good seeing you," I said as I walked in.

"So," said Randy, "how are you doing? Is everything okay with you? It's supposedly the reason I come down here, you know. To find out if you're all right, or at least *sort* of all right."

"Everything's fine. How's Mother doing? Still crackin' the whip?"

Randy sorta giggled and said, "My yes, she's the same."

In general, Randy and I usually had somewhat stilted conversations, but the subject of our mother was one thing we could find some comfortable humor about. Although we each had a completely different relationship with her, there was familiar ground we landed on when her name came up. Mother was so bossy and domineering, it was all we could do to talk about anything *but* her. She gave us plenty of material to commiserate over. But I felt kind of sorry for Randy. For his whole life, he'd put up with all of the aspects of her heavy-handed dictatorship. Hey, if it was how he chose to live, who was I to try to talk him out of it. But I gotta tell you, I'd always had the feeling he thought the same about the way I ran my life. Live and let live worked just fine with us.

We made some additional small talk, which was boring to both of us. There really wasn't anything we had in common except for Mother, so it was just a formality I met with him in the first place. He told me he'd be out for a couple of hours before returning to the room. I said that I'd clean up and maybe watch some television. I mentioned I might still be there when he came back. About half of the time I saw him during his visits it's the way things went. So it wasn't unusual to him for me to be hanging out in the room

140

when he got back.

After Randy left, I put the "Do Not Disturb" sign on the outside handle of the door. I poked my head out and looked around to see if my cronies were lurking nearby, but I didn't see any of them. After closing the door, the worry factor started to skyrocket. I had been a little anxious about the party during the whole session with Randy, but after he left I started fretting big time. I was really hoping the get-together was going to work out okay. I tried really hard to stay positive—just like I'd been told on Holidaymaker. Actually, I could have used having Cassandra or Bernard around to help me pull off the whole thing.

After about ten very long minutes, there was a tap on the door. I opened it and there they were. Not only were Sonny, Horace, and Duct Tape Sally ready to join me. That stone ugly Connie Jo, the half-crazy one, was with them. She's all I need, I thought as I quickly ushered them in. When Sally pushed her cart over the metal threshold of the door, there was a loud clanking sound from the various bottles banging around together.

"Sally," I said, "are you gonna bring your cart into the room?"

"Of course I am. Where can I leave it outside at this place? Those posh-police commandos who work here would have it tossed away in no time. It stays with me."

"Well," I said, "the room's pretty big. Just put it over there against the wall near the television."

I grabbed Sonny, pulled him aside, and in a low voice said, "What the hell is Connie Jo doing here? It was supposed to be just the three of us guys and Sally."

"Look, Mo, Connie Jo is fine. She heard about the party and wanted to join in. She even contributed an extra jug of wine."

Overhearing, Connie Jo said, "It'll be okay Mo. I want to meet your brother, too. And anyway, you know I'm just a party girl at heart. I'll add some fresh blood."

"Yeah, Morris," said Horace, "Connie Jo is just fine. She got us an extra jug of wine to make up for the second one we finished off while you was visitin' with your brother. And she got another pint of the brown liquor, too. We didn't know how long you'd be in here with him, so just we mellowed out some. Connie Jo is real nice to contribute to the party, don't you think?"

At that point, I realized during my absence they had flung the drinking into a higher gear—and it was not a comforting feeling. My anxiousness was escalating enormously, so I grabbed one of the pint bottles of the brown and took a big pull.

"Look," I said, "everybody has to cool it with gettin' too hammered. It'll be a while until Randy comes back."

"No problem, Mo," said Sonny. "Everything's gonna be fine. We'll just have a little nip every now and then to stay leveled out. Everything's gonna be fine. Don't worry about a thing."

"Yeah," said Horace, "it's going to be a good party. A real good party."

20

For me, the period of time we waited in the room seemed like an eternity. Duct Tape Sally and Connie Jo opened some of the bags of snacks and put them on the table near the window. Randy had left the curtains closed, as usual, so as not to have any passers-by see me milling around the room. No sense in letting anybody who worked at the Pier House get the notion I was burglarizing the place.

I managed to keep the gathered gang pretty much under control during the wait. There had only been one minor spill of wine on the classy-ass carpet. That occurred when Connie Jo was trying to pour the red stuff out of a big jug and into a plastic cup. The cup flipped over and wine ran off the table that held the snacks. Other than that miscue, and some dropped potato chips and pretzels—a few of which had been stepped on—the room was in pretty good shape. At least it was the way I looked at it. We had methodically and conservatively imbibed on the wine and the brown liquor, making sure there was a decent amount available for Randy when he returned. Don't get me wrong, none of us were sober, but we were holding our own. There was one short-lived disagreement between Sonny and Horace that I effectively mediated. With the two of them, there was always the potential for some sort of argument, which, in turn, could lead to a physical altercation. I figured something along those lines was the last thing we needed.

Connie Jo always has the gift of gab, but the more she drinks the looser her tongue gets. It isn't that I have anything against hearing somebody talk. It's just due to the fact she is so hard to look at when she's telling a story—or really anytime. Connie Jo is scrawny as a rail, has leathery, weathered skin, and I've already told you about her looks in the face. She is a real piece of work. To make things worse, the booze seemed to be getting to her a little more than the rest of us.

"You guys gotta hear this one," she slurred. "Last February I was up in Fort Myers visitin' with my girlfriend, Honeysuckle. Her and me and a couple other gal pals had been drinkin' grain and iced tea all day. Let me tell you, all of us were tuned up. Real tuned up...all of us. Well, they have this big-ass parade every year in honor of Thomas Edison. You know who I mean. The inventor guy. Anyway, the parade is at night and it's huge. It brings in thousands and thousands of people. Thousands of people. So we were watchin' the whole thing and I got to thinkin', why don't we join in? So, me and Honeysuckle and the other girls stepped in behind one of the marchin' bands and got in the parade. It was somethin'. We were laughin' our asses off, struttin' to the music with our cups of grain and iced tea in our hands."

"Did ya get in trouble?" asked Duct Tape Sally.

"Oh, yeah," slurred Connie Jo. "The cops got us for public intoxication and disorderly conduct and we all spent the night in jail. But it was worth it. We had a ball. Thinkin' back on that incident...I better not be goin' back to Fort Myers very soon. I never paid the fine, so there's probably an outstanding warrant up there with my name on it. Guess I won't be seein' Honeysuckle for a while. And when I do...I gotta make sure to stay away from the cops. Don't wanna end up back in jail."

"You know, Connie Jo," I said, "you are the ultimate party animal."

Just then, there was a couple of quick taps on the door and it opened. Stepping in, Randy was clearly startled as he sort of jumped, put his hand to his mouth, and gasped as he saw the group of all of us in the room. There was also another guy with him who I didn't know.

"Randy, hey Randy," I said. "I'd like you to, uh, meet my friends here. They wanted to have a little party so they could, uh, meet you. They just wanted to see you while you were here. We have drinks and snacks and everything. Uh, I hope it's okay, bro."

The guy with Randy was on the short side and trim. It was very apparent he was groomed perfectly. Too perfectly. He put his hand on Randy's forearm as he leaned over and, in a light voice, said, "Randolph, the odor in this room is absolutely vulgar. I think I may faint."

"Look, Randy," I said, trying to be upbeat, "This is Connie Jo and Sally here. And, uh, that's Sonny and Horace right over there. Everybody, this is my brother, Randy."

"Pleased to meet you," said Horace, putting his hand out toward Randy. "I'm Horace, a friend of your brother's."

With a totally blank look on his face, Randy reached forward and halfheartedly shook Horace's hand. Sonny raised his hand in the air and said, "Randy, I'm Sonny. How are ya doing? And who's the flaming faggot who's with you there?"

"What are you doin' talking like that?" said Horace. "We're tryin' to meet Morris' brother here."

"I know," said Sonny. "I was just wonderin' who the sweet little thing is. He's queer as shit."

"Cut it out, Sonny," I said. "It's okay Randy. Sonny just has a way with words sometimes. He doesn't mean any harm. Right, Sonny?"

"Yeah, don't be like that," said Horace as he gave Sonny a shove that knocked him into the table with the snacks on it. Chips, pretzels and an opened, half-empty jug of red wine went flying.

I yelled for them to stop, but it was too late. It was game on. Sonny came back at Horace and pushed him backwards onto the bed. The firmness of the mattress helped to recoil Horace back up on a rebound. He nailed Sonny with punch that landed square on the side of his neck. The blow sent Sonny backwards into the curtains hanging above the air conditioner unit. He grabbed onto them to break his fall as he was going down. A panel of the curtains went to the floor with him, pulling loose one side of the rod that anchored them to the wall above. It left one half of the window uncovered just in case anyone walking by decided to stop and catch a glimpse of the mayhem inside the room.

"Oh, how crude," Randy's friend shrieked.

As Sonny got up and barreled at Horace, he said, "I'm gonna get you now, you black bastard."

I wanted to try to separate the combatants, but the whole scene with Randy and the other guy coming into the room had, for the moment, stunned me and frozen me still. All I managed to get out was, "Knock it off, you two. Stop it."

The momentum of Sonny's lunge and collision sent Horace backward, knocking him hard into Duct Tape Sally's grocery cart. The cart then banged into the ornate pedestal that supported the fancy-ass television. The TV went to the floor facedown, shattering the screen with a loud bang. It became pretty much general bedlam in the room at that point.

"Whoa-oa!" yelled Connie Jo, "You go for it, boys. Nothin' like a good fight."

"Hey, get away from my cart, you guys!" shouted Duct Tape Sally.

I managed to get between Sonny and Horace, but most of the time while I was trying to break up the brawl I was looking back toward Randy calling, "I'm sorry Randy. I'm sorry. It's gonna be okay." I was alternating between repeating that attempted apology and hollering at the guys to stop fighting. During the whole ordeal, Randy just stood there motionless. His jaw was dropped wide open and he didn't say a word. When the hostile combat finally came to an end, Randy seemed to snap out of his daze.

"Get out of here," yelled Randy. "Morris, get them all out of here, *now*. Go!"

We beat a hasty retreat out of the room, which included Sonny and Connie Jo snatching up the remaining bottles of wine and brown liquor. Duct Tape Sally grabbed her grocery cart and led the way with two loud poundings of its wheels as it banged over the threshold of the door. "Nice meeting you, fellas," she called over her shoulder.

147

Sonny followed, with Connie Jo staggering behind him. It was a relatively swift, efficient exit considering the circumstances. Going out the door, Connie Jo tripped on the threshold and dropped one of the full pints of brown liquor, which smashed just outside on the concrete walk. Glass and booze exploded in all directions.

"Shit," she said. "I hate that." She was drunkenly wobbling back and forth as she tried to use her sandal to push the broken glass to one side of the door opening.

"Just leave it," said Randy in a stern voice.

Horace followed Connie Jo out. He turned back toward Randy and said, "Sorry about the mess. Real sorry. We didn't mean no harm."

"Look, Randy," I said. "I'll make it up to you. I'll—"

"Go!" hollered Randy, interrupting me. "Just get out of here."

As I hustled out and went along the walkway on the side of the hotel, I heard the guy with Randy saying, "My, what a horrid bunch of creatures they are. And the *women*. One was all wrapped up in duct tape and the other was just dreadful looking. And the *smell*. Oh, mercy." Then he leaned out the door, raised his voice, and called, "Uncivilized, revolting monsters."

I felt awful about what had happened. The whole deal had been a disaster from the very beginning. Randy didn't even get a chance to introduce his acquaintance. I never found out the guy's name. And we hadn't gotten to have a drink with them or anything. As I started to cross the street in front of the Pier House, I saw the others were waiting on the opposite sidewalk. Connie Jo's condition must have quickly deteriorated further because she was passed out in Duct Tape Sally's grocery cart, surrounded by the leftover bottles from the ill-advised social gathering. I stopped for a second, looked at the group of them, and thought about what Randy's friend had just said about us all. He'd nailed it right on the money, if you know what I mean.

PART TWO

21

Hello again, people. Well, two or three months have passed since the day of the debacle at the Pier House. Glad you're still there listening. And, by the way, I did just happen to pick up a bottle of the brown I can work on while we move forward and go over what's happened in the mean time. So just sit back, relax, and take it all in. Let me have a little pull here.....ahhh. It sure helps to put a soothing on the ol' vocal cords. I may feel the need for a drink and, therefore, take the opportunity to sneak a nip here and there as we proceed. You won't even know when it's happening. It'll be something kinda like when I pulled the fast one with the sherry at Suzanne's place. I'll make a determined effort to be real stealth.

To bring you up to date, Horace got his sorry ass out of jail a couple of days after his unfortunate pissing incident in front of the Fidelity Bank. I knew they wouldn't keep him in the slammer for too long. And, besides, the legal system types knew they couldn't get a paid fine out of him even if it ever came up to trial. They realized he was merely a simple citizen of the street. Horace was only taking a leak, for cryin' out loud. Not like he was one of your violent criminals or anything. And he sure wasn't burglarizing someplace or sticking up somebody with a gun or a knife. I will admit that peeing in public is not a very cool thing to do. I'm well aware of that. But it's certainly a far more minor transgression in comparison to a violent crime, if you ask me.

Now, I bet you thought I was going to tell you everything else had gotten back to normal around here on the streets of Key West. As normal as it gets for us outdoor residents, that is. But, actually, things have changed quite a bit—in several ways. Some good, some not so good. And one not good at all.

In the aftermath of the big fiasco in Randy's hotel room, there was a major adjustment to the setup I'd had at the Southern Trust Bank. To no one's surprise, least of all mine, my mother naturally caught wind of what happened at the so-called party. And, as you might expect, she got really pissed off. In a letter I received at the bank, she told me she paid the Pier House for all the damage that had occurred. As a result of the unfortunate incident, she finally decided she didn't want to have anything more to do with me. Can't say I blame her for taking that stance. But instead of just disownin' me, lock, stock, and barrel, I guess you could say she bought me off. The whole arrangement of getting money twice a week at the bank was declared over. In its place, I got a one-time lump sum payment of $30,000 from her. Now, it might sound like a sizeable sum of cash, but you have to realize it is the end of the line in my relationship with Mother. I'm talking, permanently. I'm talking, for good. She made it pretty darn clear, so that's the way I took it.

Lookin' back, I think one of the main reasons there was the twice-weekly withdrawal deal at the bank was so I could only get my hands on a total of $50 a week. With that setup, my mother most likely figured I wouldn't be able to blow a big bunch of bucks all at once on the booze—or anything else just as bad for you, or worse. She probably thought I could very likely end up killing myself by way of overindulgence in something if I had too much cash. But I think she had gotten to the point where she really didn't care about that prospect anymore. You could almost surely look at her pronouncement as a final financial farewell gesture. I got to think-ing, and calculated I could take out the same $50 a week and it would last me ten or twelve years. I said the hell with any such plan. I'm not so sure I'll live that long anyway. Seeing as I'm not planning on leaving money to anybody when I pass on, I took half of the money and bought myself a previously owned sailboat. A *very* previously owned sailboat. You wouldn't see anything like it at a boat show, if you know what I mean.

The sailboat needed a lot of work, as you might imagine. I anchored it in a mooring field on the east side of the island, not too far from the air-port. I guess you could say it was on the outskirts of town—I've always loved that expression, so that's the way I thought about it. Apparently, there's al-ways been a lot of controversy with the City of Key West over whether or not they're gonna shut down the anchorage area. Any such eventuality would directly affect the live-aboards—as the expression goes—who happen to reside there. My plan was to stay put until I got kicked out. I figured I could always sell the damn boat if I couldn't find a place

I could keep it for cheap. I'm no money bags, you know. Don't ever want to go cutting too far into the drinking reserves. That would be bad business.

You'll never guess what I named the sailboat. In honor of my acquaintances from outer space, I christened her, Holidaymaker. For the ceremony, of which Horace was the only attendee, I used an empty wine jug and broke it across her bow and everything. When Horace asked me where I came up with the name, I told him I just made it up. He did like it, though. I never did get around to painting over the old name and re-lettering her. My plan was do it eventually. In the meantime, it was Holidaymaker to me. Wasn't real thrilled with Pukin' Pelican, which was the name on the stern. Although, that name did have an out of the ordinary ring to it. I figured while it was still painted on there, it might help to scare people away—which was a good thing.

Horace stayed on the boat with me, too, on and off. Mostly on. He thought it was a great idea. Sonny didn't want any part of it. He said he'd get seasick in a heartbeat just sittin' on it, even anchored up. Horace got a hold of a couple of fishing rods and some tackle. He always got the biggest kick out of dropping a line in the water and trying to catch a fish or two. We had this little propane grill to cook our catch on, if we actually caught anything. My only worry was, hopefully, we didn't get too drunk, knock over the grill while it was cookin' away and end up catching the boat on fire. Being the tinder box that it was, the stinkin' boat would have burned up in a minute. So I tried to keep my wits about me when we were operating the grill.

Horace and I really didn't take the boat out sailing. Okay, I'll be straight with you—we never moved the boat at all, ever. It sat anchored the whole damn time in the same stinkin' spot where it was the day I bought it. I wasn't planning on taking it anywhere. Didn't know how to sail it in the first place. And the piece-of-crap motor it had, barely ran. Where the hell would I have wanted to take it anyway? I looked at it as a floating condo. Even though there were other boats nearby, it was like we didn't really have next-door neighbors. Oh, we would give a wave back and forth and all, but everybody else was sittin' out there on the water by themselves for the same reason we were. We all just wanted to be alone in our own little nautical world. No one knockin' on your front door. So, although Horace and I were living in a slightly different manner compared to the past, we hadn't changed all that much. But seeing as I was somewhat of a property owner, I guess you could say I'd taken a modest step up in the world. Even though said property happened to be a barnacle-encrusted rattletrap of a sailboat.

I do have to tell you I didn't mind Horace bunkin' on the boat with me at all. He did his part to keep stuff as orderly as people like us care to make things. He also provided me with some company and lent a hand with the slight amount of upkeep on the boat that occasionally occurred. We were actually trying to clean up our act a little. As little as possible, mind you. The step-by-step transition for a street person to go back to the regular folks' way of living is a conversion that is complex and complicated. We were taking it gradually. And, at the time, there was a fair chance a total transition would never be completed for either of us, anyway.

Along with the boat, I got this little skiff that putt-putted us back and forth to the nearby dock so we could get back on the street—which is where we probably belonged. I even took some of the money and bought each of us an old bicycle. They were those sturdy beach cruisers with baskets to carry various provisions. I bought the bikes from a bicycle rental business on Duval Street just down from Petronia. We'd take the long ride into Old Town and lock 'em up so we could conduct our characteristic form of commerce on foot. Now, the truth is, each of us did spend occasional—okay, more than occasional—nights over in town in much the same way as we used to. There was any number of times when one, or the other, or both of us, would get too juiced up to attempt to operate a bike in an effort to get back to the sailboat. Plus, even if that uncertain undertaking was accomplished without incident, there was the operation of the skiff to consider. And that little journey was on the water, usually at night, which meant it was dark. Not a sensible idea, especially if you're somewhat woozy from the day's activities.

In such cases when either of us would be staying overnight on dry land, we tried to make sure our particular bike was locked up as safely as possible. We'd then revert back to our previous sleeping practice. Horace would crash at St. Peter's Church like he used to, and I'd make my way over to the cemetery. That is, if there was no unanticipated passing out at some random location in the fair city of Key West.

You gotta believe me when I tell you I couldn't stay away from the cemetery for very long. There was no telling when Holidaymaker might show up and want to take me on board. And that, by the way, was something which has been known to happen. Be patient, I'll get around to that issue later.

22

One day not long after I got the sailboat, I was in town and decided to stop in at the Southern Trust Bank. As usual, there were two benefits achieved by going there. I could withdraw a little cash to supplement my panhandling operation. And just as importantly, I got the opportunity to talk with Suzanne. I waited my turn in the rat maze line and even let a couple of other customers go ahead of me when I got to the front. I was employing my standard technique to make sure I got to do my banking business with Suzanne. She was well aware of the change which had occurred for me regarding the previous setup at the bank. She also knew I had gotten the boat. Suzanne was looking good, as usual. However, as I walked over to her window I did notice she looked a little down in the mouth.

"How's it going, Suzanne?" I said.

"Good day, Captain Morris. I wish I could say it's going well, but it's really not."

"What's up?"

"Well," said Suzanne, "my sister called yesterday and told me our mother has taken a turn for the worse."

"I'm real sorry to hear that."

"Thanks," she said. "I'm sort of torn as to what to do. I want to go up and see her, but what if something happens to her right after I get back here? She's had setbacks before and then she came around to feeling better. I already have scheduled some vacation time and have plane tickets to go up there in about a month. To fly on short notice is expensive. Of course, I'll go up if she passes away. But extra roundtrip flights close together are not exactly in my budget. I just don't know what to do right now."

"Look Suzanne," I said, "I've got a fair amount of money in this bank. And I can get my hands on it anytime I want. Not like the way it was here before. I'll give you a hand with the cost of your tickets if you want to go up there now."

"That's very nice of you, Morris," she said. "But you keep the money in your account for yourself. You never know when you might have to make some repairs to that boat of yours. And anyway, you've helped me out before in other ways, and I appreciate it. What you did out in the parking lot a couple of months ago means more to me than money."

"I thank you for saying that, but you're welcome to any help I can give you, financially or otherwise. I mean anytime. And, by the way, how have things been going with your social life? I hope you're not still seeing my sparring partner. Well, we weren't actually sparring. I was acting more like a punching bag."

"There's good news on that front," said Suzanne. "I've finally broken it off with Curt. It took me a while to get to the point of finalizing it with him, but it's over now, at least from my view. He wasn't happy about it at all. He's just so possessive and controlling. Sometimes I still wonder if he'll flip out again on me. He's tried calling me, off and on, and leaving these long-winded messages. I don't call him back. I just hope he will eventually realize it's over for good. I am seeing the other guy I told you about. We've been hitting it off really well. I'm definitely happier about all that now."

"Well," I said, "that *is* good news. I think you are doing the right thing. If you're happy, I'm happy for you. And, anyway, I'd just as soon not have to go any more rounds with Curt. I'm not much of a fighter."

"You might not be a fighter, but you're a good guy," she said as she handed me my $25 withdrawal. "Take care."

"You do the same, Suzanne," I said. "See you in a few days. And I hope by then your mom's doing better. I'll be thinking about you. And what I said about the plane tickets is a standing offer."

"Thanks, Morris," said Suzanne. "I'll let you know how things are going."

Turning away from her window, it hit me how ironic it was to be offering to buy Suzanne airline tickets. It was pretty obvious our standing in society was light-years apart. Here was the street person, or the live-aboard, offering money to the bank teller. Although I would have done it in a heartbeat, the prospect of giving money to Suzanne kinda spun my mind, and probably hers, too. It just seemed comical to me in an odd sort of way.

As I walked through the lobby toward the front of the bank, my thought process was immediately snapped back to reality. Two guys wearing ski masks burst through the double doors and went past me into the bank lobby. One of them was holding a handgun and the other one was pulling a canvas tote bag out from under his shirt. The guy with the bag didn't appear to be armed. Although I'd never witnessed anything like what was happening, it sure looked to me like they were planning on robbing the bank.

"Everybody down on the floor," hollered the guy with the gun, "and nobody gets hurt."

As I went down to the tile floor just behind where the gunman had stopped, I saw the second guy with the bag charge the counter and vault over it at Suzanne's teller window. Just then, the bank guard, who I'd had the run-in with a while back, drew his pistol. Too bad he was a little bit late. The robber with the gun fired first and hit the guard in the shoulder, knocking him backwards and down. The guard's pistol went flying. That sure as hell got everybody's increased attention. There were shrieks all around. From the floor, I could see the guy with the bag grab Suzanne hard by her upper arm. He told her to open her cash drawer, which apparently she did. Before he started stuffing money in the bag, he gave Suzanne a stiff shove backwards and her side banged hard off the rear counter in the teller area. She let out a nasty groan, like she was hurt. That did it. I rose to my knees and called out, "HEY! The cops are comin'!"

As the gunman wheeled around toward the front door of the bank, I clasped my hands together and, as hard as I could, walloped the back of his hand that was holding the gun. The gun was knocked loose and it made a loud clanging sound when it hit the tile floor. To me, it seemed like everything was happening in slow motion. Still on my knees, I wrapped my arms around the gunman's legs and tried to tackle him to the floor. Although he didn't go down, I hung on for dear life. He got in one solid punch on the back of my neck, but I didn't let go. A second later, we both were knocked flat on the floor. Since my head was facing downward, I didn't see the hit on the robber's upper body coming from another bank customer. Next thing I knew we were in a big heap with me and the robber on the bottom. I was still hanging on to his legs, but it really didn't make much difference. At that point, there was the weight of at least several bodies on top of us. I wouldn't have been able to get up right away if I wanted to.

In a minute or two—although it seemed way longer than that—I heard loud sirens wailing. When the cops arrived they started the unpiling process, which I happened to be at the bottom of. I guess I was experiencing something like what it is to be a football player with a stack of big guys on top of you. Several of the customers immediately identified the robber. I figured that was good since, purely by appearances, the cops might have thought the guilty party was me. The gunman wasn't dressed up, but his look and his clothes were an upgrade over my standard grooming and wardrobe. I guess the ski mask that was still covering his head and face was a dead giveaway. I overheard one of the police officers say the other guy with the money bag was caught a couple of blocks away. I hadn't noticed he had run out of the bank, seeing as I was otherwise involved.

When order was restored, I started over to check on Suzanne. The paramedics had arrived and they were attending to the guard who had been shot in the shoulder. He was conscious and talking, so that was a good sign. When I got to Suzanne's window, I saw several of the other tellers talking to her, asking if she was all right. Ordinarily, I wouldn't have interrupted, but I was pretty keyed up by the whole experience.

"Suzanne," I said, "are you okay?"

Under different circumstances, the other tellers would probably have either ignored me or told me to buzz off. In general, it was kind of the way most of them normally acted toward me. I think the fact I'd saved the day, so to speak, put me at a somewhat elevated status to them. They backed off so Suzanne could talk to me. She went around through the teller's room and then came out the door to the lobby.

When she got to me she said, "I think I'm all right. I'm pretty sore on my side where I banged into the counter."

"You probably ought to get an X-ray to make sure you didn't crack a rib or something."

"I just may do that," she said. "How about you? I saw you get hit awfully hard with a punch during the scuffle."

"You know," I said, "I hadn't even thought

about it. But now that you mention it, the back of my neck is kinda hurting. It'll be alright, though. I heard the cops say they got the guy who shoved you."

"Well, that's great," said Suzanne. "As soon as you knocked the gun away, the guy with the bag jumped back over the counter at my window and took off. You sure were bold and brave, Morris. How did you do it?"

"I really didn't think about it. I guess I just kinda freaked out when I saw the guy hurt you."

"Morris," she said, "this is now the third time you've come to my defense. Two of them were right here inside the bank, and the other was out back in the parking lot. These things have got to stop happening. Although, I have to tell you, except for the time with the irate bank customer, I'm glad you were around. You're some kind of hero to me."

With that, she wrapped her arms around me and gave me a big, firm hug. It surprised the heck out of me and I didn't know exactly what to do. I just reacted by gently hugging her back. Getting hugged by a woman was something I hadn't experienced in a really long time. And, furthermore, I would definitely have to say Suzanne was the best-looking female who had ever hugged me in my entire life. It felt like I had goose bumps all over my whole body. Wow, what a thrill. I couldn't believe she had done it.

When the hug ended—which I was wishing would *never* end—I got myself a little together and said, "Thanks. I'm not going to see somebody hurt you without doing something about it. I care about you too much to let that happen. I think you're something."

"Oh, Morris," she said, "you're really sweet. It's just a shame we've had to go through these things.'

"Look, keep your head up about everything," I said, "And go get your side checked out. We've got to make sure we keep you in one piece. I'll be back here in a couple of days to check on you. And also to see how your mom's doing. Take care."

As I turned away from Suzanne, I saw Officer Keith was on the scene. He was interviewing several of the witnesses, but stopped when he saw me. With a big smile on his face, he came over.

"Well," he said, "how about all of this. From what I'm hearing, you're the courageous citizen who foiled the bank robbery. How about that? What do you think of yourself now?"

"Uh, I feel good, I guess," I said. "It all happened pretty fast. But maybe you ought to go ahead and take statements from those folks you were just talkin' to. If and when this whole deal has to go to trial, it'd be just as well if some of *them* went on the stand to testify, instead of *me*, you know."

"I don't think you'll have to worry about any of that," he said. "This case is pretty cut and dried. But, you were the man. Thanks for what you did."

"No problem," I said, smiling. "All in a day's work."

23

I guess you could say I was sorta walkin' on air as I left the bank. A bank robbery had been prevented and, by the way, a fair amount of the credit for it was on account of yours truly. I sure wasn't used to being involved is such stuff. I usually did everything possible to avoid confrontation of any kind. I was having a little trouble coming to grips with the change which had started coming over me. At least it seemed like a change. It certainly wasn't my regular method of operating. But, at the bottom of it, I was fairly sure it had to do with Suzanne. And then, her hug had pretty much put the whole thing over the top. Boy, if the folks on Holidaymaker could only see me now, I thought. There was one part of me that felt the subtle shift in my behavior was a good thing, and there was another part of me that still shunned the entire idea of giving much of a crap about anything. I was kinda confused.

When I walked outside, talk about being thrust into the spotlight. In front of the bank was a reporter who was talking to the bank customer who had put the football-type hit on the robber after I'd knocked the gun away and grabbed the guy's legs. There was also a photographer standing nearby. The fella being interviewed pointed me out and the reporter came right over. He identified himself as being with The Key West Citizen, the daily newspaper of our fair city. He asked me a lot of questions and, afterward, the photographer took some pictures of me alongside my tackling cohort. The scene was a little difficult to deal with, seeing as I wasn't used to anything close to the sort of attention I was getting. I normally expected people to either ignore me or, hopefully, give me a little cash. In which case, the contribution was most likely intended to encourage me to get lost. But at that point, I was still pumped up by the whole incident. So, I was cooperative with the newspaper guys and carried out my civic duty as best I could.

After the question and answer session, complete with photo opportunity, I headed up Duval Street and started making my way toward Mallory Square. Even though it wasn't anywhere close to sunset, I figured there was a good chance of running into Sonny or Horace somewhere along the way. I thought they might be interested in hearing about what had happened and, at the same time, possibly be willing to join me in downing a beverage or two. On me, of course. It would be sort of like the unwritten rule in golf that says the guy who gets a hole-in-one has to buy the drinks. I gotta say I was really feeling a powerful hankerin' for some liquid refreshment. Throat was awful dry. Plus, I needed a little something to calm me down a small tad. Maybe even a big tad, if you know what I mean.

I'd only gone about a block, and was crossing Caroline Street, when I spotted Sonny up a ways, sitting on the sidewalk and playing his guitar. He was holding court for the passers-by in his own musical way. I was pretty giddy about telling him about what a big shot I was. What had happened at the bank was not the type of stuff that normally happened to one of the denizens of the streets. While I was still the better part of a block from him I saw a kid, probably in his teens, run up and grab a handful of cash out of Sonny's guitar case. The kid darted away like a bat out of hell, straight across a busy Duval Street. Sonny put down his guitar, got to his feet, and took off after him. Sonny got across one lane of traffic, but cut it too close crossing the other lane. He sprinted right into the path of a car going pretty fast up Duval. I heard a loud screech of tires that seemed a little too short and a little too late. There was an awful thumping sound and it gave me a full-body chill. Sonny had been hit.

I ran straight to him, hoping he was okay. As I came up around the front of the car, I saw Sonny was down in the street on his back, and he wasn't moving. I had a big-time sick feeling in my gut as I dropped to my knees beside him.

"Sonny," I said, putting my face down close to his, "hang in there, man."

His eyes were barely open and there was a trickle of blood running out of the side of his mouth. I put my hand underneath the back of his neck to keep his head up a little. He opened his eyes just slightly and tried to talk. It was hardly a whisper and it was very slow.

"Busted...up," he murmured, and then after a pause, "busted...up...good."

"You're gonna be all right," I said. "Just stay still. "There's help coming."

"Kid...stole," then a pause, "my...fuckin'... money."

"Don't talk now, Sonny," I said as I heard a siren getting louder. "There's an ambulance coming."

Sonny's eyes were glazing over and there was a distant, unfocused look about them. "Come on now," I said, "come on, stay with me, Sonny. Stay with me."

I took a quick look up to see the ambulance arrive. As the piercing blare of the siren stopped, I looked back down into Sonny's face. His eyes slowly rolled back up under his eyelids, and I felt the life go out of him.

The EMS guys abruptly ushered me out of the way and went about their business. It didn't take long before the one paramedic, who appeared to be in charge, turned to his partner and shook his head. Sonny was dead. Skinny as he was, the hard wallop from the speeding car 'bout broke him and his insides in two. At least the pain didn't last very long for him. It was over pretty quick.

I shuffled through the crowd that had gathered and went over to the sidewalk where Sonny's guitar lay propped on its open case. I slumped down to the sidewalk next to his lone precious belonging. With my head in my hands, I sat there in a numb daze. Emotion did not come over me. It was more like I was frozen in disbelief. It had all happened so quickly and now Sonny was gone. Just like that.

There was a lot of commotion around the accident scene. Cars were stopped in both directions. Two cops had arrived and they were busy with the traffic issue. Plus, the paramedics had taken their time in loading Sonny into the ambulance. It was a busy scene that I was having trouble dealing with.

I did overhear a woman talking to bystanders who said she had an up-close view of what had happened. She said the guy driving the car that hit Sonny had been looking down at his seat, not ahead, when Sonny darted across in front of him. She also said the driver was holding a wrapper with a sandwich in one of his hands. Apparently, he was a whole lot more occupied with other things than holding onto the wheel and watching where he was going. Sonny had no business running through traffic like he did, but there still might have been a chance for him if the driver had been more alert. The guy was still there at the scene and was talking to one of the cops. But I knew in my mind nothing more would come of it for the distracted driver. He was well-dressed, was driving a nice car, looked like a tourist, and didn't appear to be drunk. I knew he was in the clear. After all, Sonny was just a stinkin' street person. Big deal. No loss.

After things settled down, I packed Sonny's guitar into its case. Then I carried it with me to the closest package store. I bought a tall bottle of the brown liquor and walked over to the cemetery. It was only the middle of the afternoon, but that's where I wanted to go. It was the best place for me to be. And, anyway, it was where I had locked my bike to the wrought iron cemetery fence a couple of hours earlier. I walked into my favorite Key West location and set up camp beside one of the burial crypts. I now had not only my backpack, but also Sonny's guitar in its case.

Proceeding first quickly, and then more slowly, to do away with the big bottle of brown, I tried reading some of my children's stories. I figured it might help to take my mind off Sonny. That ingenious idea didn't really help at all. I just couldn't get Sonny out of my head. Even though he was a pain in the ass at times—okay, most of the time—I liked the guy. He was one of us. There's a certain camaraderie between street folks that can't be denied. I knew it was going to take a while to get over losing him, even though I didn't know much more than the basics about him. I didn't even know any next of kin to contact. Heck, I didn't even know his last name. At one point while I was struggling with what had happened, I thought back on the incident at the bank. That whole scene seemed like ancient history—and it was fading fast. When I eventually polished off the bottle of brown, I put my head down and cried.

24

With no warning or nothin', they got hold of me somewhere during the middle of the night. Locked that darn beam onto me and snatched my sorry butt on a smokin' beeline right into the ship. I was headed to Holidaymaker. Bring it on, baby! Oh, yeaaah!! EEEEEE...HAAAAAAA!!

I was immediately transported to the circular room and the large, padded chair. As before, my clothing, physical appearance, and grooming were converted to a condition of fitness and neatness. Although I was alone in the room, I sensed a warm pleasantness, which was inspiring. There was now a comfortable familiarity for me on Holidaymaker. However, I was torn between conflicting emotions: first, recalling my last agonizing encounter when attempting to board the ship and, second, the anticipation of expectantly interacting with Cassandra once again. I felt a mild apprehensiveness that there could possibly be some form of replication of the nightmarish horror during my aborted prior visit. Gladly, the expectation and eagerness to see Cassandra prevailed over any unease. I felt a contented and confident sense of composure.

After an unmeasured period of time, one of the wall panels opened and, to my joyous delight, Cassandra entered. She appeared as enchanting and enthralling as ever before. Her lithe figure strolled toward me with a supple, yet secure, stride. Her facial features, which I had vividly chiseled into my memory, were without flaw. Her sparkling green eyes were captivating. To my thinking, Cassandra was ideal. Standing before me was my ultimate vision of beauty.

"Greetings, Morris," she said. "And welcome, once again, to Holidaymaker. We trust your passage to our vessel was a smooth and uneventful one."

The fact she made no mention of my previous terrifying experience while trying to board Holidaymaker, led me to believe, perhaps, she possessed no knowledge of it. I made the determination that I would, at least for the time being, decline to mention the frightening incident. I was content to file the entire ordeal in the far recesses of my mind, so I merely replied, "All was fine with the transition. It is with great enjoyment that I have returned to

Holidaymaker and am in your company. Cassandra, it is a pleasure to be back."

"Very good, Morris," she said. "We are delighted you are again in our midst. The experience we have designed, which may serve to be a culmination of your Holidaymaker experience, is a unique one. The previous challenges we have posed for you have been of a clinical variety—and I might point out that during those tests you have performed in an exemplary manner. However, this time we have planned to add a special aspect to the next installment that awaits you. Technical and creative proficiency will still apply, but in this case we will be adding both emotional and personal features as well. Initially, your assignment will consist of determining the location of a fellow shipmate outside the confines of Holidaymaker. That course of action is to be subsequently followed by their rescue. And lastly, you will be required to accompany the shipmate in a safe return here to Holidaymaker. The itinerary of the experiment will consist of the three successive venues of land, sea, and air. You will utilize the mechanical concepts of the assembly process as well as the engineering design facet, with which you have separately had previous success. The basic tools, as well as other extraneous materials, will be available and at your disposal to utilize in your quest. It will be your task to make use of them in an inventive and imaginative manner. Consequently, you will be tested in a variety of ways. And, once again, I will remind you that an optimistic mindset and a creative approach will be your greatest allies. Please bear in mind that there may well be any number of alternative options from which to choose in accomplishing your mission. In any event, a positive attitude will be vital to the successful completion of the experiment."

"The assignment," I said, "does, indeed, seem challenging. Nevertheless, I am prepared to give my best effort. I am invigorated with eagerness to proceed. May I ask which shipmate will require rescue? Am I familiar with the individual?"

"Being as you have had the most interaction with me during your stays on Holidaymaker, it will be me who will be the target of your rescue efforts."

I was certainly taken aback by the revelation and surprise that seeking to find Cassandra would be the goal of my pursuit. It unquestionably added a personal feature to the undertaking which awaited. I was momentarily speechless but eventually managed to respond, "Wonderful, Cassandra. I am ready to commence with the course of action at your request."

She approached me with her left hand extended saying, "The path that lies ahead will become apparent, Morris. Remain positive. You have the aptitude and ability to achieve the goal."

As she finished speaking, Cassandra placed the palm of her left hand on my forehead. It was a slightly different maneuver from the former procedure of gently lowering my eyelids to initiate my departure from the ship. At her touch, I was instantly rocketed vertically within the round cylindrical shaft through which I had originally entered Holidaymaker in an accelerated descent. I was thrust upward through the tunnel-like opening at rapidly increasing speed. My body had become a missile soaring aloft. However, I felt no anxiety for the mission which lay ahead. Instead, I was energized with anticipation to undertake the task at hand

Muted lighting illuminated the shaft as I rose ever higher and ever faster. As I gazed upward to the darkened summit of the tunnel, an eerie image of a grotesque gargoyle shrouded in smoke appeared before me. I immediately harkened back to my horrifying experience with such demons and it sent a shudder through to my core. The terrifying, devil-like monster spoke with a slow pace in a barely audible, raspy whisper, "You will never find her….You will never find her."

The gruesome figure faded out and in its place appeared the face of Bernard, the Director of Science on Holidaymaker. The vision of the white-bearded Bernard was similarly masked by a hazy veil. His voice was distant but firm as he said, "You will find her, Morris. You will find her. Be relentless in your pursuit."

25

The upward propelling thrust of my body came to an unexpected and sudden halt as I was abruptly plunked onto my feet upon a wide-ranging expanse of desolate terrain. The landscape was relatively flat, save for several rugged mountainous regions which ranged at intermittent distances. I was at a complete loss as to which direction to begin my search for Cassandra. I was discouraged to realize I possessed neither the proper means nor the correct route to seek her out. I bowed my head, closed my eyes, and conjured up all of the positive impulses I could generate.

I looked up, and with no rational justification, turned ninety degrees to my left and strode straight ahead over the span of barren territory. There was no explanation as to the selection of my course, but I had the distinct sense I was on the proper track. There was steadfast purpose in my being to seek out Cassandra, and I was optimistic it would come about. Although the resources to accomplish the undertaking remained unidentified, my resolve was unwavering.

After traversing a spacious course of level territory, which was only occasionally dotted which scrub vegetation, I came upon a steep hillside to my right. For some unknown reason, I was drawn to a cave-like cavity at the base of the rise. Upon entering the aperture, light, which cast in from outside, revealed a shabby, dust-covered trunk. There was an inquisitive interest compelling me to believe there was significance to the well-worn travel chest. Unlatching and opening the trunk, a second wooden panel was revealed only a few inches down from the top. Upon the panel sat a small, leather case whose contents I examined. A half dozen tiny metallic parts of various shapes accompanied a flat, round disk, smaller than the palm of my hand. In the center of the disk was a circular hole less than the diameter of a pencil. The plain face had only the single marking of a star, which was located near the outer edge.

I was energized with enthusiasm when struck with the recognition that I was a holding some form of a disassembled compass.

Without knowledge or prior practice of how to proceed, I set to the task of positioning the detached components into a functioning instrument. There was a self-assured manner to both the mental and physical process upon which I embarked. Positive thoughts flowed through my reasoning progression as I persisted with the delicate undertaking. My hands moved evenly and enthusiastically in precisely combining the various minute pieces until I held in my hand what I believed to be an operational, yet rudimentary, compass.

Setting down the assembled compass, I tugged at the wooden panel which was framed within the trunk, but it was securely affixed in the confines of the dusty chest. It came to me that the compass was the sole apparatus meant for my discovery. It was as if I had been deceived into opening a large gift which held simply a tiny, yet valuable, present. I picked up the compass, held it in my hand with its face upward, and walked out of the cave.

After emerging, I glanced down at the compass and noticed the arrow-like needle, which was positioned above the face, spin clockwise a quarter turn. I rotated the disk so the star on the edge of the face was aligned with the point of the needle, as one would do to locate magnetic North when using a traditional compass. I instantly felt a mild vibrating sensation surge through my hand. Regardless of whether I was being aimed North, South, East or West, I was certain the bearing to locate Cassandra had been established. Once more, a wave of optimism washed over me as I faced in the direction the needle and star indicated. With poised confidence, I proceeded to march ahead over the barren land.

The duration of time passage throughout my journey, as on Holidaymaker, was difficult to accurately judge. I experienced the distinct impression of virtually floating over the route in which I was headed. I alternated between, first, concentrating on maintaining a match of the star on the compass with the heading of the needle, and secondly, glancing sideward to see the deserted countryside trail by. It seemed never-ending, and yet, it could have been a quickly fleeting period of time before I came upon an abrupt chasm that cut a perpendicular swath across my path. I stopped at the edge of the steep ravine and gazed down on violent torrents of fast-moving water, flowing far below. The surging rapids spanned the width of the base of the ravine. As I gazed across the precipitous divide, I judged it to be no more than fifty yards wide. On the opposite side of the canyon sat a modest cottage. I held the compass upright in my hand and, once again, repositioned the star a minuscule turn so it matched the direction of the needle, which pointed straight at the small house. As the star moved to the setting under the needle, I felt three sharp pulses shoot through my hand. I was certain Cassandra was in the cottage. But how to reach her across such a sheer and wide gorge? I looked to both the left and the right in an attempt to find a suitable route to cross the gap, but to no avail. The canyon, with steep cliffs on both sides, stretched endlessly in both directions.

I turned away from the edge of the ravine and lowered my head. The slightest amount of despair began to creep over me. I closed my eyes, but before I could summon up positive and encouraging thoughts, the hazy image of the horrid monster again appeared in my mind's eye. In a hissing, taunting whisper the vile fiend repeated the foreboding threat from before, "You will never find her....You will never find her." I refused to allow the menacing message to deter me and mentally wiped the ghastly figure into obscurity. Conjuring up optimistic feelings, the foggy face of Bernard appeared to me. In a low, soft voice he uttered the previous heartening words, "You will find her, Morris. You will find her. Be relentless in your pursuit."

Raising my head and opening my eyes, I observed yet another cave-like opening in a nearby hillside. I slipped the compass into the chest pocket of my white jumpsuit and hastily made for the cave entrance. Upon entering, I found myself in a square grotto, at the far end of which was an upright, circular-shaped boulder. Being flat on the front and approximately my height, it appeared to be a solid stone wheel, six to eight inches thick. My instinctive intuition told me that behind the standing-on-edge, circular boulder laid either instructions or materials to aid me in my dilemma of traversing the gorge.

I stood to the side of the stone and put forth my utmost physical effort in an attempt to roll it away from what I surmised was a covered opening. Alas, an extreme exertion of strength and force proved fruitless in moving the stone even the slightest amount. Undeterred, I turned away and scanned the grotto for some physical means of assistance to budge the wheel-like rock. I spotted a wooden timber roughly four inches in diameter and about eight to ten feet long lying to the side. Its usefulness in serving as a lever instantly flashed through my consciousness. Something to act as a fulcrum was all that was needed. Among the various rocks which lay scattered in the cave, I chose one seemingly appropriate in size. With great effort, I rolled it to a location on the side of the large, circular stone. I wedged the end of the timber at the bottom of the stone and then rested it on top of the rock, which was placed several feet away. I grasped the timber near the middle and pulled down with all my might. There was still no movement of the stone wheel. I reached higher, toward the end of the timber, and pulled down hard once again. Exerting the downward force further from the fulcrum provided better leverage and the stone moved several inches.

I repositioned the rock, which was serving as the fulcrum, closer to the stone wheel and pulled down again while gripping near the end of the wooden timber. Once more the stone rolled away a short distance, revealing a partial opening behind it. I repeated the process several more times until a door-sized entrance to another chamber was exposed. With dim light barely streaking in from the outside, I entered and managed to distinguish that the second cavity contained several organized stacks of tubing. After a moment, my eyes adjusted to the lower level of light and my vision was enhanced. The diameter of the tubing was four to five inches, which was similar to the thickness of the timber that had acted as my lever. The tubing was made of some form of synthetic material with which I was unfamiliar. The tubes were all identical and approximately six feet in length. I pulled one off of the top of a stack and quickly realized its weight was bearable. I carried the tube back through the first chamber and to the outside.

I noted that one end of the tube was flared to a slightly larger diameter while the other end was not. Upon returning to the inner chamber, I allowed my eyes to adjust for a second time to the lowly lit cavity. To the side of the stacks of tubing, I then saw a tarp covering a mound on the floor of the chamber. Pulling the tarp aside, I could make out some hand tools, a stack of two-by-four-inch lumber of a similar length as the tubing, a cylindrical canister, several small containers, and, among some unidentified items, a pad of graph paper and a pencil.

All of the objects that had been under the tarp I methodically carried outside and arranged in an organized fashion. I was certain I had come upon the materials intended to provide me a means of crossing the gaping chasm. It was now my task to determine the purpose of each item and to make use of them in such a way so as to negotiate the intimidating ravine separating me from Cassandra. Although the undertaking was daunting, I had attained a higher level of self-assurance than at any time during my previous Holidaymaker experiences. I was prepared to carry out whatever course of action was necessary to achieve the crucial goal of crossing the gorge. I was enthused with inspiration.

With my mind racing, I determined that the primary means of bridging the divide lay in connecting the synthetic tubing. I examined the assorted equipment spread about. The cylindrical canister was marked with a label, showing it contained propane gas. There was also a round coil of a flux-like material. The means of joining the lengths of tubing was set forth before me. I could insert the standard end of one tube into the flared end of another and solder the sections by heating the flux to create a seal. But I realized, by merely linking the tubing and then advancing it to the opposite side, its overall weight would cause it to bow downward as I moved it forward across the canyon. Thus, the bridge of tubing would reach below the height of the ground on the far side.

After taking stock of the rest of the materials, which included the two-by-four lumber, hand tools, nails and large spikes, I seized the pencil and the pad of graph paper. Even though all of my calculations were based on estimates of distance and weight, I maintained a high level of confidence that I was following an accurate process in my computations. The planning and engineering phase prior to the construction of the bridge seemed unforced and methodical. I sketched out both plan and elevation drawings in a deliberate manner and without effort.

I designed an angled platform, rising toward the opposite side of the gorge, which would be constructed with the lumber and hand tools. The platform would have an elevated, reinforced ring through which the fused sections of tubing would be fed. The platform would be anchored to the ground with spikes to secure it while supporting the weight of the bridge. I was not as concerned with the overall weight of the load that the platform would be bearing, as I was with the increasing flexibility of the connected tubing when it traveled away from the supporting ring. My biggest apprehension lay with establishing the proper upward angle of the tubing as it moved away from the platform. Would it be sufficient in height to arrive above the cliff when it reached the opposite side? Although the prospect of the bridge ending up below the level of its intended destination was vexing, I carried on with the construction stage of my project while maintaining a positive mindset.

One by one, I carried the sections of tubing out of the inner chamber and systematically stacked them in crisscross fashion adjacent to the location where I had chosen to construct the platform. With what seemed like ease, I erected the platform using the lumber and assorted tools. I was precise in my building of the raised, reinforced ring, through which the tubing would be threaded. Nailing together successive two-by-fours at wide angles created an octagon. Using a rasp, I then scraped off portions of each interior side of the octagon to form a rough circle. That process was then followed by a series of shavings and sandings in order to hone a round opening. Although the available tools were basic, it seemed as though there was a suitable one for every need which arose. I made certain the ring would accommodate the diameter of the flared end of each tube, also allowing a small amount of additional clearance. Each of the steps of construction flowed quickly and efficiently. The many-faceted procedure progressed with what seemed minimal time and effort.

When the platform and ring were complete, I set to the task of fusing together the sections of tubing. Lighting the propane torch with a flint-like device, I proceeded to connect the tubing by heating the flux to seal the progressive segments. What should have been an arduous and lengthy process flowed at a remarkably swift pace. The lengths of tubing were soldered and advanced through the ring rapidly and with ease.

Though there was some downward bowing of the bridge as it neared the opposite side, I was flooded with enthusiasm at the sight of the end of the tubing crossing several feet above the level of the distant cliff. While traversing the bridge, I realized the weight of my body would lower the plane of the tubing somewhat, so it would rest on flat ground not far from the cottage. I added several extra sections of tubing and pushed it ahead so the bridge extended well past the far edge of the precipice. The back end of the tubing, which was well behind the reinforced ring, I firmly secured with a lumber boot. I was now, from an engineering standpoint, prepared to cross the newly erected bridge. But by what means and method?

Pondering the possibilities, I retrieved the wooden timber I had used as a lever to move the round stone inside the cave. By holding it in my hands horizontally, I reasoned it could serve as a balancing pole while walking across the bridge. On the near side of the tubing, which led to the platform, I practiced striding with what I felt was capable proficiency. In preparation of the bridge crossing, I stepped over the reinforced ring with the balancing timber in hand. As

I stood there peering at the modest cottage sitting beyond the gorge, I once again mustered all of the positive feelings I could render. The goal was in sight.

26

Filled with controlled confidence, I took several steps forward with steady results. Just as I reached the point on the bridge where it began to pass over the near side of the cliff, my left foot slipped and I lost my balance. I instantaneously comprehended that the bridge was my lifeline. I released my grip on the balancing timber and, falling, wrapped my arms forcefully around the tubing. I also managed to hook one of my legs over the bridge as I was going down. Hanging precariously on the tubing, I glimpsed downward and saw the timber fall away for what seemed an extended period of time. At last, it plunged into the raging rapids, which surged violently at the bottom of the deep canyon.

With great angst, I powered my body to a prone position on the top side of the tubing. My heart raced and my breathing was deep and rapid. After minimal deliberation, I made the firm decision to shimmy across the bridge on my chest and stomach. Though there had been a traumatic turn of events, I maintained a greater determination than ever to continue on my quest to locate Cassandra. I was possessed with resolve and tenacity.

Inch by inch, foot by foot, I gradually moved on my chest and stomach across the bridge. I coordinated the use of my arms, which were wrapped around the tubing, to reach and pull, followed by a backward push of my legs. The crossing was onerous and demanding, both from a physical and mental standpoint. The former from pure muscular fatigue, and the latter by an ill-advised glance downward in the early stages of the crossing. The furious flow of whitewater seemed yet a greater distance below than it had previously. For several moments my body was frozen motionless. Closing my eyes and forcing my psyche to a higher level of reassurance, I made the determination to not look down again during the balance of the journey.

The assumption that the weight of my body would lower the far end of the bridge to the ground was proven correct when I reached approximately the midpoint of the crossing. However, after touching ground, the tubing out over the gorge bowed downward. Thus, the second half of the journey was on an ascending angle. With every ounce of exhausting effort, I pressed on undaunted.

Upon finally reaching the intended destination, I drew myself up over the precipice and crawled to my feet. The crossing had been grueling, but I was infused with a newfound energy. Without delay, I rushed to the cottage and burst through the open front door. Entering the foyer, I stole momentary glances left and right to small rooms that revealed nothing but emptiness. Then, as I looked up the flight of stairs to the second floor, my heart leapt. At the top of the stairs stood Cassandra. Instead of the usual strapless white gown I was accustomed to seeing her wear, she was dressed in a white jumpsuit similar to mine. And her long dark hair was draped down over her shoulders as opposed to being twirled up upon her head.

I tried to call to her but was unable to utter any sound whatsoever. Nor did she address me. Feeling certain the objective of my quest was within reach, I bounded up the stairs, two at a time. As I reached the landing at the top of the flight, she was gone. Frantically, I turned and stared down a long hallway containing scores of doorways. Six or eight doors away, I caught a trailing sight of Cassandra's lustrous brunette hair vanish into a room. As I rushed down the hall to follow her, I was dumbfounded by the unusually large size of the second level. From the exterior and the first floor, the house appeared as simply modestly-sized. But upstairs, I found myself pursuing Cassandra in a cavernous dwelling of extraordinary dimensions. Undeterred, I raced after her.

When I turned into the doorway I assumed she had entered, I was met with yet another corridor containing ascending stairways to the left and right. My eyes darted about, seeking a sight of Cassandra. As I twisted my head to look up the stairs to the left, once again I caught a fleeting glimpse of her beautiful brown hair. In neither case since she had taken flight had I seen any other portion of her body. Only the gleaming dark flow trailing behind her. I followed Cassandra at a frenetic pace, up stairways and down stairways, through what seemed never-ending halls. The only sign telling me I was still within some form of contact with her was the sporadic, yet momentary, view of her luminous locks flowing in her wake. The chase was maddening.

Like dozens of times before, I rushed into a room where the trail of her dark brown mane had vanished. But on this occasion I staggered to a stop. Through open floor-to-ceiling glass doors I saw Cassandra standing outside the house on the far end of a broad wooden deck. She stood facing me with her back leaning against the railing of the deck, which cantilevered outward several floors above a massive body of water. With her arms spread to each side, her hands rested placidly on the flat rail. Sunshine glinted off her slender form. She was the perfect embodiment of beauty, and I had, at long last, reached her.

As I strode slowly toward Cassandra, I once again attempted to call out to her. But hard as I tried, I could emit nary a sound. There was a great agonizing frustration in being unable to verbalize any words at all. Not speaking either, she continued standing motionless at the railing. In peculiar fashion, she displayed an impassive expression on her face. Not the welcoming warmth from her striking features I had come to know on Holidaymaker. Even though I desired to sprint to her at maximum speed, I was somehow restricted to mere slow, short steps. All the while, the distance to reach where she stood appeared to diminish only infinitesimally. The unidentified restraint to which I was inexplicably subjected was exasperating. It seemed as though my forward movement was reduced proportionately further with the greater effort I exerted.

As I closed the expanse to just beyond arm's length of her, Cassandra turned and vaulted up upon the wooden rail. She then dove gracefully off of the railing, down into the far-ranging, but calm, sea below. I reached the edge of the deck in time to see Cassandra create virtually no white splash upon entry. Her lean form slipped into the aqua body of water flawlessly. Without trepidation or consideration of the risks which might lie ahead, I leapt up onto the railing and dove headlong after her.

After what seemed a prolonged time airborne, I penetrated down through the surface of the water and entered a clear marine environment. There was a calm serenity in the water, which contained a colorful array of both coral and plant life. In addition, there were ample numbers of tropical fish swimming about in a multitude of sizes and colors. Oddly, all of the usual factors of being a human under water no longer applied. Breathing was not a difficulty or concern— nor was the fact that I continued to wear my jumpsuit and boots. Furthermore, I became immediately adept at propelling myself forward at a relatively swift rate by simply the gentle up and down kick of my legs. It was as if I wore enormous flippers on my feet. And stroking was not required to swim in the undersea world. I simply kept my arms relaxed at my sides. I could change direction with a minimal turn of my head. In essence, I had taken on the physical characteristics of the other fish, and was moving about with them as a peer.

By far, the greatest source of any unease was in locating the elusive Cassandra. I had made no sighting of her since entering the water. Even worse, I had not the vaguest clue of her whereabouts within the depths of the aquatic environment in which I found myself. Briefly closing my eyes, I rallied the utmost inspiration I could generate. When I reopened them, I observed an undersea rock formation off to my flank. Instinctively, and on impulse, I adjusted my direction to investigate. My intuition told me I was on the correct course. As I navigated to the port side of the submerged, mountain-like edifice, I viewed an opening near its base. I was driven to explore the interior. Unlike the previous caves I had examined during the land segment of my ordeal, I entered an underwater tunnel perhaps ten feet in diameter. I maintained a strong suspicion I was on the proper track as I probed the passageway.

After continuing through the tunnel on a straight course for roughly one hundred yards, I turned on a sharp, left-handed angle into an intersecting passageway. I immediately came to an abrupt halt. Ahead of me huddled a cluster of menacing sharks—all of which were significant in size. As I turned to withdraw, I caught sight of Cassandra just beyond the horde of sharks. Dressed as before in the white jumpsuit, her long and full dark hair floated out away from her head as a peacock fans its feathers. Once again, her face was devoid of expression as she lingered behind the intimidating pack of hostile executioners. It became instantly clear amid the perilous fight-or-flight circumstance in which I found myself that immediate retreat was the prudent course of action.

Keen, fierce vigor flooded my mind and body as I turned and propelled myself back toward the

191

opening of the tunnel with great exertion. Staying as low as possible, I used my arms to alternately stroke and then dig with my hands into the mucky sediment on the underwater bottom. Gathering speed as I swam, my objective was to scoop up mud and fling it backward into the trailing water to create a cloudy shield. It was my only hope to impede the pack of sharks that I felt certain had commenced their pursuit of me. Again and again, I tossed gobs of the sea floor behind me while I forcefully kicked my legs to accelerate. My intent was to hinder the sharks' advance as best I could. It was an agonizing and distressing departure from the passageway. I had no way of knowing if I would be overtaken by one or more of the menacing group, which I expected was close on my trail. I put forth a frenzied life-or-death effort to flee.

As I exited the tunnel, I made an abrupt turn and stopped. Without doubt, I clearly grasped there was no chance of hiding from, or out-swimming, the herd of aggressive assassins in the open under-sea water. The only likelihood of my survival lay in driving them off one by one. Frantic, my eyes darted down to the marine floor where I viewed a fossilized stone. It was shaped in the irregular form and size of a primitive club. Picking it up, I was pleasantly surprised it was of manageable weight to wield. As I stole a quick look back into the brown muddiness I had created, a shark burst forth through my restricted vision. As it roared out of the tunnel, I pulled back and delivered a forceful wallop with my club across its open jaws. The blow sidetracked its hostile mission, causing it to turn away and draw off. Within a heartbeat, another shark appeared out of the opening from which murky cloudiness gushed. I managed to recover from the first encounter in time to clout down on the head of the second shark with a powerful thump. It also was effectively warded off.

Over and over, as each shark emerged from the tunnel opening, I used the club to pound either the jaw or head area of the beasts with as severe an exertion of strength as I could bring to bear. And, over and over again, each successive would-be slayer was coerced to leave the vicinity—much to my relief. After I battered countless sharks with repeated violent assaults, there came a distinct break in the convoy-like procession that had poured out of the clouded tunnel. With great caution, I swam into the opening while maintaining a firm grip on the club, which had been my savior. My deep-rooted desire to reach Cassandra overwhelmed any sense of fear.

I swam the full length of the straight portion of the tunnel through near-zero visibility, ever vigilant of a lingering shark. As I reached the point just before the distinct ninety degree turn, the muddied water cleared. With the improved visibility, I experienced a dramatic reduction in my level of anxiety. I also gained the encouraging sensation that the last of the sharks had departed their submerged lair. With calm determination, I turned the corner of the tunnel where I had previously seen Cassandra at a distance. I experienced an immediate gut-wrenching shock as a lone remaining shark lunged toward me from some ten yards away. Its jaws heaved open as it swiftly closed the gap between us. The confined dimensions of the tunnel left me with essentially no options. As the shark charged at me, I thrust the club, large end first, into its gaping mouth. Letting go of my grip, I rolled off to the side of the tunnel as the shark flashed past. It vanished around the corner and into the darkness, at what appeared to be increasing speed. I wished, hope upon hope, I had seen the last of that intimidating predator.

Trembling with both cautious and fearful alarm, I turned to look forward in the clear waters of the advancing tunnel. To my elation, I saw Cassandra floating perhaps fifty feet away. She was upright and treading water in a serene manner. Her facial expression, however, was featureless as before. Re-energized, I accelerated toward her in the sunken marine world in which we subsisted. I was filled with enthusiasm as I closed the expanse between us. When I reached a distance of perhaps ten feet from Cassandra, she turned and darted away through the extended tunnel. I pursued, but my speed fell far short of matching the effort I exerted. Within a short distance, the tunnel split into two forks. I barely caught a fleeting glimpse of Cassandra's white boots as they disappeared into the passageway to the left. Surging after her with all the might I could rally, I, once again, suffered from some sort of intangible restraint. The velocity of my forward movement continued to be strangely limited. Oh, how hard I attempted to overcome the unknown force holding me back. The struggle I underwent was incredibly wearisome.

As I continued my quest for Cassandra, there were ever-increasing undersea corridors serving as alternative routes. Where there previously had been two options of tunnels to follow, with each succeeding intersection, the number of selections continued to increase. Three, then four, then five and six possible passageways presented themselves. The only indication of which one to choose lay in the momentary sight of Cassandra's white boots disappearing as she headed away.

27

After what had been a seemingly endless quest, the tunnel in which I had been trailing Cassandra opened into an enormous underwater grotto. On the floor of the massive space sat dozens of vertical black tubes, each alike in size and shape. They appeared to be about six feet in diameter and stood at least twenty to twenty-five feet high. At their base, each tube had a vertically-shaped aperture with a hinged portion of the tube serving as an open door. The entry of the tubes was of dimensions easily accommodating the size of a human being. Gazing far upward in the cavernous water-filled space, I noted numerous round openings which perforated the domed ceiling of the grotto. Even though the height of the upper limit was possibly one hundred feet, it was peculiarly interesting that each tube seated on the floor appeared directly aligned with a similarly-sized, corresponding opening above. Only many feet of open water separated the tops of the tubes and the equivalently-shaped holes. With no basis to have such knowledge, I was struck with the comprehension I had come upon an underwater launching complex. The tubes were some form of missile silos, I reasoned.

With frenzied agitation, I sought after any sighting of Cassandra. I swam about the silos as if I was scurrying through a forest, searching for her around huge black trees. On several occasions I saw her white boots dart away behind the tall tubes. At last I came upon Cassandra as she was disappearing into an entryway of one of the silos. Almost reaching her, I watched her swing the entrance closed, which, in turn, served to encapsulate the tube as a sealed structure. I pounded my fist over and over again on the closed door, to no avail. Hearing and feeling a deep, muffled rumbling, I pulled away from the silo. The resonance and vibration increased to an explosive roar and a pulsating tremor. Looking to the top of the silo, I saw a black capsule burst upward and away from the black cylinder at great velocity. As it ascended, the water in its wake was swirled and churned into a bubbly torrent. I moved away far enough to see the capsule exit the submerged cavern and surge up through the opening in the vaulted ceiling far above the silo from which it had been launched.

Invigorated with commanding energy, I was determined to seize Cassandra and bring this exasperating enterprise to an end. I turned and bounded into the opening of the nearest black tube. I pulled the curved door closed behind me as I climbed in. Narrowly fitted within the silo was a vertically pointed missile into whose cockpit I compacted myself.

With no concept of what course of action to take, I spontaneously grasped the basic scheme of things within the cabin area. As I positioned into the molded seat with my back down and legs up, I observed the release handle for closing the capsule door. I grasped the handle and slid the door downward and shut. The securing of the door also served to immediately empty the cabin of water. Automatically, an air supply activated, ventilating the interior.

Having no prior experience with such matters, I proceeded instinctively—all the time sustaining a positive burst of eager enthusiasm. It was as if I possessed prescient and perceptive knowledge of each successive and appropriate step in everything I undertook. Before me, attached to the control panel, was a clear plastic pouch. Unzipping the pouch, I pulled papers, the first of which was a schematic diagram of the capsule's power source. Scanning it briefly, I engaged the energy supply by flipping two toggle switches on the forward panel. A potent rumble vibrated the capsule while at idle. I examined a second document which was an elementary map, the apparent objective of which was to locate Holidaymaker. After quick scrutiny, I comprehended the fundamental concept of the intended destination. Other papers contained in the pouch dealt with the procedures required to maneuver the capsule in space. There were concise instructions for managing the parameters of pitch, yaw, and attitude of the craft while in flight. Even though I possessed no former training in the genre, I easily absorbed all of the information with uncommon rapidity. Yet, there was a controlled uneasiness about me, realizing the distance to reach Cassandra was increasing with each passing second.

I momentarily closed my eyes and braced myself with an optimistic drive and a spirited will. After locking the safety harness which secured me snugly in the seat, I was set to go. Advancing the lever controlling the throttle, the thunderous vibration of the engine increased to a deafening roar. When the needle on the gauge registering the available torque had reached its zenith, I flipped the switch on the instrument panel that engaged the power supply. With astonishing force, the capsule thrust hastily upward and then out of the surrounding silo which had encased it. The craft accelerated at such a rate that the passage through the water up to and into the aligned tunnel in the upper dome seemed almost instantaneous. There was multiplied gravitational force applied to the capsule as it ascended, causing it to shake and shudder with severe tremors. I was compressed backward in the seat of the cockpit with increasingly weighted downward power. It was both a startling and exhilarating experience.

The vessel rocketed vertically into and through the upper tunnel with incredible speed. Through the side windows of the capsule, the walls of the passageway soared past in an indiscernible blur. The view through the forward window gave no distinguishable vision, save an ever-enlarging dark hole, as I was propelled upward at rapid velocity. In what seemed mere seconds, I emerged into the vastness of space. Coinciding with exiting the tunnel, the quaking and thunderous reverberation of the capsule ceased. A peculiar calm silence ensued. In addition, the restraining force of gravitational pull came to an end, causing the craft to soar ahead with tranquil ease. Had it not been for the restraint of the safety harness, my body would have floated about in a state of weightlessness.

Gazing at the distant stars and the infinite darkness of space, I was at a loss as to how to proceed. As I was about to glance down at the paper on which the map was printed, a meteor-like object with a trailing flame sailed diagonally across my path. Although the distance had not been at close range, I instinctively applied a more firm grasp on the steering control. Once again, before I could look down at the map, another flaming ball cut an angle ahead of my projected direction. It was quickly followed by yet another and then another. Seemingly without effort, I steered the capsule so as to easily evade the small shooting stars. The fiery displays escalated until dozens of streaming missiles crisscrossed in advance of the spacecraft. Oddly, there was a reverse effect on my anxiousness as the brilliant balls of fire continued to increase in number. I came to sense no fear of them. I viewed the experience as a dazzling light show, which created more of a distraction than a danger. Instead of being frightened, I was entertained as I maneuvered through what seemed an endless chicane of streaming lights.

At one point during the scintillating display, I was able to observe a flashing green light emanating from what appeared to be a distant craft. With no specific rationale to presume the vessel held Cassandra, I pressed on through the maze of zigzagging meteors in pursuit of the flashing green light.

I was convinced it was not a phantom signal, but a beacon I was intended to follow. I activated the display screen on the control panel, locked onto the source of the flashing light and homed in on its constantly-changing coordinates. The blazing flares crossing my path ahead were a diversion, but I was not deterred.

During my quest to track down Cassandra, I noticed the direction-controlling instrument had the propensity to pull the craft to the left of my projected course. I continually made manual adjustments to the joystick in an attempt to override the drift that was occurring. It became so unwieldy, I scrutinized the paper which displayed the schematic diagram of the components controlling the bearing of the ship. After quick examination, I grasped the make-up of the control instrument and then set about to make adjustments. With little effort and in no time, I reconfigured the wiring in the grid at the base of the joystick. My modifications corrected the guidance mechanism and, at once, control of the craft became sound.

Using as much power as the engine of the vessel could provide, I gradually—oh so gradually—closed the gap separating me from the spacecraft emitting the flashing green light. The flurry of fireballs continued, helter-skelter, as I rocketed ahead. Nevertheless, I navigated through them with little difficulty. Onward, ever onward, I flew. At times I tracked the course of my intended target on the display screen—at other times I used physical sightings to make manual corrections in evading the flaming meteors. It was an intense and concentrated undertaking, seemingly without end.

Continuing in determined pursuit, I observed what I believed to be Cassandra's capsule slow its forward speed and, in a deliberate manner, veer upward. I did a swift scan of the map, which was spread across my lap. Although I was a novice at interpreting such a chart, I noted the object of my chase had adjusted its course on a direct attitude toward the North Star. En route on that line was the indicated location of Holidaymaker. An excited joy swelled in my chest as I seemed to close the space separating me from Cassandra. As we continued on a northerly track, there came a point where I clearly sensed the power and steering of the craft leave my control. I was within striking distance of the capsule with the flashing green light, but command of my vessel had come under some sort of superior control. The instruments with which I had been flying my spacecraft became utterly ineffective. As my vessel slowed, it appeared the same controlling influence was affecting the capsule I was trailing.

Both ships continued methodically upward until I saw the dark, round globe of Holidaymaker become illuminated by surrounding stars. A panel at its base slid open and the two capsules, by no visible means, were precisely ferried, one by one, into the lighted bay within. Once again, I was confounded by the comparable size difference between the two capsules and Holidaymaker. It did not seem possible the mother ship with its diminutive size could possibly hold the capsule I had been flying, much less two such vessels. Nevertheless, the craft I had been tracking proceeded to dock against a circular walkway in the spacious bay. My vessel followed suit. As I reached for the lever to open the door of the capsule, I heard the thud of Holidaymaker's payload panel shut with authority below. At the same moment, the exit access of my spacecraft glided inexplicably open prior to any contact by my hand.

Flushed with excitement, I climbed out onto the grated, metal walkway and turned to see Cassandra emerge from the capsule she had flown. She was dressed as before in a white jumpsuit, and her long dark hair remained down over her shoulders. The vision of her beauty overcame me, and I was unable to contain a broad smile as I approached her. Unlike her expressionless face during the arduous adventure, she also was beaming with a wide smile.

"Cassandra," I said, "at last we are reunited. It was a truly grueling undertaking."

"A grueling undertaking, indeed," she said. "You showed unwavering persistence throughout, and for that you should take great pride. It is apparent that you followed the guiding instruction of Bernard. With no doubt, you were, in fact, relentless in your pursuit."

"I remain at a loss," I admitted, "as to how virtually all of the means and manner were accomplished."

"The methods you employed," she said, "are of little concern. The progression of your thought development, coupled with the creative concepts you utilized, allowed you to overcome the many obstacles which were presented. Furthermore, you deserve the utmost praise for your steadfast adherence to maintaining a positive mindset throughout. That devotion to the affirmative allowed you to be resourceful and to prevail."

"I am overcome with elation," I said.

"Morris," said Cassandra, "you have achieved the ultimate honor attainable here on Holidaymaker. You have realized élan vital—that is, you have demonstrated that you sustain a vigorous spirit and enthusiasm. You are filled with vitality. It is a decisive tribute for us to bestow our admiration upon you. Based on your hard-earned accomplishments, please allow me to demonstrate the warm affection we here on this vessel wish to present to you."

Having said that, Cassandra approached me, wrapped her arms around my waist, and embraced me. Although I was caught off guard by her action, I returned the embrace. I held her close, then yet closer. By that act, I experienced a euphoric sensation throughout my entire body that was akin to making love in an earthly way, but on a far grander scale. A mystical and thrilling ecstasy raced through me from my core to my extremities, rising to a crescendo of both mental and physical pleasure. A stirring sense of delight reached every recess of my mind and every cell of my body. Pure, unadulterated bliss filled me throughout. I was inundated and exhilarated with perfect happiness.

Cassandra released her grip of me and stepped back. I stood momentarily motionless in stunned serenity as she said, "Morris, you have succeeded in carrying out the comprehensive challenges we have presented. You have realized the potential we envisioned in you. To use a colloquial term, with which you will be familiar, you have passed the tests with flying colors. Congratulations."

"Thank you," I managed to utter. Then after a pause, "I have been a willing participant in the agenda you have presented. I feel privileged to have taken part."

She stepped closer and extended her left hand, index and middle fingers forward, as she said, "Morris, it has been gratifying for all of us here on Holidaymaker to have had you in our midst. We bid you a fond farewell."

Before she reached me, I interrupted, saying, "But, Cassandra, is this my final visit to Holidaymaker? Will I ever have the opportunity to return?"

"We like to think," she said, "there is always a potential to revisit. We deal with a variety of individuals. There is a harmony in that for us. Because, despite differences, there is a blending of diversity. Here on Holidaymaker we value diversity. With a candidate who has been successful here—which is practically without exception—yes, a random few have later returned for, shall we say, follow-up analysis and therapy."

"I look forward," I said, "to any prospect of coming back. In fact, it is something I would eagerly relish."

Over Cassandra's shoulder, I perceived a hazy vision of Bernard's face appear in the open air of the cargo bay. Slowly nodding his head up and down several times, his distant yet firm voice echoed, "You have done well, Morris. You have done well."

Before I could speak, Cassandra leaned toward me and said, "Be at peace." She then extended her fingers and touched my eyelids. With a slight downward motion, I was far, far away.

28

Holy freaking shit. I felt like I'd been blasted into the stratosphere and plopped right back down to the ground all at once. I'm talkin' about right now. I could see it was daylight in the cemetery, and I heard this whirring sound, but I had more important things to think about—I could hardly breathe. Actually, it was the complete opposite. I was breathing way too much. I was lying on the ground next to the vault where all my stuff was, but the air that was going in and out of me wasn't doin' any good. I guess you could say I was gasping heavily. I was back on Mother Earth and alive, but it seemed like I was on the extremely distant edge of alive. I was heaving air so forcefully that I couldn't get any. A good bit of alarm set in when my fingers and toes started twistin' up like I had the worst case of arthritis of all time. My head was spinning and I wasn't thinking clearly at all. I was fucking crippled.

I looked over and realized what the whirring sound was. The maintenance guys for the cemetery were cutting the grass and one of them, who was close by, was edging around the grave stones with a weed trimmer. He could see I was in the throes of some kind of seizure, or whatever the hell I was having, and he shut off the motor.

"Okay, señor?"

"I...I don't...know," I gasped.

He set the weed trimmer on the ground and trotted off. At that point, I was startin' to think I was having a stroke or at least something close to it. My fingers and toes were all locked up in cramped criss-crosses and I was panting like an out-of-breath dog. I was really hoping somebody would come along and give me a hand. That was because not only was I unable to get to my feet, but also, for some reason, I was beginning to curl up in a fetal position. I started thinkin' that it was gonna be a hell of a way to go, right there in the stinkin' cemetery. I guess you could say I was in a severe state of panic.

The Hispanic maintenance man came back with another guy who was dressed like he was a supervisor. The crew boss knelt down beside me and propped me up so I was sitting with my back against the vault that had my backpack on it. Sonny's guitar case was on the ground right next to me.

"Talk to me," he said.

"What?" I wheezed.

"Just start talking to me. What's your name? What color shirt and pants am I wearing. Just start talking."

"My...uh...name's...Morris Scott," then a pause for more heavy breathing. "Your shirt...is white...and your pants...are green."

"Keep going," he said. "Where are you from? Tell me about yourself."

"Well," I said, "I'm from Phila...delphia... Philadelphia. I got one brother...name's Randy." I could sense my breathing was startin' to get better and my extremities were starting to relax some.

"Keep on talking," he said. "Tell me about something that happened here in town. Just keep talking."

"Okay," I said. "Yesterday...or I don't know exactly...my friend got...hit by a car...got killed...it was bad. And...I was at the bank that got...robbed." My breathing was getting back to normal and the cramping in my fingers and toes was over. "How'd you get me...fixed up like that?"

"Piece of cake," he said. "My wife gets these kinds of panic attacks all the time. She's the nervous type. I've got the cure down pat. You just have to get talking. It helps regulate your breathing. You were hyperventilating. By slowing down and talking, it lets the carbon dioxide get back into the blood in your body. All you were doing with all that heavy huffing was losing all your carbon dioxide. You all right now?"

"Yeah," I said. "Thanks for the help. I was startin' to think I was done for. Guess I was just comin' out of a bad dream or something. I don't know. Feeling better now, though." I was starting to stand up as I said those words, but I was really a little unsteady on my feet. I decided to take it slow.

"You'll be all right," he said. "Now get yourself together and get moving on. The higher-ups around here don't much care for people camping in the cemetery. And, by the way, I read about both of those things you said happened yesterday. I thought I recognized you. You got your picture on the front page of The Citizen this morning. You're some kind of hero they say."

"Really?" I said. "Don't know if I'm up for all that...don't know about that."

"Yeah, it was very cool. Real good work you did to bust up the robbery. But I'm sorry about your friend. That's too bad."

"Yeah," I said, "It was awful...really awful. Maybe I was kinda sick here just now 'cause of all the excitement yesterday. I'm okay now. Thanks again for helpin' me out. Don't know what I would have done without you guys giving me a hand."

"No problem at all," said the supervisor. "Glad I could help you out."

The Hispanic guy raised his hand and nodded his head as both of them turned to walk away. I was still feeling a little shaky as I leaned over to grab my backpack. I stuffed the large and empty bottle of the brown in it and collected my kids story book and an extra t-shirt that were all scattered about. When I picked up Sonny's guitar case I held it up and called after them.

"This was my friend's guitar that's in here. The one who was killed." The guy who had talked me back to life turned around and lowered his gaze. He shook his head slowly back and forth a couple of times. Then he turned and walked off.

As I left the cemetery, I got to thinking about what I'd said about Sonny's guitar. Heck, I knew I couldn't play it a lick. I was wondering what the heck I was going to do with it. It occurred to me I could pawn it, but there was no way in hell I'd ever do that. It was not gonna happen—I'm talkin' about never, ever. I needed to come up with somethin' good to do with it. It struck me that I ought to take the guitar on over to the church where Sonny slept. I figured I could donate it. After all, Sonny had said the priest at St. Paul's Episcopal Church had always been real nice to him. Plus, I figured I could maybe talk to him a little about Sonny. I didn't have the slightest idea of what the heck was gonna happen to Sonny's remains. I was thinkin' maybe the priest could help me out. I left my bike where it was chained to the fence outside the cemetery and headed on foot over to the church.

On the way, the same freakin' thing happened that had always happened after a trip to Holidaymaker. I got a song in my head and couldn't get it out. It was "I'm Your Captain." I'd never even known all the lyrics of the damn tune. But I sure remembered the part near the beginning that went, "I'm your captain, I'm your captain, though I'm feeling mighty sick." It kinda had a pretty relevant meaning for the way I had been feeling a little earlier at the cemetery, for sure. The song kept going round and round in my mind about the story of a captain who doesn't want to lose his ship. I picked up the tune again in the middle where it goes, "Am I in my cabin dreaming, or are you scheming, to take my ship away from me?" I was stuck on the song as I walked to the church. I got to the end part where the line keeps repeating over and over, "I'm getting closer to my home, I'm getting closer to my home." I didn't know why the song issue kept happening after I was on Holidaymaker, or what it all meant, but it was starting to bug the hell out of me.

When I got to St. Paul's, I went in the unlocked side gate to the courtyard where Sonny used to crash at night. I went over and sat down on his favorite bench. When I set the guitar case down on the pavers, I thought about how I'd seen it right there anytime I'd happen to come by and had caught Sonny before he got up. I was feelin' kinda down until I thought about the ghostly voices of the kids that supposedly haunted the courtyard. Sonny had never had a problem with any of that sort of thing. Instead of thinking it was eerie, he seemed to feel it was pretty neat whether it was just a myth or not. As I sat there, I made up my mind I was gonna ask the priest if maybe Sonny's ashes could be placed in the courtyard somewhere.

I got up and went into the church office and asked the secretary if I could talk to the priest. Probably because of my appearance, she seemed a little reluctant to offer assistance. She seemed like the real prim and proper type. But when I mentioned I wanted to talk to the priest about Sonny, she turned and marched with quick steps down the hall. A couple of minutes later, she came back and escorted me to the priest's office. He was a lot younger than I expected, probably not any older than me, if that. He was dressed casually and, right off, he just plain acted like he was a nice, easy-going guy. Didn't seem like he was puffed up about himself at all. As I walked toward his desk, he rose and extended his hand.

"I'm Father Raymond," he said. "Very nice to meet you."

Shaking his hand, I said, "Name's Morris Scott. I wanted to talk to you about Sonny. I think you know who I mean. He has spent a lot of nights out in the courtyard and sometimes in the Fellowship Hall when the weather's bad."

The priest hesitated for a second and then said, "Of course I knew Sonny. He's been around here longer than I have. Regretfully, I saw in this morning's paper that he left us yesterday in that terrible accident on Duval Street. I was hoping someone might come by in his regard."

I was kinda relieved the priest hadn't brought up anything about my picture apparently being on the front page of the newspaper. He must have not recognized me like the maintenance guy at the cemetery had. "Yeah, but I don't know if *accident* is the right word about what happened. I know Sonny shouldn't have run out into the street and all. But if the driver of the car that hit him had been paying more attention to his driving, Sonny might still be around."

"It's a terrible shame," said Father Raymond. "Is there any way we, here at the church, can be of assistance?"

"Well," I said, "for starters I'd like to donate his guitar I got right here. Sonny always said you and the rest of the folks at the church were real nice to him. I believe he'd think it would be the right thing to do. I bet someone would be able to play it. Maybe even let some of the young kids practice on it."

"This is a very nice gesture, Morris," he said. "I'm sure we can put the guitar to good use. Now, I know this is still very recent, but do you have any information regarding the disposition of Sonny's remains? Does he have any family in the area?"

"You got me, Father," I said. "I don't know of any—close by or far away. I don't even know what his last name is. At some point, way back when, he had been married and had a child, I think. But it was up north, and I'm not sure whereabouts. Think it might have been North Carolina, but I don't really know for sure. Us folks livin' on the street usually don't get into a lot of details regarding our former lives."

"I can understand that, Morris," he said. "I'll contact the police department to see if I can get any information. And they will probably direct me to the Health Department."

"When you check with the police," I said, "Ask for Officer Keith. I'm sorry, but I don't know his last name either. But, anyway, Keith knew Sonny and he never had any problem with him that I know of. He'll help out, if he can."

"Thanks," he said as he jotted down a couple of notes. "I know who you mean. Keith Brown is a fine police officer. I've had the opportunity to deal with him on several occasions. I'll see what I can find out. If no relatives can be located, the Health Department will, more than likely, pick up the cost of cremation. Then the ashes will be held until such time as some form of next of kin comes forward to claim them."

"Well," I said, "that was the other thing I wanted to talk to you about. I was thinkin' about how Sonny really liked to spend his nights out there in the courtyard. He really felt like he had a connection with this church. So, I was wondering if maybe we could bury his ashes out there with that old sailor and the rest of the old time crowd from back in the 1800s. And plus, Sonny thought it was pretty neat about the voices of the kids, whether it's true or not. He told me one time that he'd never really heard the voices, but he thought the legend of it was comforting in an odd kind of way. Overall, he just felt like this place was a home to him."

"As rector of this church," he said, "I would certainly be willing to see to your request. But I would have to get the approval of the Bishop's Committee of our congregation. That course of action could, in a discreet manner, be avoided altogether I suppose. It's best, though, for me to follow the proper protocol. Let me give it some thought, Morris."

"Look," I said, "I wasn't suggestin' we break any rules or anything. But maybe if you could find a little spot off to the side or something, under a brick somewhere, Sonny would have a final resting place, you know."

"Tell you what," he said, "give me a few days and then check back. If Sonny was really all alone in this world, I think we can work something out. I'll see what I can do. Come back and see me."

"Thanks for any help, Father," I said. "I'm sure Sonny would appreciate anything you can do. And, besides me, he had some other friends here in Key West...from out on the street."

"I bet he did," he said. "And thank you for donating Sonny's guitar to the church. It was very thoughtful of you."

After we said our goodbyes, I left the church and went out through the courtyard. I lingered there for a few minutes and looked around. For just a second, it struck me that the song I'd had going round and round in my head had stopped. I decided it was good to let it go and concentrate on the matters at hand. I was hoping Father Raymond could find a little spot for Sonny. It would be better than his ashes just lying for eternity in a vault at the Health Department or somewhere. The church was the best idea I could come up with. I made a mental note to stop back in a couple of days and check with Father Raymond. I felt pretty sure, if anybody could figure things out, he could.

29

I left the courtyard and started walking up Duval Street. With all that had happened since I'd come around with my medical event and whatnot in the cemetery, there hadn't been a chance to reflect on the whole deal on Holidaymaker. And during my walk to the church, the stinkin' song had monopolized my thinking. But, man oh man, my head had cleared up and I was all over it. The extended trip had been even more realistic than the other times. I didn't know what to make of it. How the hell could I have done all the stuff I'd done? I couldn't see how it was possible. Chasing after Cassandra on the land, underwater, and up in space. And then the hug she gave me. Holy guacamole. Beyond words. I tried to control myself because I knew I'd go straight off my rocker if I let everything that had happened start to consume me. I decided to try only to think about it a little bit here and there. It was way too complex. And it was also vivid as hell, if you know what I mean.

I didn't even feel hungry, so when I got up to Fleming Street I hung a right and went over to the library. Thought some down time in an educational environment was a good idea. I stashed my backpack in the bushes and went on in. I saw Bill, the guard, at his regular post near the checkout desk and, as I went by, we exchanged friendly waves. I went into the reading room and saw Duct Tape Sally studying the Wall Street Journal. It never ceases to amaze me that she is interested in anything that damn paper has to say. But I've seen her reading it a ton of times.

I took a chair across the table from her, and in my normal library tone of voice said, "Hey there, Sally."

Raising her head, she said, "Well hey there yourself, Mr. Hero. You're pretty darn famous around here. Got your picture on the front page of today's Key West Citizen. It's over there on the periodical rack."

"Naw," I said, "I'm just a guy who was at the wrong place at the wrong time. No big deal. The big deal is Sonny."

"Yeah, I know," she said, "I've been trying not to think about it. Found out late yesterday from Horace when I saw him up near Mallory Square. News travels pretty fast around this little ol' town. Somebody had told Horace you were on the scene right after it all happened."

"Yeah, I was there, alright. It was bad, real bad. I've been a pretty big mess ever since…in a lot of ways."

"Well," said Sally, "Horace wasn't exactly doin' so good himself yesterday when he told me. You know, it kills me the way it seemed like those two were always fighting. You would never have known it by the looks of Horace yesterday. He was takin' it pretty hard. Kept sayin' how we'd lost one of our own."

"That's for sure," I said. Then after a pause, "I just went by the church where Sonny liked to sleep…St. Paul's. I talked to the priest and he's gonna do what he can to find out if any relatives are coming to get Sonny's ashes. The guy seems really okay. I'm supposed to go back and see him in a couple of days. If no kin turns up, I suggested maybe his ashes could be buried in the courtyard there at the church."

"Great idea, Morris," said Sally. "With our type, you never know whether any relatives really give a crap anyway. That is, even if anybody can find any relatives. In a lot of cases, it'd be like findin' a needle in a haystack. Let me know if anything turns up, though."

"I will," I said as I started to get up. "Think I'll take advantage of the complimentary facilities here at the library."

"Take a look at the front page of The Citizen on your way," she said.

I stopped at the periodical rack on the way to the men's room and picked up the newspaper. Damned if there I was, big as life, on the front page standing with the other guy who had put the heavy hit on the bank robber. I only looked at it for a second. I flipped through a few pages until I found what I was looking for. My eyes went straight down to the bottom of Page 4 to a small headline that read: "Homeless Pedestrian Killed by Car on Duval." As I scanned through the short article about it, I started to get royally pissed off. The cop who was quoted just said Sonny ran in front of the car and the driver didn't have a chance to stop in time. No charges were being filed against the driver. Son of a bitch, I thought. Sonny gets himself wiped out by some distracted driver, and all they can say about it on the bottom of Page 4 is a stinkin' homeless person got himself killed. The way I read the article, it was like they were sayin' Sonny brought it all on himself and was entirely to blame. And between the lines it was implying that it was no big deal anyway. He was just a homeless bum. It didn't even mention he was chasin' after some young punk who had stolen his money. I dropped the newspaper down on the counter and stormed off to the men's room. I was so mad I couldn't see straight.

When I came back to the reading room I sat at a different table than Duct Tape Sally. I needed some solo time to get myself calmed down. Didn't want to start talking about Sonny and get upset and loud. Especially not in the library. So I opened up a magazine that was laying on the table, looked down, and held my forehead in my hands. I had no clue what the magazine was about. Might have even had it upside down for all I know. I just sat there looking down and focusing on nothing. I did make a point of moving around a little bit every now and then. Didn't want to get tossed out if it looked like I was sleeping.

Thinking about Cassandra and Holidaymaker helped me come around from my pissed off funk. Boy, what a distraction that subject was. I kept going over in my mind all of the stuff I'd been through on the visit. I worked on itemizing everything in my head so I wouldn't forget anything. What a freakin' amazing trip. I couldn't tell what happened to me to the people I knew, 'cause they'd probably just start laughing. And if I tried to tell anybody like the cops or the press, I figured I'd be taken less seriously than Sonny had been. Knowing I'd have to go the whole thing alone didn't do anything to squelch my curiosity and interest in the entire deal, though.

After a while, I got up and went to the reference area where I pulled out some more reports on UFOs and The Bermuda Triangle. As I devoured everything I could get my hands on, I kept on thinking how there was a correlation with so much of the stuff. There had been this disorientation I'd been through with time, space, place, self, you know, everything really. And there had been land, sea, and air all in the picture. I got to thinkin' on the concept that maybe it all had to do with some weird parallel universe I'd been skipping over to. I was open to any explanation, logical or not, to somehow justify what the hell had happened. I read an awful lot of information, but all it managed to do was get me even more confounded. At the same time, I was so fascinated by the crazy thing I wasn't about to let it go.

When it got to the middle of the afternoon, I put back all of the stuff I'd been going over and waved goodbye to Duct Tape Sally. She was still reading away and looking silvery as ever. When I'd been talking to her earlier, I hadn't even noticed how the tape she had all over her was brighter than usual. Must have gotten herself a fresh roll of duct tape, I thought. I said goodbye to Bill, the guard, and started walking up toward Mallory Square.

30

Just before I got to Sloppy Joe's Bar, I looked across Duval Street and saw Horace milling around on the opposite corner. He was doing his well-polished, low-key impression of a needy street person lookin' for a handout from the passersby. Horace has a certain way about him that tourists can hardly refuse to give in to. Since I have known him, I've always thought if I ever started a business, Horace would be perfect for my chief salesman. It's amazing how he has such a familiar way with strangers. On the street, he's so good at it he ought to have a title like, "Ambassador of the Asphalt" or "Maestro of the Macadam." He has a natural ability for the street-business profession.

When I reached the corner in front of Sloppy Joe's, I waited patiently for the light to change before I crossed over Duval. After what had happened to Sonny, I had a new-found respect for making a major effort to keep from getting run over by a car or any other form of motor vehicle. Even after the light changed and it was okay to cross, I made a point of watching for turning traffic until I got to the opposite sidewalk. Being nearby to experience somebody on foot being popped by a car can make you somewhat of a paranoid pedestrian afterward. I knew that feeling was gonna stay with me for quite a while.

Horace didn't see me coming, so when I got within about ten feet of him I disguised my voice to a higher-pitched level and called out, "Excuse me, sir. Could you direct me to Mallory Square?"

He turned, with the expectant look on his face of an upcoming encounter with a potential financial contributor. When he saw it was me, he said, "Aw, Morris, don't go foolin' me like that. I thought for sure I could pick up a couple of bucks for givin' out that sort of information."

Then we both just stopped for a second. It was like a wave crashed over both of us at the same time. It was the first time we'd seen each other since Sonny had been killed the day before. Without a spoken word from either of us, we gave each other a big ol' bear hug. It didn't cross my mind, and I'm sure it was the same for Horace, how crazy it must have looked to see two street types hugging each other in broad daylight on Duval Street. But, in Key West, you're liable to see something comparable, or even way stranger, any old day of the week.

"Can't believe it, Morris," said Horace, choking up a little.

"I wouldn't either," I said, "if I hadn't seen it myself. It was real bad. Real bad."

We broke apart and then we each kinda just looked down and around at nothing. Neither of us could think of anything to say for a couple of minutes. Most civilians might figure if you're nuts enough to live on the street, then you're probably immune to emotions. In some ways that can be true. But, at least that wasn't the case with Horace or me while we were thinking about how Sonny went out.

After a minute or two, I said, "Look, what do you say if we call it an early day and get on back to the boat while it's still daylight. I think we could use a little down time after what's happened."

"That sounds just fine to me," he said. "Maybe I can hook me a catfish or somethin' to give us some supper. Let's go. My bike is locked up a couple of blocks down Duval."

On the way to Horace's bike, we stopped at a package store and got a jug of red wine. We were hoping to use it to wash down some freshly caught fish. Also, we each picked up a pint of the brown liquor for a nightcap. We were thinking ahead. I sat on the back of Horace's bike and straddled his carry baskets while he gave me a lift over to my bike at the cemetery. Two characters like us riding on one bike must have made for a sweet-looking sight to any of the tourist types along the way. The black guy steering and the white guy hanging on behind. When we got close to the cemetery, I told Horace our setup on the bike made it look like he was my chauffeur. I even called out the old expression, "Home, James, and don't spare the horses." He actually thought the whole thing was funny. I think we were both just looking for something, anything, to laugh about.

I unlocked my bike and we rode as a team over to the east side of the island where the run-about skiff was tied up. As we approached the dock, we both hit the brakes of our bikes hard enough to cause skids on the pavement. Out in the mooring field, my sailboat sat halfway submerged. The ass end, which included the motor, was completely under-water. The front half of the boat was raised up out of the water on a diagonal. It was not a pretty sight.

"Oh, no, Morris," said Horace. "This is not a good thing to see."

"That's all I need right about now," I said. "What the hell is going on?"

"What are we gonna do?" said Horace.

"I'd run the skiff over to her," I said, "but it would be just like me to step on the front end and have the whole damn boat go under. I can't deal with this right now. I'll think about it tomorrow. I'm going to be like Scarlett O'Hara at the end of 'Gone with the Wind' and say, 'After all…tomorrow is another day.' Or a line something like that."

There was still an hour or two of daylight, so we walked our bikes through some underbrush and went over toward the Salt Ponds. We picked an opening, laid our bikes down, and made a makeshift camp. We were out of the sight of traffic, which was the primary concern. Being very close to the airport, every now and then there was the loud roar of a plane either landing or taking off. I grabbed the jug of wine and cracked open the twist-off top. Handing the jug to Horace I said, "Go ahead and take a nice big pull, 'cause like Ernest Hemingway once said, 'People in the Southern climates drink for pleasure, and people in the Northern climates drink to avoid depression.' And right now I'd say we gotta be doing a lot of both, my friend. I'm kinda startin' to wax philosophic with all these quotes I'm laying on you, huh?"

"Okay by me," said Horace as he hoisted the full jug and nodded at me. "And thanks, Morris."

Then after a long drink he said, "Mighty fine, mighty fine. There's sure some bad news goin' on for us. Some horrible stuff...some real horrible stuff."

"Maybe it has to do with that 'Robert the Doll' over in Old Town."

"What are you talkin' about?" said Horace in a serious tone. "Who the hell is 'Robert the Doll' or what the hell is 'Robert the Doll?'"

"Don't you know about that doll? It's supposed to have been around Key West for at least a hundred years. Was owned by some artist who lived here back in the1800s. When the artist was a kid, he got the doll as a present. But when anything would go wrong, he'd blame the damn doll. So the doll ended up gettin' put in an attic window. From then on, as legend has it, 'Robert the Doll' supposedly taunted kids when they'd walk by the house. Scarin' them and all. It's been goin' on ever since... at least that's what they say. I've heard the tour guides on the trolleys point it out to the vacationers. But I couldn't tell you where the hell the house is. Can't remember."

"Don't go tellin' me these kinds of things," said Horace. "This ol' doll you're talkin' about and then them ghosts of kids at Sonny's church. All that stuff gives me the creeps. Don't be tellin' me nothing 'bout 'Robert the Doll'....Robert the stinkin' Doll. Don't need to be hearing about that kind of stuff. Too much of that in this town. I don't wanna know anything about it."

"Okay, okay," I said. "No more scary stories. Just trying to get my mind off all the bad news. That's all."

We sat for a while and drank quietly until Horace said, "But I did see your picture in the newspaper this morning. It must have been some mess of a time at the bank. How'd it all go down?"

After I took a couple of big gulps, I gave Horace a brief rundown of the events in the thwarting of the bank robbery. Even though it had only happened the day before, it was a subject that seemed a long time ago to me. And it seemed pretty minor considering what had happened since. I also filled Horace in on the meeting I'd had at the church with the priest. He seemed to think I had done the right thing and he was eager to hear any additional news about Sonny.

Because of the boat incident, Horace had missed his chance to do some fishing for dinner. And although I hadn't had anything to eat all day, I still didn't feel hungry at all. Having some wine— and knowing there was some of the brown liquor in reserve—was all that really mattered. A liquid diet was fine with me. Time passed as we continued to share the jug.

"You know," I said, "it's not right about Sonny. It's just not the same with only the two of us passin' this jug of wine back and forth."

"Not the same at all," said Horace. "You know, I'd fight with that redneck son-of-a-bitch any ol' time. He was such an asshole sometimes...lots of times. But I do miss him...I miss him. He was one of us. One of us."

"Yes he was," I said. "I miss him, too……….. and he was an asshole a lot of the time. But maybe we ought to start reconsiderin' what being one of us means. Maybe we ought to start workin' on getting back into the regular way of living. Or at least give it a try. With all that's been happening, we only got one way to go if we're gonna survive. And that's gotta be up. Anything else, and we're not gonna be around for too awful long...for one reason or another."

"That's all good, Morris," he said, "but what are we gonna do? I mean, who'd give us a job?"

"I don't know," I said. "But there's gotta be a way...got to be a way. What the hell do we have to lose?"

31

The next couple of days passed quietly. I decided to just let the sailboat go. To use the jargon associated with these types of matters, I was going to let the boat become a "derelict." There really wasn't much anything of value on it, so I figured I might as well abandon it. It would probably take the authorities quite a while to figure out who the owner was. And when they finally did, how the hell were they gonna find me anyway, seeing as I didn't have what you would call a permanent address. Paying the salvaging cost to move the boat somewhere to either junk it or repair it was not an expense that was in my modest budget. No sense in throwing good money after bad was the way I looked at it.

I decided to symbolically donate the half-sunken rust bucket to the City of Key West. Until something was eventually done with it, I was gonna think of it as a semi-floating monument to the street people of our fair city. The only regret I had about the whole deal was that I never had gotten around to changing the name on it to Holidaymaker. Since the boat was technically still named Pukin' Pelican, it made walking away from it slightly less painful, though. The concept of me being a boat owner was a little over the top anyway. A fair amount of us street types aren't cut out for those sorts of undertakings. Probably wasn't the best idea to buy it in the first place, if you know what I mean.

I'd spent the last few days employing the panhandlin' practice and the last few nights in the cemetery. In a way, I looked at the sinking of the sailboat as a blessing in disguise. With it out of the picture, I could spend as many nights as possible in the cemetery. I didn't want to miss any additional chances to hook up with the folks on Holidaymaker, just in case they happened to stop by for a return visit. By the way, one particular member of that crew was of primary interest in my mind. And I'd bet you people followin' along here have a pretty good idea of who I mean.

I'd also remembered to stop by St. Paul's Church and see Father Raymond. He hadn't heard any specific word on Sonny's remains, but he had contacted Officer Keith and felt sure he'd be hearing something from Keith before too long. It made me feel good they both were on the case. They each had a whole lot more contacts and influence around

Key West and with Monroe County than I would ever have. Somebody looking like me was not going to get the kind of straight answers that a priest or a cop would get from the administrative authority types. Street folks aren't known for getting a whole lot of respect in a number of ways.

Father Raymond mentioned that when he was checking out Sonny's guitar I had left with him, he noticed there was a small amount of cash in the bottom of the case. It was something like twelve dollars. He had it in an envelope and wanted to give it to me. It was apparently the leftover money that the punk kid didn't manage to grab out of Sonny's case during the robbery. I hadn't even noticed the money when I packed up the guitar right after Sonny was killed. I guess I wasn't thinking very clearly at that point. I told Father Raymond to keep it and to consider it a donation from Sonny to the church. I sure as heck wasn't gonna take the twelve dollars from the priest. It seemed like the right thing for me to do and Father Raymond happily obliged. I told him I'd check back with him the following week regarding Sonny, and he assured me that nothing would be finalized until he talked to me.

As I headed up Duval Street, I thought about how I really liked Father Raymond. It seemed like he was treating me like he would anybody else, even though I wasn't a member of his church who was putting a lot of money in the till every Sunday. Heck, he'd allowed Sonny to camp out in the courtyard at night, and even let him sleep inside if it was raining. It seemed like Father Raymond cared for everybody, regardless of their station in life. It reminded me of the way Suzanne treated me at the bank. None of that haughty, "I'm better than you" or "you're a loser" crap that street folks are used to getting—said or unsaid—from most civilians.

I noticed the finances were getting a bit low, so I swung by my bank to make a withdrawal. Plus, I wanted to catch up with Suzanne on how her side was feeling from the slam into the counter she had taken. I also wanted to check on how her mother was doing. It was the first time I'd been back since the robbery had been foiled. There were only three or four customers ahead of me in the rat maze line. When I got to the front and Suzanne called to me to come over, she and the other three tellers all stopped what they were doing and started applauding. Word quickly spread to the customers at the teller windows and then to the few people in line who had come in behind me. They all started clapping, too. Since everyone was standing, I guess you could say I got a standing ovation. There were even a couple shouts of "Yea" and "Way to go." My long hair and beard hopefully hid most of my face from what I'm sure was blushing. As I walked toward Suzanne's window, I turned to the assembled group, raised the palm of my hand and silently mouthed "Thank you."

After a smiling Suzanne stopped clapping, she leaded forward and, with enthusiasm, said, "Aren't you the brave man, Morris! It's good to see you."

"Good to see you, too, Suzanne," I said. "This is a little embarrassing, you know."

"Oh," she said, "you deserve a little embarrassing. You're a hero around here. It's all we've been talking about."

"Well, thanks," I said. "But what's more important is how your side is doing where you hit the counter. And how's your mom making out?"

"Good on both counts," she said. "I got x-rays taken and nothing is broken. I've got a couple of bruised ribs, though. And Mom's doing some better. She's tricky that way. She goes along doing okay, then she goes down some, and then she makes a comeback. It's happened quite a few times before. I still have my plane tickets to go up to see her next month. It's a relief she's bounced back."

"That's good to hear," I said. "About your side and your mom, both. And I meant what I said about helping you out with some money if you had to fly up there a couple of times in a row. Now, when it comes to your bruised ribs, I guess I can't do much to doctor you the way you did me before. I would if I could, though."

"Oh," she said, "you've done so much to help me. I can't thank you enough. Everything is going to work out. I just know it."

"Well," I said, "you take care of yourself. I'll be back in a few days, as usual."

"Oh, Morris, I almost forgot. A letter came for you yesterday. It looks like it's from your brother."

I took the letter from Suzanne, put it in my pocket, and said, "Thanks. I wonder what in the world he's got to tell me. We're kind of estranged, you know. Ever since we had the change in the way we work the finances here at the bank." I'd never told Suzanne about what had happened with the incident in Randy's room at the Pier House. It was something I was not exactly proud of and I didn't want her to think any less of me because of it. There was no sense letting her in on the details.

"See you soon," she said.

"Take care, Suzanne."

As I left, my curiosity about the letter got the best of me. I went around to the parking lot in back of the bank, sat on a parking stump near Suzanne's car, and opened it up:

Morris,

I'm writing to tell you that Mother passed away a little over three weeks ago. It was very sudden. She had a stroke and was gone very quickly. There was a nice gathering at the funeral and the service was well done.

There is a sizeable inheritance. In view of the fact that there are only two of us, I just don't feel right about not including you, even though Mother had removed you from her will. I'm willing to put the disaster at the Pier House behind us. I'm certain that you did not intend for things to turn out as they did.

Consequently, at the beginning of next month, and every month thereafter, there will be an automatic deposit of $500.00 made into your bank account. There will be no restrictions, as there had been before, with the limits or frequency of making withdrawals.

230

It is my intention to continue to visit Key West from time to time. I will still stay at the Pier House and will notify you in advance of my scheduled arrival. I would welcome seeing you under the same arrangement as we had previously, with these restrictions: No other friends, no parties—just you, and only you.

I trust all of this is satisfactory with you. I feel sure that Mother would be at peace with our understanding. Will be in touch in a few months.

Randy

Well, reading that little ditty pretty much stunned the heck out of me. First off, I was sorry my mother had died—who wouldn't be. But the bottom line was: Mother was gone, and Randy, to my way of thinking, was being awfully fair and big about everything. My allowance, if you wanna call it that, had been roughly two hundred bucks a month before. Now it was getting kicked up to five hundred and I could get any amount of it any old time I wanted. That sure was some mixed news to digest. On top of it all, I felt good about Randy and me getting back on reasonable terms with each other. Although, I still felt bad about the mess that had split us apart. Heck, even though we were a lot different, he was my brother, after all. I didn't want to go on through life thinking the link between us was broken forever. That happens with families sometimes—and sometimes with real good reason—but I didn't want to be cut off from Randy on account of a trashed motel room. Even if it was the Pier House. It struck me, from this point on, Randy wouldn't be telling me any new stories about Mother carrying on and being the way she could be. But I figured we had enough ones from the past we could swap to last us a very long time.

32

A couple of days later, I stopped by the bank to grab a little cash. Suzanne was off, but the teller who handled my business gave me a large envelope that Suzanne had left for me in case I came in when she wasn't there. There was more weight to the envelope than just papers would make. When I got outside, I tore it open. There was a note inside, but what made the envelope heavier was a pair of scissors. I couldn't get to the note fast enough to find out what the heck the scissors were for. At first, I thought she must have dropped them in there by mistake. But knowing Suzanne and her detailed way of life, that didn't seem likely.

The note informed me that on the upcoming Friday, which was two days away, there was going to be an event at Mallory Square to honor local citizens who had recently done heroic deeds in Key West. She had even included an announcement for the ceremony that had been cut out of The Key West Citizen. The guy who helped me corral the bank robber and I were two of the honorees. In fact, we were getting top billing. Seeing as I didn't read the newspaper every day, I didn't know anything about the observance that was planned. At the end of the note, Suzanne had added a cute little P.S.: "Thought maybe the enclosed might be helpful in sprucing up for the ceremony." I laughed out loud. Suzanne had never been one to seem critical, or to care, about my appearance. She'd never made a comment about it at all. Since I'd gotten to know her a lot better in recent months, I figured she wasn't really telling me what to do. She was just trying to help me out with a friendly suggestion about cutting my hair and beard so I'd look more presentable, so to speak. I didn't take any offense in the least.

By Thursday, I'd trimmed my beard some and had Horace give me a hand with cutting my hair. Nothing terribly radical had gone on or anything. I didn't look like I'd just joined the Army, but my grooming was a good bit neater. I'd even rinsed out what was my best tee shirt in preparation for the event. Although, I wasn't all that satisfied with the amount of wear even my best shirt showed. Overall, I tried to clean up my act to a reasonably acceptable level.

On Friday morning, I hadn't woken up at the cemetery quite as early as I had hoped. I checked the time as I was walking up to Mallory Square and realized I was cutting it close to be on time for the ten o'clock start of the show. Since I was hustling all the way up Duval Street, by the time I got to the Square I was sweating up a storm. The speaking had already begun, but I felt pretty sure I was only a little bit tardy.

To give you an idea of the seriousness of the event, there was even one of the local radio station vans set up off to the side. They were doing a live remote broadcast and, on top of that, they were distributing new tee shirts advertising their station. Since my shirt was soaked, I got one of the complimentary ones and made a quick change. I figured a bright, white, brand new tee shirt was way better than an old sweaty one. It didn't bother me one bit that the front of the shirt said boldly: "B-100.5—The Big Talker."

I wasn't sure who was doing the speaking up on the stage, but he was introducing the Mayor of Key West to a fairly good-sized crowd. If it hadn't been for the reason I was there, I felt sure I could have easily worked the gathered group for a fair amount of bucks. I looked around and recognized quite a few people I knew. It was easy to spot Suzanne as tall and good-looking as she was. I could have picked her out from a hundred yards away. She was standing with the security guard who had been wounded by a gunshot in the bank robbery attempt. And I was fairly sure that the branch manager of the bank was with them. Officer Keith wasn't far from me, so I went over and stood next to him.

"Hey there, Morris," Keith whispered. "This is your big day. When it's over, I'd like to talk to you. I've got the word on Sonny's ashes. It's all good."

"Okay," I said. "But it can only be so good. I mean, what happened to Sonny with that driver—I don't like it, I just don't like it."

"I don't like it, either," he whispered back. "But, at this point, there's only so much we can do. If you recall, we were stretched a little thin that day on account of the bank robbery. We just didn't have enough officers available to do a thorough investigation of what happened and why. It's not a good explanation for what happened, but it's the only one I've got."

The Mayor was now up on the podium, speaking away. He was, as is the custom for politicians, taking the opportunity to get as much camera time, and talking time, as possible. He was going on, and on, and on. I was almost sorry I hadn't gotten to Mallory Square even later than I had. There were several presentations recognizing heroic actions of various locals. One guy had saved a tourist who was a novice at scuba diving and had almost drowned. Another was for a woman who was a clerk at a local convenience store. Apparently, a teenager, acting as if he had a gun, had tried to stick up the business. The clerk had basically put the kid in a wrestling hold until the cops got there. In the back of my mind, I was hoping the kid was the same one who'd stolen Sonny's cash. But if you saw this gal who was the clerk, you wouldn't be surprised that she could have handled the situation. She was another example, like Officer Keith, of someone you'd want on your side if you ever got involved in a street fight.

The highlight of the public ceremony was the recognition of two local citizens who had put a stop to the attempted robbery at the Southern Trust Bank. It was the first time I ever found out the other guy's name when they called John Reader and Morris

Scott up to the stage. I left my backpack on the ground next to Officer Keith. The branch manager of the bank, Suzanne, and the security guard were also asked to come up. The Mayor presented John and me with framed Certificates of Recognition from the City of Key West. The certificates were pretty swanky and very official looking. It struck me sort of funny that I didn't have a wall to hang the thing on. I figured I'd carry it around in my backpack until I came up with somewhere to put it. I was thinking I'd ask Suzanne if she thought it would be okay to put it up in the bank someplace, even if it was out of sight in the teller's room. I just wasn't used to getting an award or anything.

After the Mayor spoke for about five times longer than he should have, the bank manager was asked to say a few words. He introduced the guard who had been wounded and he also recognized Suzanne who had been injured during the incident. They both got a nice round of applause. The bank manager was followed at the podium by my tackling partner, John Reader, who was reserved and modest about his involvement. John even said that if I hadn't knocked the gun out of the guy's hand, he wouldn't have done anything. He said he'd played some football in college and it seemed easy for him to come in for the big hit seeing as I had the guy propped up and under control. I thought to myself that, at the time, it wasn't exactly how I felt about the situation. I was basically just hanging on for dear life, if you know what I mean.

Then they asked me to say a few words. I was probably about as embarrassed as I could get.

But with my hair and beard trimmed, not to mention the brand new radio station tee shirt, I felt okay about my appearance. I decided to give it a go. As I walked up to the podium, I caught Suzanne's eye at a glance and she smiled and nodded her head.

"I'm not used to talking in front of a group of people," I said into the microphone. "So, if I seem a little nervous, I am."

I hesitated for a minute and thought about all the things that had happened in my life in the recent past. It started with the bank robbery episode, which was the reason I was up there at the podium in the first place. Right after that, Sonny had been killed in a crazy kind of way. On the same night, I'd had the biggest Holidaymaker adventure ever. Then I'd had the hyperventilating incident in the cemetery that made me think I was possibly gonna die. I just kept thinking about everything. The sailboat sinking—or really half scuttling itself. And then the note from Randy telling me that our mother had died. Man, the weight of it all really came bearing down on me. It put me in the frame of mind to say a few things. I guess I just felt like using my voice to vent some of the frustration I was feeling.

"I want to thank you for having me here today. It's a very nice ceremony. And I want to also thank John Reader for what he did to help put an end to the robbery. The only reason I did anything to begin with was because of my friend, Suzanne, over there. She was introduced a few minutes ago. When the robbery started, Suzanne was in danger almost from the beginning. She got pushed hard into a counter by the second bank robber. I could tell she got hurt, and that got me very upset. I guess you could say it was just a natural reaction to try to help her. Heck, if I'd gotten hurt somehow, it wouldn't have been any big deal. But I just can't stand to see a friend of mine get hurt. That's why I did what I did. I didn't even think about it. I'm usually not one for any confrontations, but when I saw what was happening, it really pissed me off. Excuse me for using those words, but it's the truth.

"Now there's something else that happened right afterwards that day that got me upset, too. Another friend of mine, his name was Sonny, was hit and killed by a car on Duval Street. You may not have heard about it. It was in The Citizen, but it was a very small article that was buried on the fourth or fifth page. Well, Sonny lived on the streets, so maybe that's why there wasn't much of a fuss about it. He had some faults, there's no denying that. But Sonny didn't have to die. He was chasing after a kid who had stolen his money that he'd made playing the guitar. Sonny ran out into the street and was hit by a car. What I heard from people who saw it happen up close, was that the driver of the car wasn't paying attention to his driving. The guy wasn't watching where he was going. He hit the brakes too late and plowed right into Sonny. Couldn't stop in time. And that was the end of that. Nothing ever came of it, and probably nothing ever will. All I'm saying is—it didn't have to happen. Like I said before, I hate to see a friend of mine get hurt—anybody really. I'm sorry if I've been rambling on here. I just had to get all that off my chest. I'll say it again—it didn't have to happen."

As I hesitated for a second, I recognized Horace's voice call out from the crowd, "Tell it, Morris! Tell it!"

"Thank you for giving recognition to all of us and for letting me speak here today," I said, finishing up.

Because my head was spinning as I walked off the stage, I didn't get to fully appreciate the loud round of applause I'm pretty sure I got. It was the second time in less than a week people were clapping for me. Was hard to believe. I walked over and stood between Officer Keith and Horace. While the various dignitaries got in their last long-winded remarks, I put the framed certificate into my backpack.

"Sorry I'm late," said Horace, leaning closer to me. "But I heard the last part of what you said. And it sounded great to me. Real great."

"You did a good job up there, Morris," said Officer Keith.

"Thanks," I said. "Not used to doing all that public speaking. I guess I got a little carried away."

"Not at all," said Keith. "You said what you had to say. Nothing wrong with that. Now, look, Morris, here's the lowdown on Sonny's ashes. Father Raymond at St. Paul's asked me to look into what was happening. I checked with the Health Department and they were coming up with blanks on finding any of Sonny's relatives. So, that agency went ahead and covered the cost of the cremation. I told them Father Raymond was prepared to take possession of the remains. He's got it under control, now. Just check with him for any other details."

"Thanks again," I said. "I'll do just that."

When the event was finally finished, a beaming Suzanne came over. "Wow, Morris," she said, "you were something. You gave a great speech. But I didn't know about your friend. I'm so sorry."

"I just had to say some things about it," I said. "It was a shame he was killed. A real shame. But I'm glad you're okay. How's your side doing?"

"Oh," she said, "it's almost better. The black and blue marks are just about gone. And it's not sore anymore. But I want to tell you how impressed I am with you for all the things you said today. You were wonderful. I feel proud to say you're my friend."

"Well, thanks," I said. "You know I feel the same way about you. And it's good to hear you're almost healed up. I'll be seeing you soon at the bank. I bet you gotta be gettin' back there."

"Yes, I do," she said. "See you the next time you come in."

As she was walking away, I called after her, "And thanks for the scissors. It was a good idea."

She turned and gave me a smile I could have looked at all day. Wow. And, on top of that, Suzanne had just told me that I was something. Man, in my mind, she was the one who was *really* something.

33

Horace and I left Mallory Square and walked down to St. Paul's Church. We both were interested in what was going to happen with Sonny's ashes. But, as usual, Horace was reluctant to set foot on the grounds of the church. I had to twist his arm a little to convince him to see Father Raymond with me. After sufficient encouragement, I persuaded him to come along.

Father Raymond told us he had gone to the Health Department that very morning and had taken possession of Sonny's remains. It was a little humbling to see the small cardboard box that held Sonny's ashes sitting on his desk. Written on the outside of the box was what looked like an inventory number and the name, Ralph Andrew Coverdale. Below his full name was "Sonny" in parentheses. It was the first time I ever learned what his real name was. I had no idea how the authorities found it out. Maybe they compared his fingerprints to a computer data base or something. It wouldn't have surprised me at all if Sonny had spent some time in the Big House at some point or another during his time on earth.

Father Raymond told us he was available in the middle of the afternoon on Sunday to have a little memorial service for Sonny. Even though it was Friday, it wasn't like anybody needed a lot of time to make elaborate preparations. We settled on three o'clock on Sunday. Father Raymond was a little disappointed to let us know we wouldn't be able to actually bury Sonny's ashes in the court-yard. The priest had checked with the committee that oversaw those matters at the church and they had denied the request. So, when Father Raymond suggested we scatter the ashes on the flower garden in the courtyard as an alternative, Horace and I agreed.

After we left the church, I was more than ready for a little liquid refreshment. Heck, I'd spoken in front of a big group of people, plus the media, and then had kind of a serious meeting with the priest. I was thirsty as hell. We stopped by a package store and picked up a big jug of red wine and a pint of the brown liquor. I bought. Then we made our way over to the empty lot behind Steamers Restaurant and proceeded to relax.

"I gotta tell you, Morris," said Horace, "you were the real public speaker earlier today. Wish I'd gotten there in time to hear everything you said. I was runnin' a little late."

"No big deal," I said. "I was just explaining what happened during the bank robbery. And then I guess you heard the rest of what I said about Sonny."

"Yes I did," he said. "It was some good stuff. Some real good stuff. And how about this? I got some other good news today. The priest at St. Peter's Church, where I sleep most of the time, received a letter addressed to me. My cousin from up near Cleveland, Mississippi was trying to track me down. He'd heard I lived on the streets in Key West, so he took a chance and mailed a letter to the only black church in town. He figured the priest might maybe know of me, seeing as there aren't a whole lot of black folks here on the island."

"Well, how about that?" I said. "That's some kinda coincidence and some good luck."

"I'll say," said Horace. "And my cousin had

some bad news, but some good news, too. He said that his mother, who's my aunt, is not doing all that well with her health. He was inviting me to come on up to their place and stay with them. They live just outside of Cleveland, not far from the Sunflower River. Some good, good fishin' up there. He even said he thought he could get me a job. Not many good-paying jobs in the Delta but, man, that's the place to fish and hear some good blues music. Cleveland's right on Highway 61 between Clarksdale and Greenville. And Greenwood's not all that far away, either. It's the heart of blues country, the Delta is. I lived there for a while when I was growin' up. Haven't been back in many, many a year."

"Well," I said, "maybe it's time to give it a try. You'd be with your kin and all. In the long run, it'd probably be a good move."

"Oh, yeah. I got a mess of cousins around that area. Never really told you about them. When I left there, I sorta decided to forget about them and everything else. But, in the last few years, I've been thinkin' about getting back up there some day."

"Then this is your chance," I said. "Like I said one other time, what do you have to lose?"

"I'm gonna give it some serious thought," he said. "Some real serious thought."

We proceeded to drink away the rest of the afternoon. The chance to move to Mississippi and be with relatives sure seemed like a good opportunity for Horace to get off the streets. I decided I'd continue to encourage him. Although it would mean losing a friend, I was starting to look at the big picture and become a little more aware of the reality of things. There is only so long that Horace, me, or any-body else can make it following the street lifestyle. Although you could say the pace is slow out here, it really is an accelerated pace in terms of aging and using up your life. I was starting to realize that.

We talked some about the service at the church for Sonny. We each agreed to tell Duct Tape Sally about it if we saw her in the mean time. Horace even talked me into letting Connie Jo in on it. In the back of my mind, I was hoping she wouldn't get the word. Although, what the heck, I thought. Why not? After all, when someone dies, there's no reason to keep somebody from being able to pay their last re-spects. Even if it was Connie Jo. I was just hoping she wouldn't make a scene or anything—like she was known to do more often than not.

Horace and I traded the jug and talked until the wine was gone. Horace was very upbeat about the prospect of moving to Mississippi, and I was happy for him. It was a way out. As we took turns on the brown liquor, I got to thinking about my future, which is not a subject most citizens of the streets give much consideration. It just seemed like ever since I'd made the trips on Holidaymaker, I'd had a better outlook on things. The positive attitude that was so customary there had a way of being con-tagious. With the other stuff I'd gone through in my life in a short period of time, I'd had a chance to see what *good* can happen and what *bad* can happen. And it seemed like I was better off going with the good things. I decided that even though there would be more money coming through from Randy, I was still gonna make an effort to find what you might call a more conventional occupation. Soliciting money from strangers, by way of the panhandling game, can work on your core after a while. It either beats your self-esteem down to a pulp, or you turn things around and come out of it somehow. I was starting to think I really didn't want to do the begging routine all that much anymore.

34

Sunday afternoon rolled around and I went over to St. Paul's. I got an early start so I wouldn't be late. I'd say I was at least an hour early for the three o'clock service. I sat on Sonny's favorite bench and thought about how I couldn't believe what was gonna happen there in the courtyard before long. I thought about a lot of other stuff, too. The last several days I'd been considering, and reflecting on, more things than I could ever remember. I was starting to become the real cerebral and analytical type. It hadn't come to the point of contemplating the meaning of life, or anything. But it was close. I was starting to get a little restless with myself.

After about thirty or forty minutes sitting in the courtyard, the church secretary came out of the office door and walked over to me. She hadn't been at the church several days earlier when Horace and I had met with Father Raymond. She was as strait-laced and proper as the first time I met her but, this time, she seemed friendlier than before. Maybe it was because she appreciated the reason I was there and she was showing some sympathy.

"Father Raymond," she said, "will be out in fifteen or twenty minutes. Would you care for a cold drink while you're waiting?"

"No, thank you," I said. The thought of a good pull on some of the brown liquor went through my head. But I knew for sure that wasn't close to what she had meant. I'd been good about not having anything to drink before I showed up. "There probably will be several other people coming shortly," I said.

"That's fine," she said. "We won't get underway until they arrive." She turned and with short, quick steps went back inside.

After a few minutes, Horace, Duct Tape Sally, and Connie Jo came in the gate to the courtyard. I was glad they had made it, although Connie Jo seemed a little unsteady on her feet. It wouldn't have surprised me if they'd done a little pre-event tailgating, so to speak. Duct Tape Sally had her grocery cart with her, as usual. After she wheeled it through the gate, she pushed it over to the side behind a decorative fountain, which partially hid the cart from sight.

As they approached me, Horace said, "Well, we made it. Not late at all."

"Good job, Horace," I said. "Hi there, girls. How's everyone doing? Nobody's tipsy or anything, are we?"

"We're fine," said Duct Tape Sally. "We just needed to have a little bracer before the service. No problem at all."

Horace, who seemed a little bit antsy, said, "I hope all this doesn't last very long. This place gives me the creeps."

"You'll be fine," I said. "Just hang in there. You're in good company."

Connie Jo hardly spoke a word other than a quiet "Hello." For once, it seemed, she had decided to display a little etiquette and be on her best behavior.

Before long, Father Raymond, the church secretary, and a teenage boy emerged from the church. The boy had Sonny's guitar strapped over his shoulder, and the church secretary was carrying the cardboard box with Sonny's remains. Father Raymond motioned for us to come over to the edge of the courtyard flower garden. He greeted us and I introduced him to Sally and Connie Jo. He also acknowledged Horace, who he'd met a couple days earlier at the church. Father Raymond was as casual and relaxed as the other times I had talked to him. The guy was genuine.

Beginning the service he said, "Good afternoon, everyone. I'd like to welcome you all to St. Paul's Church. It's a beautiful day that I hope will strengthen your spirits. Although this is a somber occasion, I'd like this experience to be both comforting and uplifting as we celebrate the life of Sonny Coverdale. To begin, one of the newer and younger members of our church, Jason, will play 'Amazing Grace' on Sonny's guitar."

I could tell the boy was a little nervous. Heck, he probably wondered what the hell he was getting into, standing outside and playing the guitar in front of a rough-looking bunch like the four of us. Of course, my hair and beard had been trimmed some for the awards ceremony at Mallory Square. So that contributed to improving our overall appearance a little. And I was even sporting my new white tee shirt from the radio station. But we sure didn't come off looking like a typical congregation of mourners, if you know what I mean.

Jason strummed a couple of notes on the guitar, stopped, and then started again. During the hymn, he made more than a few mistakes, but he got through it. Considering what was happening, and who was there, it almost seemed fitting that his performance wasn't anywhere near perfect. When he finished, Connie Jo got in a few hard claps of her hands before Duct Tape Sally grabbed Connie Jo's arm and shushed her.

"Thank you, Jason," said Father Raymond. "We are here today to honor Sonny Coverdale and his memory. I've known Sonny for the past several years, so I feel grateful to speak today on his behalf. Sonny spent many nights here in this courtyard and also occasionally in our Fellowship Hall. He was never a difficulty in any way for anyone here at the church. And he treated our facilities with the utmost respect. While here, Sonny was reverent of all things at St. Paul's. He was an accomplished musician on the guitar, which gave listening enjoyment to many. Although he led his life in a singular manner, it was his life to lead, and Sonny lived it in his own unique way. He ran *his* race. He fought *his* fight."

While I was listening to Father Raymond, I looked up and saw Officer Keith standing outside the gate to the courtyard. He gave me a little knowing nod and I did the same. Father Raymond must have let Keith know about the timing of the service. What a good gesture on both of their parts.

"Please let us bow our heads," said Father Raymond. "Heavenly Father, bless these ashes of Sonny Coverdale as we commit them to the ground. And bless his spirit as a child of God. May he rest here in peace for eternity. Let there be a moment of silence as we reflect on Sonny's memory."

During the quiet, Connie Jo was noticeably sobbing. Duct Tape Sally was trying to console her, but Sally wasn't doing much better. I was dealing with some tears, too. Matter of fact, I don't think there were too many dry eyes around. Glancing up, I even saw the church secretary dabbing her eye with a small handkerchief.

"Morris," said Father Raymond, "While Jason plays two hymns, would you spread Sonny's ashes throughout the flower garden?"

As I walked over to the secretary and took the box from her, Jason began playing, "Higher Ground." I wasn't sure how well his rendition was of that hymn. I was busy leaning over, trying to lightly and evenly spread the ashes around the base of colorful flowers that filled the rectangular-shaped garden. It struck me that Sonny's ashes had the look and texture of fertilizer you would use to feed plants. In a way, I guess that's what was happening. Jason followed up with "How Great Thou Art" as I finished my mission. During the benediction, I again looked over to the gate where Officer Keith had been stand-ing, but he was gone. I thought it was a pretty kind and caring effort on his part to come by at all. There was no doubt he had a heart.

Following the ceremony, Father Raymond invited us all to stay for some light refreshments. I thanked Jason for his playing before we started to walk toward the Fellowship Hall. When I got to the door, I looked back and saw Jason carrying a large bag of mulch over to the flower garden. I stood there for a couple of minutes and watched him scatter a light coating of the mulch around the base of the flowers where I had spread the ashes. If the wind kicked up before it rained next, Sonny's ashes would be safely covered. Father Raymond had thought of everything.

Inside the Fellowship Hall, there was a small arrangement of coffee, soft drinks, and some pastries on a table. The church secretary managed to disappear unnoticed. The four of us mourners were all very polite and had a few snacks with Father Raymond. But I was sure what was on my mind was on the minds of the rest of the street folks in attendance. We were all in need of something stronger than coffee or cola. I realized Connie Jo had come prepared for such a necessity when I saw her trying to take a discreet pull of brown liquor from a pint bottle she'd brought along in her backpack. Duct Tape Sally immediately pounced, grabbed the bottle, and stashed it away in her handbag. Sally then proceeded to give Connie Jo a quiet scolding.

After a reasonable amount of socializing, we all said our goodbyes. I would have thought Father Raymond would have been in just the same amount of hurry to part ways as the rest of us were. After all, he wasn't getting any compensation for his handling of the service, and he was dealing with a group of folks who were about as opposite from church people as you could get. But he sure didn't act that way. It seemed like he would have been happy to stand around and talk with us for the rest of the afternoon. It was very clear he wasn't picky about the people he dealt with at the church or anywhere else—you could just tell. He treated us with sincerity and warmth. After he got to know you, Father Raymond would be the guy you'd want speaking at your own funeral.

35

The four of us walked back through the courtyard on our way out. Duct Tape Sally retrieved her semi-hidden grocery cart while Horace hustled out the gate. Seeing as being in the courtyard made him anxious, I could tell he didn't want to spend any more time on the grounds than necessary. I lingered for a few minutes and gazed at the flower garden where I'd deposited Sonny's remains. With the fresh covering of mulch over the ashes, you would have never known what we had done a little while earlier. It was like it never happened.

It crossed my mind that after Father Raymond got the thumbs down from the higher ups for actually burying Sonny's ashes, he masterminded what we did without telling anyone else at the church. I'd be willing to bet that he and the church secretary were the only ones in any kind of authority who were in on the deal. But it was awful nice of him to conduct the ceremony, regardless of how it was handled. It was also nice to know Sonny got a special sendoff in his special place. I knew for sure I'd think about him every time I went by St. Paul's. Heck, isn't that what cemeteries and headstones and plaques and all that kind of stuff are really for anyway? They're just a physical reminder of someone's memory. At least for a handful of us, that intended aim had been accomplished.

The others were waiting for me when I got out on the sidewalk. It was quickly decided we would pool our money and obtain some liquid refreshments. We did just that and made our way up to the empty lot behind Steamers. Rounds of red wine were interspersed with an occasional shot of the brown liquor. Considering the drinking she'd done before the service, plus the emotional toll it had taken, it wasn't long before Connie Jo became royally shit-faced. Duct Tape Sally was right behind her in the same fashion. In Sonny's honor, they had moaned and cried and hugged and drank until they both passed out in the late-afternoon shade on what little grass was in the lot. It gave Horace and me the chance to talk uninterrupted.

"I wanted to tell you," said Horace, "I've been giving a lot of thought to my cousin's offer to move up to Mississippi. A lot of heavy thought. And I've decided I'm gonna give it a shot. I've been gettin' a hankerin' to move on."

"I think that's great," I said. "I'll miss you, but I feel good for you. I really do. And I know what you mean. I've been feeling the same way lately. There's got to be something else. Something else to do than what we've been doing with our lives. Then, after what we just went through today, it gets you thinkin' that way even more."

"Yeah, it does," said Horace. "It sure does."

"I mean," I said, "what happened to Sonny was a freak thing. But, you know, if we keep on like we've been doing, there's no telling how long we're gonna make it. We don't eat right, we drink way too much and, overall, we're not taking very good care of ourselves in a lot of ways."

"You're right, Morris," he said. "I'm looking at the move to Mississippi as a chance to get a new start on things. It's been a long time since I've been around my kin up there, but they're still kin. I don't think my cousin would have bothered to take a shot at gettin' in touch with me unless he was wantin' to help me. I guess he figured I could help him and his mom out, too. Maybe we'd all be better off. That's how I'm lookin' at it."

"I think it's good," I said. "I think you're doing the right thing. Now all I've got to do is come up with something to get *me* off the streets."

"You can do it," said Horace. "You can do it. You'll figure somethin' out."

"Yeah," I said, "as long as I don't do like you and I have done a couple of times before. You know what I mean. We were gonna go try to get a job and we decided to have a couple of drinks to get our nerve up to do it. Then the couple of drinks turned into a bunch of drinks and we never went to wherever the hell it was we were going in the first place. I can't be doing that. Not anymore."

"You'll get it right," he said. "I just know you will. Me, I'm gonna just go on up there to the Delta and get myself squared away. I figure I can get to doing somethin' to make some money. Then I'll work on gettin' me hooked up with one of them young soul sisters. That's what I'm gonna do. And if I can pick up enough cash to make it so I can go fishin' when I want, have a woman to look after me, and listen to some good ol' blues, I'll be just fine... just fine."

"You go for it, man," I said. "You'll be ruling the roost up there in Mississippi before you know it. And, thanks, I do appreciate you encouraging me like you did. I'll find something."

We sat quietly for a spell until I was struck with a thought for a place to get a job. "You know, my friend, I just came up with somewhere I could work. What if I go see the guy who runs the bicycle rental joint and ask him if he could use a hand workin' on the bikes?"

"That the place where you bought our bikes?"

"Yeah," I said, "it's the same business. I've fiddled on ours some. I know how they work. I could become a regular ol' bicycle mechanic."

In the back of my mind, I was thinking about the different engineering tests I'd had on Holidaymaker. I'd passed all of those with flying colors—just like Cassandra and Bernard had told me. I knew I could do okay working on bikes. I just knew it.

"Well, that sure sounds like a good idea to me," he said, starting to laugh. "Now just look at us, sittin' 'round here plannin' out all this stuff. Who woulda ever thought that? Lordy, Lordy. Who woulda *ever* thought that?" Then in a more serious tone, "But we can do it, Morris. We can do it."

"Here's to you," I said as I took a hefty gulp out of the bottle of brown. I passed the bottle to Horace and he said and did just as I had. It was our informal street-folk way of having a toast.

EPILOGUE

A couple of months have passed since that day. And I gotta tell you—things have worked out pretty darn good. As a special treat for myself, I picked up a little ol' bottle of the brown to work on while I bring you people up to date. I've been doing a lot better keeping the drinking under control, but I know I'll need a few pulls here and there to get me through the rest of what I've got to tell you. Need to take care of the throat with some soothing, you know. You won't even notice.

Shortly after the day of Sonny's service, Horace caught a bus up to his cousin's place in Cleveland, Mississippi. He had scraped together as much money as he could, but came up a little light on the bus fare and some spending money he'd need along the way. I withdrew seventy-five dollars from my account at the bank and gave it to him as a contribution to his new effort to change his way of life. Duct Tape Sally and Connie Jo even chipped in ten bucks apiece as a sendoff gift.

Horace is with relatives up there, so that's a good start. It should sorta give him a support group while he's getting his feet on the ground. Maybe some day I'll go on up there to Mississippi and catch up with him—if I can figure out exactly where he's livin'. He did tell me I'd be welcome to come up and do some fishing with him. Said we could kick back with some drinks and listen to some blues music. That'd be fun. Now, this is all assuming Horace got there okay in the first place. As you might expect, us former street people aren't exactly very good at communicating either by phone or letter.

You'll notice I said *former* street people. That's right. I landed a job at Davis Bicycle Rentals on Duval Street. It's the same place I bought the old beach cruisers for Horace and me. I work on repairing bikes and also cleaning them up when they're returned dirty. Sometimes it's simple things like fixing flats or broken chains. Most of the bikes are the basic beach cruisers that only have one gear anyway. But some of them in the inventory have multiple gears. With those kinds, I've gotten the hang of repairing the derailleur that moves the chain from one set of gears to another. The business also rents out a few motor scooters. They're more complicated to work on than bikes, but I'm getting the hang of them, too. I like to think that my experiences on Holidaymaker have helped me figure out a lot of the mechanical stuff. I try to keep a positive attitude if I run into a difficult repair job—and it usually seems to help.

Ed Davis, who owns the business, has been great to me. Not only has he coached me along with learning how to do different repairs, he even has let me take up residence in the bicycle warehouse. It's more like a big shed, but there's a cot and a bathroom with a shower in the rear of the building. Plus, there are a couple of windows I can keep open, and there's a big-ass upright fan that keeps the air moving. It may not sound like much, but the setup is fine with me.

One of the funny things about the location of the business is the bar right next door at the corner of Duval and Petronia. It specializes in drag shows. Just about every night there are two shows, at seven and nine. I'm telling you, the performances are a hoot. You wouldn't believe some of the acts. If I'm a little bored for something to do in the evening, I'll walk over there and catch part of a show featuring men dressed up like women—and acting crazy. Most of the time, I laugh my ass off. The good part is I'm only a matter of yards from where I live and work.

The job doesn't pay all that much, but when you figure I can sleep and shower there, it's a pretty good arrangement. It's way more than I had going for me before, that's for sure. From Ed's standpoint, having me sleep overnight in the warehouse has several benefits. For one, I'm around to keep an eye on the place at night when we're closed. But it also means I won't be a no-show for work. I'm already on site in the morning. A couple of times, though, he's had to prompt me about getting up. But, I don't think he has any big problem with it. It's not like I didn't come in to work at all. And I'm actually getting better about being on time, in general—if you can believe that.

I gotta think that Ed was taking a chance by hiring me in the first place. Even though I'd been a customer earlier when I bought a couple of bikes from him, it didn't necessarily mean I could work on bicycles or be a dependable employee. Heck, I couldn't even come up with any recent work experience or any references that would do me any good. I had a notion to mention Suzanne's name, but then I thought better of it. There was no sense in getting her involved with my attempt to get a job. Oh, I'm sure she would have said some nice things about me, but probably not the kind of comments an employer would be looking for. What could she have said? Something like, "Well, Morris is a really kind person who comes into the bank to withdraw money that his family has deposited for him. And he's gotten into a couple of fights defending me." I had decided it was best to just let that all be.

As a form of reference, I did show Ed the nice framed certificate I got at the awards ceremony. When he saw it, he said he remembered me from seeing my picture in The Key West Citizen the day after the thwarted bank robbery. So, getting the award was a plus. I've even hung the certificate on the wall in the bike warehouse above the cot where I sleep. The fact I'd trimmed up my hair and beard for the ceremony probably also helped out with my appearance as a prospective employee. I can give Suzanne credit for coming up with that idea. Looking back, if it hadn't have been for what I did at the bank robbery, my mini-cleanup might never have happened. It's funny how it turned out that way.

Speaking of Suzanne, I guess you could say she had some good and bad timing going for her. Just before she was going up to New York, her mother took another turn for the worse. And then, a couple of days after Suzanne got up there, her mom passed away. She stayed on for an extra week to go to the funeral and to help out her sister. Maybe the friction between the two of them that was caused by Suzanne not being around to help with their mother will fade away now.

Some other good news for Suzanne—but not for me—is that the guy she's been dating has asked her to marry him. The day she told me the news, she made a big deal of notifying me I'd be invited to the wedding. Imagine that, me—former street person, Morris Scott—getting invited to a wedding. Six months ago, I would have told you something like that would never happen in a million years. But I guess you could say I had the good fortune of making a friend of Suzanne over the last couple of years and it ended up turning into something even better. And now since I'm making a few bucks at the bike shop, along with my increased funds from Randy going into the bank every month, I figure I can afford to buy a few new clothes. Still, it's hard to picture me at a wedding. I can just see me now, most likely sitting in the back row during the ceremony. And then, at the reception I'll probably get something to eat and take off. But you never know—stranger things could happen. Maybe I'll meet somebody I can talk to, and take it from there. I'm keeping an open mind about it. Not all that long ago, I would have looked at the wedding scene as an opportunity to hit on the attendees for a few bucks here and there. But, for now, I've made up my mind to retire from that former lifestyle. Mind you, I haven't sold out completely by going with the regular way of living. But I'm getting the gist of it.

I'm happy for Suzanne and I know I'll still get to see her and talk to her at the bank. I feel lucky about that prospect. And I always knew deep down there was never gonna be anything romantic between us anyway. But she's still the nicest-looking and nicest-acting girl I've had the pleasure of being around—Cassandra on Holidaymaker notwithstanding. Since I'm making some money at the bike rental place, I don't need to go to the bank as often as I used to. But I still do. Sometimes I'll take out a little less cash than I did before. I even just make up excuses to get over to the bank a couple of times a week. Can't go much longer than that to get a chance to see, and talk with, Suzanne.

I'm doing a little better with the personal hygiene stuff and I'm eating better, too. I'm still not near the robust fitness level I had when I was on Holidaymaker. Probably won't ever be. I mean, I haven't grown back my missing pinky toe and part of the finger I lost to frostbite. But I feel healthier and just plain better in general. I've even been controlling the drinking thing during the hours I'm working at the shop. So, it's a start. And, overall, I guess I don't feel as lonely as I used to. I think having the job at Ed's place has given me more confidence in dealing with other people one on one. I sense I'm getting closer to being on an even level with other civilians, if you know what I mean.

With the job and all, I don't go to the library nearly as much I used to. But I do run into Duct Tape Sally every now and then. She even occasionally makes it by the bike place to say hi. She tells me she still spends a lot of time at the library, getting her reading in. Sally has got to have her regular fix of the articles in the Wall Street Journal. Who knows, maybe Sally's got a fortune stashed away somewhere, and nobody else knows about it. She might just be livin' on the street as a cover for being a millionaire, for all I know. Stranger things than that can happen. Especially in this town. The first couple of times she stopped by the shop, Ed, the owner, gave her some crazy looks. I clued him in on the fact that Sally is harmless. Heck, if you live or work in Key West you aren't too surprised by anybody's appearance. Ed had noticed her on the street a number of times before, but he was still awful puzzled by all the duct tape. To check her out up close, kinda blew his mind. He finds her, her duct tape, and her grocery cart all very fascinating.

I haven't run into Connie Jo much lately. And, actually, that has had a soothing effect on my eyesight. By merely being a resident of our fair city, she accounts for a goodly amount of the hard-looking women population—all by herself. Duct Tape Sally has kept me up to date, and she tells me that things are about the same with Connie Jo. Which basically means that she's continuing to get drunk and disorderly on a regular basis. Thinking of Connie Jo in some kinda sports terminology, you could say that you can't control her—you can only contain her. I guess that job goes to the law enforcement types such as Officer Keith. He and his police force co-workers have their hands full when it comes to Connie Jo. Not only do they have to arrest her every now and then, they get stuck having to actually look at her up close. I'm wondering which is worse.

Officer Keith is still steady as he goes. He'll occasionally stop by the bike shop and pass the time of day. It makes it not so secretive for him to talk to me like he used to now that I have an actual job. I've even done a few minor repairs to his bike when he's been in. I know he appreciates the effort. And Ed doesn't mind that I'm doing a little freebie fix up. He's glad to see a police officer hanging around every now and then. Keith has got to be the most even-keeled cop ever. To deal with all the lunatics that come and go in this town, and not to go stark raving mad, is beyond me. He does his job in a firm and serious way, but he carries it out with a patience that amazes me. Keith must have some kind of screw loose to do what he does in the first place, if you ask me.

I just got a letter from Randy at the bank the other day. He's coming down in a couple of weeks for a long weekend like he used to. He doesn't know anything about the new deal I got going. Man, is he going to be surprised. He's gonna start picturing me in a whole different way. With my somewhat new grooming, along with the fact that I'm actually employed now, he'll flip. I can't wait to go up to his regular room at the Pier House and knock on the door. I wouldn't be surprised if Randy would even be willing to go out to a restaurant or something with me. Man, that would be a far cry from me buying some food and sittin' down in an alley to eat with the chickens like I used to. I'm a good bit more presentable and all, now. Not quite up to Randy's level of grooming standards yet, but a big improvement for me, even so. Something tells me, with the changes I've made, in addition to our mother's passing, he will look at me in a whole new light. I think, in some ways, she had a strong influence on the way he has always thought of me. Maybe we can interact in a better way now. I sure hope so.

I'm still not completely over Sonny. May never be, for all I know. Time has been making the ache a little less sore. But I'm still not at peace with the way he died. It just seems to me that it could have been avoided. I would really like to wring the neck of that little bastard who got the whole thing started by stealing Sonny's money and then running away. It wasn't like Sonny was killed just because he was a street person. He was only conducting his little musical business like any other vendor-type might. Although, if Sonny's diet was a little healthier, and he had more meat on his bones, he might have taken the impact from the car better than he did. I guess that's not really an endorsement for gaining weight, though. Or maybe if he was in better shape in general, he might have outrun the impact. Anyway, I still continue to feel like it was something that didn't have to happen.

Okay, there's one little item I haven't let you in on yet. Even though I have the place to stay overnight in the bike warehouse, I'm still not forgetting about Holidaymaker—not one bit at all. If I have the following day off, or if I don't have to start working at the bike shop until later in the day, I still go over and spend the night in the cemetery. Don't want to do that if I have to start work in the morning, like I usually do. I don't want to oversleep at the cemetery and be late for my job. I'm not taking that risk. But I just can't stay away from the cemetery for too awful long. Any opportunity to get back on Holidaymaker is something I'm looking forward to with a ton of eagerness. And any additional chance to be with Cassandra is something I can't wait for. For me, every experience

265

I had on that spacecraft is still as vivid and valid as it ever was. And nobody's gonna make me think otherwise about the whole deal. Holidaymaker is real as far as I'm concerned. I'm so sure of it, most of my limited time at the library these days is spent doing more ongoing research on UFOs, The Bermuda Triangle, and stuff like that. In my spare time, it's become somewhat of an obsession with me. So, I intend to make it over to the cemetery at nighttime every chance I get. If there's ever a possibility to go up with Cassandra and the rest of them, I want to be there. I still have the strongest feeling they'll be coming back again sometime. It could happen any night now.......any night now.

Acknowledgements

To my better half, Gayle, for encouragement, critique, seemingly endless editorial support, and without whom this would not be possible

To my brother, Gus, for editorial assistance, suggestions, and a wealth of educational experience

To Sidney H. Christie, D.M.D., for editorial assistance

To Sherri Moore, Parish Administrator, St. Paul's Episcopal Church, Key West, Florida, for friendly and kind help